Colde &
Rainey

R. E. BRADSHAW

Titles from R. E. Bradshaw Books

Rainey Bell Thriller Series:
Colde & Rainey (2014)
The Rainey Season (2013) Lambda Literary Awards Finalist
Rainey's Christmas Miracle (2011) (Short Story-ebook only)
Rainey Nights (2011) Lambda Literary Awards Finalist
Rainey Days (2010)

The Adventures of Decky and Charlie Series:
Out on the Panhandle (2012)
Out on the Sound (2010)

Molly: House on Fire (2012)
Lambda Literary Awards Finalist

Before It Stains (2011)

Waking Up Gray (2011)

Sweet Carolina Girls (2010)

The Girl Back Home (2010)

Colde & Rainey

A Rainey Bell Thriller

R. E. BRADSHAW

Published by
R. E. BRADSHAW BOOKS

USA

•R.E.B.BOOKS•

Colde & Rainey
By R. E. Bradshaw

© 2014 by R. E. Bradshaw. All Rights Reserved.
R. E. Bradshaw Books/April 2014
ISBN-13: 978-0-9903760-1-9

Website: http://www.rebradshawbooks.com
Facebook: https://www.facebook.com/rebradshawbooks
Twitter @rebradshawbooks
Blog: http://rebradshawbooks.blogspot.com
For information contact rebradshawbooks@gmail.com

This is a work of fiction. Names, characters, businesses, places, events, and incidents are either the products of the author's imagination or used in a fictitious manner. Any resemblance to actual persons, living or dead, or actual events is purely coincidental.

Acknowledgments

Michelle, Curtie, Kate, Terry, Henriette, and Toni—Thank you.
To the readers who continue to ask for more Rainey Bell—Thank you.
To my support group, and you know who you are—
THANK YOU FOR KEEPING MY BUTT IN THE SEAT!

About the book...

If you have crossed paths with a malignant psychopath, you have my condolences. Unfortunately, one taught me a great deal about trusting my instincts and in some ways inspired this book. A cunning and cold psychopath has no boundaries. Rules are for others. Empathy and remorse are nonexistent. Difficult to spot under the masks of the fiction created to hide true intentions, they wear a different face for every occasion. If you're among the few that see the real personality under the psychopath's façade of normalcy, good luck convincing others who have not yet comprehended the illusion. Still, as Rainey says in this book:

> *"It takes a different skill set to interpret the behavior of a known person as opposed to that of an unknown subject. I wasn't looking for a psychopath, and even if I was, I saw only what I was allowed to see. I can see more at a crime scene of a criminal's true personality than I can across the dinner table from them. Hence, the reason I am always armed. You just never know."*

Colde & Rainey is a different look at the behavioral analyst role in solving crimes. It is also not the edge of the seat thriller that was *The Rainey Season*. As a plot line needs moments of calm in order to build to the next heart-pounding moment, Rainey has taken a break from the sadists trying to murder her—or has she? Trouble has a way of finding Rainey Bell, even at a funeral.

REB

Dedication

Deb, thank you for never giving up on me.

"All truths are easy to understand once they are discovered; the point is to discover them."
~Galileo Galilei

Chapter One

February 10, 2000
Jordan Lake, Chatham County, NC
9:30 a.m.
Scattered Clouds, 47°F, High today near 70°F

William "Billy" Bell sat behind the steering wheel of a beat-up Chevy truck with more dents and rust-tinted primer than original paint and missing its tailgate. It was his most recent "incognito accessory," as he called the series of old jalopies he employed to catch bail jumpers.

"Come on, Rainey Blue Bell," Billy beckoned across the truck's bench seat to his daughter. "Your friendly neighborhood bail bondsman needs to blend in today."

His green eyes exactly matched hers and glinted with the mischievousness of a schoolboy. A cloud of dust lifted from the sun-cracked dashboard, as he patted it like the head of a good dog.

"Don't judge her by her looks. If they can outrun this three-twenty-seven small-block, they deserve to get away."

"Good point," Rainey commented, brushing dirt off the seat before climbing in. The door rattled into place after a second good hard slamming. She immediately hunted the seatbelt she hoped still existed, and asked, "Exactly, how fast do you plan on driving? I'm a federal agent. I can't just willy-nilly go on high speed pursuits."

"What if we are the ones being pursued?" Billy asked, deepening his one cornered grin.

Rainey held half of the seatbelt in one hand and dug between the seat cushions for its mate. "Now, that's different. The question then becomes can you out run them?"

"There are fast vehicles and then there are fast drivers. It's good to be in one driven by the other."

Billy reached for the sunglasses stuck in the thick curls of his graying chestnut-brown hair and slid them down over his eyes. He put the truck in gear and pulled away from Billy Bell's Bail and Bait, located on Jordan Lake in Chatham County, North Carolina. To her relief, Rainey found the other half of the seatbelt before her father was tempted to gun the engine and prove his point. She snapped the two parts together and then lightly clapped her hands in front of her to clean them of dust.

"I suppose this layer of dirt is part of your attempt at subterfuge, though I'm not sure how the bright yellow Hawaiian shirt over the thermal underwear ensemble"—she paused to take in the full effect of her father's clothing choices before continuing—"with cargo shorts no less, is going to blend in, considering it's February."

"Vietnam vet, that's my undercover persona and I have the scars to make it work for me," he said, grinning at Rainey. "Never wander too far from the truth on your fake identities."

"If you're going for breezy vet that never really left China Beach, you nailed it," Rainey replied, "but how are you going to explain me? This Academy tee shirt might be a dead giveaway and I've been told I reek of cop."

"You're on the take," Billy deadpanned.

"Got it," Rainey said with her own one cornered grin. "So, who is this guy we're going to meet?"

"An old friend. He needs a favor and he might have a line on a guy I've been looking for. I also thought it might be time for a father-daughter drive. There's been a lot going on with you since our last one."

"'A lot' doesn't quite cover the last eighteen months," Rainey noted.

Rainey and Billy had been taking long drives together since she started visiting on the weekends at age ten, after her mother finally came clean about his existence. They drove back roads, drank too many sodas, and ate boiled peanuts. The memories piled up like the salty shells discarded in the rumpled old newspaper resting on the seat between them. Rainey loved that her father was interested in what she thought and the happenings in her childish world. The conversations changed over the years along with the menu—peanuts became the carrot sticks of an athlete in training and the whys of a child turned to the why nots of a teenager—but their drives remained a constant, just as Billy's concern for her well-being persisted.

"You conked out in the recliner pretty quickly when you got home. They keeping you too busy to sleep up there at Quantico?"

"I just finished seventy-two hours in the field with a critical incident response team, not many of which were spent with my eyes closed. I guess I hadn't caught up yet," Rainey offered as an excuse.

She was twenty-nine years old, a veteran federal agent, and still she didn't want her father to know she was having trouble adjusting to the dreams that came with knowing the deepest depravities of humanity. Rainey had listened from her room, enduring the sounds of his fight for life, as Billy Bell's nights filled with jungle combat terrors. A man who suffered through his own horrors would worry about his daughter doing the same, and she didn't want that. Rainey was glad when he moved on to another subject.

"You went back to the academy for sixteen weeks and then did eighteen months in supervised BAU training—you haven't talked about it much."

"I'm still making sense of it all, I guess. I thought I'd seen a lot," she paused, blinking the sudden and unwanted images from her head. "When I first started training, I heard one of the old guys say he always has a moment before each case when he wonders if he's going to see something more depraved than he's already seen. His meaning is quite clear to me now. I'm learning how to compartmentalize better. It will take time."

"Crazy shit you see," was Billy's simple but accurate assessment.

"It's not like people outside the BAU don't see horrid things. It's just that we witness so much of it. A cop might get one case like that in a career. We see it every day, in one form or another. If I wasn't reading the details of an old case, I was looking at a new one. What human beings are capable of doing to one another will never cease to amaze me."

"Now what?" he asked. "Have they decided where to put you?"

"They wanted to know my preference, but I will be told where I best suit the Bureau's purposes when I return from my five days off."

"In other words, you have no input in the matter," Billy said with a chuckle.

Rainey nodded in agreement. "They could assign me to counterterrorism, white collar computer crime, even put me with VICAP entering and evaluating data, something along those lines. I think my computer forensics degree was the reason I was chosen for the program to begin with."

"So, you think that's how it will go? Computer crimes?"

"There are lots of computer-related jobs in the various Behavioral Analysis Units. My last six weeks of mentored training were with the crimes against children section, tracking a sadistic pedophile ring's online activity."

Rainey shook her head and shrugged off the images that popped into her mind. She was thinking she needed to get handle on this compartmentalizing thing soon. Having ghastly images simply appear at will was not acceptable.

She added to her previous answer, "I know I don't want to focus on abused and murdered children, not for any length of time, not yet."

"Not yet?" Billy took his focus from the road and glanced at his daughter.

"I think I can harden to it, but what they do to them—that just crawls under my skin and I can't seem to shake it loose. I can't sustain that level of anger and still function. It's part of learning to set aside what I feel and see the evidence. It is a disconnect I have yet to master when the case involves children."

Billy stared straight ahead, as he commented, "Never harden to the pain and suffering of a child."

He had that thousand-yard stare again, and Rainey knew they both had seen things they would rather not remember. She spoke to break the spell.

"I really want to work with the adult victims unit, but they'll probably say I need to increase my knowledge base. There is so much information to process. I'm young compared to most of the more experienced candidates," she paused and smiled at her father, "but I'm good at it, Dad. I can improve, no question, but I'm absolutely sure this is what I'm supposed to do. I just need a chance."

"Stay patient and your opportunity will present itself. 'He who knows when he can fight and when he cannot, will be victorious.' "

Participating in a father-daughter ritual as old as their relationship, Rainey answered with her own *Art of War* citation, "The supreme art of war is to subdue the enemy without fighting."

Billy's smile deepened the wrinkles peeking from under his sunglasses. "That bit of wisdom might save your ass one day." He glanced at her again, which Rainey noted he seemed to be doing often, and then asked, "So, how close are you going to get to these psychos? You look like hell, by the way. Are they in your dreams already?"

He knew. He always knew. She didn't have to tell him. Rainey often wondered if they actually shared a brain. She spent the first ten years of her life not knowing Billy existed, but genetics will out. There was more than a little truth in Rainey's mother's lament, "You're just like your father." Constance Lee Bell Herndon may have meant those words as an insult, but Rainey never felt the sting. The pride would surge through her veins and her green eyes would sparkle, usually followed by a smartass remark that sent her mother stomping away, harrumphing as she went.

Rainey tried not to look as worn out as she felt, making an effort to smile. "I'm just tired, Dad. This is the first time I've been off the clock for more than twenty-four hours in six weeks. I'll be fine. I need some home cooked food and rest." She reached across the seat and playfully punched him in the arm. "And you know what? I'm starving. I thought you said this truck was fast."

"Well, just don't let those monsters follow you home. Set your boundaries, Rainey. You're going to need them."

And with that, Billy hit the gas and the old beater roared to life, throwing Rainey back against the seat.

"Woo-hoo," she yelled and gripped the armrest on the door, grinning from ear to ear. They were on a straight stretch of two-lane highway with not a car in sight. "Let her eat," Rainey shouted, which was NASCAR fan lingo for "step on the accelerator."

"I can't. Got a law enforcement official in my vehicle."

Rainey laughed and tightened her grip on the armrest. "Right now, I'm just a girl riding with her dad. Hammer down, old man. Let's see what ya' got."

#

Hominy Junction,
Dobbs County, North Carolina
11:00 a.m.
Mostly Cloudy, 57°F

Wellman Wise was the sort of man not easily forgotten. He stood six feet four inches from the bottom of his clown-sized shoes to the top of his pampered, bald scalp. Rainey was five feet ten inches tall, taller if the height added by her thick mane of chestnut curls counted, but she felt small next to the Kodiak bear of a man. Wise reached to clasp Billy's hand in a firm, welcoming grip. His voice boomed out of a barrel chest.

"Master Sergeant Bell, thank you for coming."

"Captain," Billy said, accompanied with a respectful dip of his head. "I'll put it on your bill," he added with a chuckle.

"I'll owe you the rest of my life," Wise answered and then turned his attention to Rainey. "And it is very much a pleasure to see you again, Special Agent Bell."

"Captain Wise," Rainey said, offering her hand with a smile. "I had no idea you knew my father or vice versa," she added, glancing back at Billy.

"If I told you I knew the Captain, I would've had to kill you," Billy said, feigning sincerity.

Rainey knew that meant the two of them were somewhere they should not have been doing something for the United States government the average person was never to know. Covert and top secret were words Rainey learned early on, when discussing her father's military career.

"I think as long as the conversation stays in the present, we're okay," Wise offered, not too successfully suppressing a smile. "Please, have a seat," he said, as he stepped over to a worn Formica-topped table and pulled out a wooden ladder-back chair for Rainey.

"Thank you," Rainey said, taking the seat and a look around.

They were in an old diner in what was left of Hominy Junction, a living monument to the whistle-stop tobacco-farming hamlets that dotted the train tracks southeast of Raleigh, North Carolina. One in a line of little settlements built along the rails leading to what was once the "World's Greatest Tobacco Market," the town had gone to seed, turned back to the earth, its houses and people decaying to extinction. Rainey looked beyond the faded wallpaper, sepia-stained from years of tobacco smoke and bacon grease, through windows clouded with layers of farm dust and nicotine to the abandoned downtown storefronts.

A covered wooden sidewalk remained intact along one side of the main street. A lonely drug store still operated in the middle of the block on the other. It looked like the kind of place kids used to gather after school for a scoop of ice cream or a malt. The windows advertised specials for arthritis pain relief and incontinence pads now; the younger generations having long since abandoned the quaintness of the small town soda fountain for the mall. The post office was at the other end of the block, identifiable by its red bricks and the blue mailbox out front. The

Stars and Stripes and the North Carolina flag drooped from the flagpole, as lifeless as the town. A small branch bank occupied the lot across the street. The rest of the businesses were boarded up, replaced by the big box stores in the larger cities just a few miles away in any direction. Evidently, someone thought a fresh coat of white paint on the empty storefronts could disguise the decay. It did not.

Possibly reading Rainey's assessment of the town's bleakness in her expression, Captain Wise offered, "Not much left of it, but at one time, this was a hopping little place. I suppose we'll wait around for the cities to grow into us. Some more hip folks will move in, renovate the old homes, and open up quaint village shops down Main Street. At least, that's what the Mayor keeps telling everyone."

"You live here?" Rainey asked, turning her attention back to the men at the table.

"My wife and I were both born and raised right down the street, just a couple of blocks," Wise answered. "We came back home when I retired from the Air Force. I do a little part time work for the Sheriff to keep from driving Harriet crazy at home."

"Was taking a class at Quantico part of your work for the Sheriff?" Rainey remembered Wise in class and grinned at him. "Are you the new cyber crimes expert for the county?"

Wise chuckled. "As you can attest, computers baffle me, but I did learn quite a bit. I appreciated your help and patience. The instructor is an old buddy of mine. I audited the class for pretty much the reason I took the part time work with the Sheriff—to stay busy."

Rainey filled her father in. "I assisted some of the less computer-savvy members of the Captain's class as part of my training time in the cyber crimes unit."

"He might have mentioned something about that," Billy said, just as a rotund little woman stepped to the table to take their orders.

Billy, Rainey, and Wellman Wise were the only occupants in the dining area. A few old farmers sat at a countertop nearer the kitchen, nursing coffee and swapping tales. They were identifiable by the dirt embedded in the cracks of their well-worn brogans and the tanned-hide appearance of their deeply wrinkled necks. They each had a pale stripe of skin across the forehead, where Rainey imagined a soiled feed and seed cap usually blocked the sun. A quick visual survey of the hat rack by the door confirmed her suspicions.

The woman with the order pad appeared to be a rosy-cheeked grandmotherly type, until she opened her mouth and snarled down at the table occupants. "We got a hot plate and a cold plate, no substitutions. If you want a burger, you're too late. I'm out of meat. Preorders beat you to it. Water, iced tea, or coffee, and no it ain't fresh. Made it this mornin'. Wise, you want the usual?"

"Doris makes up for her lack of personality with a talent for cooking a good plate of food. Hot or cold, you will not be disappointed. I'd shy away from the coffee though."

Doris curled her snarling lip around, "Wiseass, you can kiss mine."

Wise chuckled and said, "The usual will do just fine."

In Rainey's experience, food in this type of diner was heavily steamed, boiled, or fried. The high cooking temperatures offered some protection from food poisoning, she surmised, and ordered the hot plate just in case Doris's nasty attitude carried over to her kitchen cleaning habits.

Once Doris had everyone's order, she exited, saying, "I'll be back when I get back."

Wise slapped his thigh and laughed aloud. "She's ornery, but a damn fine cook. Don't let the looks of the place fool you. Half the town and most of the senior class from the high school down the road will be here within the hour to pick up lunch."

The bells over the door jangled as a teenaged girl slouched in. Rainey watched the dark-haired, pale-faced, young woman hang up her coat and then peek from under her bowed brow to see if anyone had noticed her entrance. She saw Rainey watching her and shrugged further into her slouch, just as Doris reentered with drinks for the table.

"It's about time you drug up," Doris spat at the young woman. "Start them burger patties 'fore those kids get here."

"Sorry, Mom. The test took longer than I thought it would," the girl said.

9

Doris shook her head. "It's always something, Leda, always something," she said, as she turned her back on her daughter.

The girl made eye contact with Rainey again, as she stepped behind the counter. This time she seemed to be saying, "Do you see what I have to live with?"

If Rainey understood anything, it was the dynamics of bad mother-daughter relationships. She and Constance had been going at it for as long as she could remember. Rainey had not resided with her mother since she was fourteen, but that didn't make their relationship any better. She sympathized with young Leda and silently wished her a way out of town. *"Distance. That's your only chance,"* Rainey thought, watching the girl disappear behind the swinging kitchen doors.

Doris put three glasses of sweet iced tea on the table, though Rainey had ordered water. She didn't bother to complain, or rather, she had no time to do so. Doris was gone as soon as she got there. The bells clanged again and more customers entered. Three tall, blush-cheeked, athletic young men pushed through the door, still laughing at a joke no one inside the diner heard.

"Fallon is the funniest guy ever on Saturday Night Live," one of them said.

Rainey remembered the original cast and chuckled at the poor deprived youth of the day. Her father and Wise were talking about some fugitive Billy had been trying to flush out for a few months. Rainey wasn't particularly interested in the pursuit of some career criminal named Chauncey Barber. Her people-watching habit kept her busy. It had been honed on many stakeouts and refined during her recent behavioral science training at the academy. Rainey could tell a lot about a person, just by how they walked into a room.

The three new diner occupants carried themselves with the swagger expected from young men of their age and obvious social status. They were handsome in their leather and wool letterman jackets. The large entwined H and J on their chests glinted with gold-plated achievement pins and marked these young men as exceptional—in case there were doubts as to where they stood in the high school food chain. These were the alpha males, the top dogs, hometown heroes with whom girls like Leda never stood a chance.

Rainey noticed Doris was kind, maybe even a little sweet, when she spoke to the new customers, "Hello, boys. Have a seat. Leda will have those cheeseburgers right out," and then with a whoosh of the swinging kitchen doors she disappeared again.

The three old farmers at the counter brightened at the young men's arrival and added their welcomes. One simply dipped his head in a silent show of fine regard. The other two spoke in rapid succession.

"Good to see you, boys."

"How many points you gonna score tomorrow night, Skylar?"

The shortest of the teenaged trio, by only a few inches, but handsomest by far, showed his perfectly aligned teeth behind a dimple-bracketed, Hollywood-worthy smile and responded, "Well, Mr. Harris, I hope I score just enough to help the team win the game."

The taller ginger-haired teen spoke up, "Don't worry. He'll get that season scoring record. Now that Ely's out, it's a done deal."

"Shut up, G." The one named Skylar rebuked his larger friend, adding, "It's not about that."

The last of the trio joined in, punching G in the shoulder. "Yeah, it's about winning the conference, dickwad." He noticed Rainey at the table, adding quickly, "Sorry, ma'am."

"No problem," Rainey assured him.

The three boys moved on to one of the booths lining the back wall, as Doris whooshed back through the doors, heading for Rainey's table. The old gal was quite the marvel, balancing three dishes with two hands, including silverware rolled tightly in a white paper napkin. She clanked a plate and serving set down in front of each of them, pulled out her order pad, and started tallying up the ticket.

Rainey looked down at a steaming mound of ham, cabbage, and little red potatoes, with a splash of pickled beets in the middle of the pile. The beet juice ran trails of deep red veins down the cabbage leaf quarters and pooled at the edge of the plate. Rainey blinked away another unwanted image and tried to

11

focus on Billy's plate of chicken salad on a bed of lettuce, sliced tomatoes and boiled eggs on the side, served with two packages of saltine crackers. She had to focus on the details of the here and now—any detail would do—anything other than the horrific ones her mind seemed to throw at her with no notice and without provocation. Control. Rainey needed to gain control and master the locks on the mental boxes she created to store those images.

Doris's shrill voice brought Rainey fully back to the room, as she slapped the ticket down by Wise's hand, "If you want more crackers or refills on your tea, fetch 'em from the counter over there," she said. "I'm busy."

Evidently, the service Doris was to provide had just ended. The rest, a customer had to find and fend for themselves. Doris moved on to chat with the teens in the booth, but not before Wise thanked her for his "usual," which turned out to be a plain ham sandwich on white bread with a pickle on the side.

Wise smiled over at Billy. "The wife won't let me have white bread. It's the only decent sandwich I can get anymore."

"One more of the many reasons I do not have one of those," Billy said.

Rainey chuckled and picked up her fork, as she said, "There's not a decent woman that would have you. Ernie is the only reason you're semi-civilized."

"Ernie is not civilized," Billy said of his longtime office manager and friend, Ernestine Womble—the only woman he seemed able to tolerate for more than a week or two.

Wise interrupted the family banter with, "I suppose you're wondering why I asked your father to bring you here."

"I was not aware that you had," Rainey answered, while slicing off a piece of ham.

Her plate no longer harbored unwanted imagery, just smelled delicious, and the first bite confirmed that Doris could indeed cook a mean plate of food.

"Need to know basis. I didn't think she needed to," Billy offered as an explanation for why he dragged her an hour and a half from home on the first day of a much-needed vacation.

Rainey shot him a closed-lip smile while she chewed. Billy Bell was secretive and a bit paranoid, in her estimation. He had raised her to share the same feral cat defenses, cautious and suspicious, constantly checking her surroundings.

raised her to share the same feral cat defenses, cautious and suspicious, constantly checking her surroundings.

"Have fun," he would say, "but always, always be aware. If you see them coming, you got a chance."

These traits served both of them well in their chosen professions, but made for interesting relationship dynamics. Neither father nor daughter could sustain a romance beyond the "get to know me" stage. No one was getting in that vault. Luckily, as far as her father was concerned, Rainey didn't "need to know" more than he was willing to tell most of the time.

Wise reached under his jacket and produced an envelope. He placed it next to Rainey's plate. "Billy told me you attended that school shooter conference up in Leesburg last July. I wish you'd have a look at this and tell me what you think I'm dealing with. What personality type wrote it?"

Rainey swallowed a forkful of cabbage and ham, then picked up the envelope and took out a folded sheet of copy paper. Unfolding it revealed a page covered with doodles and scribbling, including some that obscured parts of the single-spaced typed paragraph at the top. The copier even picked up the creases in the paper where it had been folded and refolded dozens of times.

"You know one writing sample isn't enough to make a recommendation, right? Kids blow off steam, say things they shouldn't. It takes more than a few written rants and some violent imagery to make a school shooter." She pointed at one of the black ink doodles depicting a heavily-armed stickman mowing down a row of stick figures, blood dripping, piles of stick body parts at the stickman assassin's feet. "But I can see why you have cause to be concerned."

Wise nodded. "I didn't think this was run of the mill angst. That paragraph will make the hair stand on the back of your neck."

Billy leaned over to see the page. "Anything that would make Wise's hair stand up, makes me curious." He read over Rainey's shoulder.

> I kill who I don't like, I waste what I
> don't want, I destroy what I hate. My
> belief is that if I say something, it

goes. I am the law, if you don't like it, you die. If I don't like you or I don't like what you want me to do, you die. Dead people can't do many things, like argue, whine, bitch, complain, narc, rat out, criticize, or even fucking talk. So that's the only way to solve arguments with all you fuckheads out there, I just kill! God I can't wait till I can kill you people. I don't care if I live or die in the shootout, all I want to do is kill and injure as many of you pricks as I can, especially a few people, like:

Skylar Sweet
Gordon Terrell
Adam Goodwin
Burgess Read
Benjy Janson
Ely Paxton
Cassie Gillian

"& Ellie" was hand-written beside the name Ely, along with "fuck you....shutup....and die" at the bottom of the list of names.

"Whew," Billy whistled. "I do hope you have eyes on this child."

Wise was focused on Rainey when she looked up from the page. His brow rose in question, but he said nothing.

"Is this a test?" Rainey asked, only slightly amused at the links the old boys would go to rattle the new girl. "Did your friend at the bureau put you up to this?"

A confused expression replaced Wise's questioning one. "I'm not sure I know what you mean."

Rainey refolded the page and slipped it back into the envelope. "This is copied from an online rant written by Eric Harris, one of the Columbine shooters. The names aren't right, but the words are almost verbatim, except for some spelling corrections. Nice touch with the creepy artwork."

"You recognized where that came from in the time it took to read it. I'm impressed," Billy said.

"Well, I'll be damned," Wise said, not really listening to Billy. "I knew it. I knew that kid didn't write that."

Rainey froze in the middle of sliding the envelope back to Wise. His reaction was sincere. He had no idea what she was talking about and she could say the same about his declaration. Wise dug into his other inside breast pocket for another envelope, which he then held out for Rainey to take.

"My friend at the bureau did suggest I contact you, since you were close by, but no, Special Agent Bell, this is not a test."

She opened the second envelope to find another piece of copy paper. This page contained a single paragraph decorated with an inked illustration of a black bleeding heart, a dripping dagger thrust through it. The artistic style resembled the drawings from the first envelope, however, the thoughts contrasted greatly.

> *As Lancelot to Guinevere, until she comes to me, I shall wait, guarding her honor from the shadows. One day, she will know that I am the only one who sees how special she is and that fate has brought us together. She will know our souls are bound as one. I see her pain and I will save her. I will save us both. If I could only break free of these self-doubts. Who am I kidding? I can't save her. I can't save myself. I am what they say, a weakling, a runt. You know what they do with runts on the farm. They kill them, so they don't waste the feed. I'm a drain on society. I am a waste of feed. I want it to end.*

Billy didn't whistle this time. He just shook his head. "That boy's a bit overly dramatic and has read entirely too many English romances."

Rainey stated clinically, "Depressive personality, inward loathing, unrequited love, self-depreciation—typical teenage angst or a cry for help? It's hard to tell without more information and a thorough workup by a mental health professional. I see none of the same contempt for humanity or blaming as in the first one." Noting the smug look on Wise's face, she asked, "How can I help you, Captain Wise?"

"Like I said, I do a little part time work for the Sheriff. He asked me to take a look at this case, make sure nothing was missed. There is a shy fifteen-year-old in custody—well, in a coma and in custody. He isn't going anywhere for a long time. He's accused of double homicide and attempted murder. He was shot in the head and chest by one of his intended victims, ten days ago."

The bell above the door jangled every few minutes as more town-folk and students came and went. Wise lowered his voice. What he had to say, he appeared not to want the others to overhear.

"By some miracle, he survived. The first note was found in his pocket at the scene of the crime. The second, and many more like it, were found on his computer, in notebooks, on scraps of paper all over this kid's room, his locker, in books, but nowhere did I find another hair-raiser like that first one. It led me to believe someone else might have been involved."

"So, you don't think he simply borrowed Harris's words from the Internet? He may have felt it but been unable to express that level of rage. Maybe he admired Eric Harris for doing so," Rainey suggested. "Like lyrics to a favorite song, we often find that type of transcribing in a school shooter."

"I didn't hear of any school shooting," Billy said.

"He never made it to the school. He went next door to kill the neighbors first. The daughter, Ellie, she shot him after he had already pulled the trigger on her mother and father. Ely, her twin brother, was wounded in a struggle with the gunman. We're pretty sure Ellie was the object of the shooter's affection and that's why he went there first."

"What about his own parents?" Rainey asked.

"Alive, well, and completely shocked at their son's behavior," Wise answered. "So are the family therapist, his school counselor, his teachers—nearly everyone that knew him says they are surprised Graham would do something like this. I tend to agree, but the evidence points to him and him alone."

"But you were not convinced of that, because of the first note," Rainey said.

Wise glanced around the filling diner. "I can't afford to be wrong."

"You mentioned family therapy. Any specifics there?" Rainey couldn't help but be intrigued.

"Teddy, Graham's father, came back from Afghanistan physically wounded and mentally—" Wise hesitated, casting a knowing glance toward Billy. "Let's just say, PTSD is a family problem, but they are dealing with it head on, responsibly. Teddy and Susan are involved parents. They truly can't believe this happened."

"You said the shooter was shy. All of his other writings indicate self-esteem issues and difficulty with interpersonal relationships. There is a wounded warrior in his home. I'm assuming he had access to firearms, since he shot his victims." Rainey was beginning to see a familiar pattern. "Next you're going to tell me he was bullied by the kids on that list."

Wise sat up a little taller in his chair, ready to defend his townspeople's actions or non-actions, as was often the case. "He was not an outgoing kid. His shyness was debilitating according to his mother and his teachers. He was awkward socially, and yes, he was the object of some teasing and pranks. But the neighbor kids, Ellie and Ely, sheltered Graham when they could. Ellie said they had done that since his family moved next door in sixth grade. Until he walked in her house with a rifle and started killing her family, Ellie Paxton thought Graham Colde was her friend."

"Jesus, that's rough," Billy commented.

Rainey concurred with a nod of her head. "Is her brother going to make it?"

"Yes," Wise answered. "His promising college basketball prospects are probably over, but he is alive."

Rainey summed up her observations thus far, "So, Captain, you have a suspect in custody, two living witnesses, and what's bothering you is a note you found in the shooter's pocket. The

17

students on the list, have you talked with them? What do you know about this kid and his relationship to his actual victims?"

Wise swept the room with his eyes and leaned in for his fervent but whispered delivery, "Graham was exceptionally smart with math and computers, an above average student in all of his other classes. He displayed advanced intelligence as compared to his peers, which also separated him from them more. Socially, he lagged behind his age group. You know the type."

Billy and Rainey nodded that they did and Wise continued.

"If I read him right, after going through his online correspondence, his video game activity, his journals, listening to his music, interviewing everyone that knew him—I do not think this boy was about to pull off a school shooting alone. Had he committed suicide or become a famous computer genius, I would not have been surprised. Becoming a potential mass murderer on his own? That is a real stretch."

"But there is no evidence of a partner, other than that one sample of writing that seems out of place with the others. You've mentioned no substantiation of a planned attack. All you have is a list of names—a list that could mean anything. Maybe this kid isn't a school shooter at all. He could suffer from a personality disorder and the girl next door was part of some fantasy or obsession. The parents may have been obstacles to his final goal, possession of the daughter." Rainey concluded with, "It would take a lot of hours poring over evidence to give you any kind of real answer."

Wise had nothing more to offer than, "You're right. I suppose I am making a lot of fuss over a done deal. That boy is going to be in a hospital or prison for the remainder of his days. I just had this gnawing at my gut that says there is more to this story."

Rainey understood the Captain's need to comprehend. No one wanted to face the reality of murderous rage in a child, particularly one that lived down the street. People wanted to know why these things happened so it could be prevented. Sadly, there would be a next time and the warning signs would be clearly visible, yet no one would put it all together until it was too late—after the fact, when the bodies were counted.

She cleared her throat and said, "The people out there in Colorado are still trying to understand how that happened, even though the shooters left video-taped confessions of their plan and the reasoning behind it. If your shooter comes out of his coma with any cognitive abilities remaining, you can ask him. Nonetheless, you may have to resign yourself to never knowing what he had planned and what finally set that plan in motion."

"That isn't very comforting," the dejected Wise said.

Rainey could not give him the answers he wanted, but she could offer him tools. "If there was a partner and a planned attack on the school, something went awry. It will be a person with whom your coma patient spent time alone. This person will show signs of distress right now, wondering if coma kid will wake up and expose him."

Wise listened intently to Rainey's suggestions. His intensity convinced Rainey that his hunch was real and warranted.

"Captain Wise, could you write down your address for me. I'll send you a copy of the report from the school shooter conference. It will help you in your investigation. In the meantime, watch and listen for leakage. If there was a plan, it's already been leaked. They truly cannot help themselves most of the time. They tell in words or deeds; it's compulsory for the majority of these school shooters."

"I'd sure appreciate that report and thanks for talking with me. Knowing where that anomaly in the writing came from helps ease my mind some. He probably was just copying something he saw on the Internet. Still, I'd hate to miss a clue and leave these kids in danger." Wise glanced around the diner again and then let out a sigh. He seemed ready to let the matter drop. "I've kept you from your plate long enough. Go on, eat up before your cabbage gets cold." He nodded at Rainey, adding, "If Graham Dean Colde ever wakes up, you can bet your last dollar I'll be there to ask him what in the hell he was thinking."

Rainey forked a piece of ham and smiled at Wise across the table. "If he has even the slightest clue, give me a call."

#

19

Tar Heel Trace, Edgecombe County, North Carolina
2:06 p.m., Mostly Cloudy, 63°F

"Come here, you little prick."

Billy Bell grabbed the blue-haired young man's leather trench coat lapels and bent him backwards over the hood of the truck. Rainey stood by watching, sipping sweet tea through a straw, and thinking how the constraints of constitutional law were not necessarily part of country road justice.

"What the fuck is wrong with you old man?" The kid shouted, drawing the attention of others in the parking lot and those that had followed Rainey out of the store.

She watched the young man's friend carefully and inched closer to her father, in case he needed backup. Thus far, Billy had not asked for assistance and appeared to have things well in hand. Rainey had the advantage of being a bystander for now. No one noticed her. They were all too interested in her father and the spike-collared youth in his grasp.

She saw the vein bulge in her father's neck and heard him growl at his captive, "Where are your grandfather's legs?"

This all started because Rainey wanted something to drink on the way home from meeting Captain Wise. They had taken back roads, caught up on their separate lives, and ended up at a little crossroads store. The signage and appearance indicated a local hangout, where one could acquire essentials, such as fuel for any number of things, cigarettes and chewing tobacco, ice and beer, and some barbecue made from the pig roasting out back. What else could country folk need? The gravel and sand parking lot was wide and long, leaving room for the carpoolers that parked there every day. This place wasn't in the middle of nowhere; it was just between somewhere and somewhere else.

When he pulled up and parked, Billy turned to Rainey and said, "Don't act like you know me. You'll ruin my rep with that tee shirt."

"This from a man dressed like Magnum PI," Rainey replied.

Billy looked down at his clothing and commented. "My shorts are longer and nowhere near that tight."

"Thank God for small miracles," Rainey quipped.

She teased him, but understood his warning. Billy was a bail bondsman. She probably shouldn't have worn the Academy tee shirt, but she had been rushed and not thinking. Her father moved in circles that might be a bit suspicious of a federal agent. His network of informants, usually former clients, was vast and a valuable asset in the bond business. Billy was known for his fairness and ability to bring skips in without violence and with their dignity intact. Should he encounter a bond skipper or someone that knew how to find one, he wouldn't want them to spook and run because of Rainey's presence.

In some instances he let a skip run, as he had explained to Rainey years ago, "That man was ready to die rather than let me take him back to face prison time. I know this guy. He's a desperate man, not an evil one. I'll keep him running. He'll get no rest. He'll see me on every corner. Eventually, the fight will leave him and he'll be resolved to turning himself in. It's important to know the difference between the scared rabbits and the cornered wolves."

Other times, things did not go so well. If a criminal were bad enough to require deadly force to bring in, Billy would say, "I shouldn't have bailed him out." Still, Rainey had seen skips run for their lives or attempt to scratch her dad's eyes out over a three-month stint in jail for shoplifting. Force was the last resource Billy Bell would choose, but it was often chosen for him.

Rainey went into the store before her father, who said he needed to check on a pickup he saw in the parking lot. She found the drink dispenser and filled a large white foam cup with crushed ice and sweet tea. The shopping area and cash counter were crammed into the front of the store with the beverage coolers. A few old rickety men played checkers at the back of the store, seated at wooden tables in not much better physical condition. Through the screened door at the rear of the store, she could see several men drinking out of plastic cups near a smoking barbecue made from a fifty-gallon drum. Rainey thought they were probably consuming an alcoholic beverage of the illegal variety. She made her way to the counter and paid for her tea.

A kid with earrings and other shiny objects sticking out of his nose, lips, eyebrows, and even his ears came rushing in. "Hey, there's some old dude out here threatening to kick Squib's ass."

The alarm sounded; the store occupants, including Rainey, rushed into the parking lot. Squib turned out to be the young man Billy held in his grasp.

"I asked you a question," he said, smacking the kid's head on the hood of the truck for emphasis. "Where are your grandfather's legs?"

"At home, dude, chill."

"You piece of shit," Billy snarled. "That man lost his legs defending your country and you steal his money and meds. I ought to rip your throat out."

Billy put the fingers of his right hand under the boy's jawbone and squeezed. The boy gasped and fought. Billy gripped tighter. He whispered, making it hard for anyone other than Rainey to hear.

"If you fuck with Corporal Darden again, I will hunt you down. There will be no place you can hide. Do you understand me, you little prick?"

Rainey took a step forward, but she stopped when Billy slowly relinquished his grip on the boy's throat. If scaring this kid was Billy's intention, she was quite sure that had been accomplished. She also knew the mistreatment of a veteran was one of the few things that could make Billy Bell angry enough to show it.

"Where are the keys to your grandfather's truck?" Billy demanded.

"In m-m-my pocket, sir," the kid said in a shaky voice. The cocky punk attitude was gone.

Billy let him up and held out his hand, palm up. The kid produced the keys quickly, his face white with fear.

"The money too," Billy said.

The kid turned out his pockets and gave Billy a wad of bills and every coin he had.

Billy looked at the crowd. "If this boy comes up here to cash another check from Steve Darden, call the police." He pushed the kid away. "Get the fuck out of here, before I change my mind about letting you breathe another day."

"How are we supposed to get home?" Dog-collar-boy's pierced friend asked.

Billy turned and glared at him. "Walk, you fucking cowards. You've got two legs."

The boys took off running and the crowd dispersed. A couple of the old checker players, one sporting an Army veteran's hat, shook Billy's hand and thanked him. Rainey stayed back, out of the way, until everyone was gone. When her father finally acknowledged her presence, he was smiling again, the anger having subsided. He tossed her the keys to his old truck.

"Sorry to interrupt our father-daughter day, but I need to drive Darden into the VA hospital. He's in pretty bad shape. Take the truck home. I'll get Mackie to come pick me up."

"Do what you need to do," Rainey said, and then spontaneously hugged him. "I love you, Dad."

"I love you, too, Rainey Blue. I love you, too."

Some girls loved their fathers for what they could provide for them. Rainey loved hers because of the character of the man. At that moment in time, standing in a parking lot just south of somewhere, sipping sweet tea through a straw, she could not have loved Billy Bell more. He was her hero and always would be.

Chapter Two

Fourteen Years Later,
Tuesday, February 11, 2014
The Bell-Meyers Home
9:00 p.m.
Mostly Cloudy, 30°F, Windchill 23°F

"Rainey, what are you doing?"

From her vantage point, Rainey could only see her wife's thighs. She raised her head to see more, saying, "I'm trying to make you a happy camper."

"I can think of other ways to get that done. What are you doing down there?"

"I'm almost there, hang on."

"I'm hanging, but you better hurry up. I hear the pitter patter of little feet."

"I thought they were in bed," Rainey said with a grunt. The sound of a splash followed immediately and then a, "Yuck!"

Katie squatted down, blocking the light under the master bathroom sink, where Rainey's shoulders and head were. "I told you I called a plumber," she said, holding out a hand towel.

Rainey took the towel and used it to wipe the dripping water from her chin, as she slid out from under the sink. She held her closed fist in front of Katie. "Yes, but you wouldn't want to have to kiss the plumber." She opened her hand to reveal Katie's ring in her palm.

"I can't believe it was still in there," Katie exclaimed, and threw her arms around Rainey's neck.

They had no time to celebrate further, because their two-year-old triplets crashed into them, forming a giggling dog pile in the bathroom floor. Freddie, Rainey's cat, who had been observing from the sink above, bolted at the triplet's appearance.

"What are you guys doing up?" Rainey asked, laughing too. "Look, I saved Mommy's ring."

Weather came toward Rainey, opening and closing her little hands. "Ring, ring," she whispered, like Gollum.

"And I have a good idea who put it in there," Rainey said, profiling the culprit's obsession. "Miss Lord of the Rings here."

Timothy lost interest in the dog pile and was halfway under the sink. Mack, who was hopelessly devoted to Katie, clung to his mother, pointing at his sister.

"Wedder. Wedder," at least that is what Rainey thought he said.

Katie chuckled. "She's going to be called Wedder her whole life."

Weather repeated her new favorite word, "No, no, no," for no particular reason, other than she heard it often, and Rainey assumed the little klepto knew she wasn't getting the ring back.

Rainey held the ring out to Katie, "Here, put this on."

Katie took the ring, while Rainey towel dried her hair and watched Weather follow the ring.

"Where does she get this obsession with sparkly things?"

Katie corrected her, "Expensive, sparkly things."

Rainey chuckled, knowing exactly where their daughter acquired her eye for the finer things in life. She needn't point that out to Katie though. Instead she asked, "Did you ever find your diamond earrings or the necklace?"

Katie slipped the engagement ring back over her wedding band, saying, "No, I haven't and since we know from the x-rays she didn't swallow them or feed them to her brothers, I'm assuming I'll find her nest one day."

"Quite the haul she's made so far," Rainey commented and pointed at Mack. "You could always get him to rat her out. He'd do it for you."

The sound of banging came from under the sink. Rainey turned to see Timothy with the channel-lock pliers, preparing to take another big swing at the cold-water valve.

"Whoa there, Mr. Plumber-man," she said, removing the tool from the toddler's hands. "We don't need to knock that off the wall."

"Okay, back to bed," Katie said, trying to pry Mack off her shoulder so she could stand. "Let go, honey. Mommy needs to get up."

"I read the clingy stage only lasts a few months," Rainey offered as solace for Katie, who though extremely patient, looked tired these days. "At least it's not all three of them at once."

"My mother says there will come a day when I'll wish they clung to me more. At this point, I really don't see how that could be possible."

Rainey pulled Mack away from Katie, tickling his ribs to distract him from his true love. The largest of her children, Mack weighed in at an astounding thirty-three pounds at twenty-six months, large for his age, especially for a triplet. His siblings were smaller, but all were very healthy and advancing normally. The Bell-Meyers triplets were doing well, even if their parents wore thin.

Katie took only one step after standing, before Mack tore away from Rainey to attach himself to his mother's leg. "Come on, baby boy, let's get you in bed," Katie said, with no hint of aggravation.

"You are the perfect mother." Rainey complimented Katie, while grabbing Weather before she climbed onto the toilet.

"I'm a tired mother, right now," Katie said, scooping up Weather from Rainey's grasp.

"Hang in there, baby. I'll bring the plumber in a minute. He can help me put this pipe back on."

Katie moved off with Mack stumbling at her side, as he began to whine and pulled on her nightgown. Weather peeked over her mother's shoulder, waving and saying, "Bye, bye, Nee Nee,"

Rainey waved back at her, "Night, night, baby girl." She turned to Timothy, "Okay, let's put this elbow joint back where it goes."

Timothy liked hanging out with Rainey. He was the quietest of the triplets. He observed more and took his time pondering the world. Unlike the other two, he could sit still and focus on a task for long periods. He was the cerebral triplet. Rainey liked to watch him process his environment. While Mack and Weather flew headlong into new things, Timothy had a more reserved approach. Katie worried some at first, but Rainey told her to relax.

"He's just a thinker, Katie. He's fine."

He smiled at Rainey now and crawled further under the sink with her, as she ducked back in to reattach the pipe. Her kids were very different, but she loved them all the same and found it fascinating how that worked. She had enough love to go around and then some. Katie and the kids, the businesses, it was all working out perfectly. Life was good. It wasn't just a slogan on a tee shirt. Rainey only wished for one thing.

"Timothy, I was quite a bit older than you when my dad taught me how to do this. I wish you could have met him. Your granddad was a cool dude."

Timothy tried to mimic Rainey. "Coo doo."

"Yep," Rainey answered. "Cool dude."

#

Wednesday, February 12, 2014
7:30 a.m., Overcast, 25°F, Windchill 13°F

Rainey backed the van out of the garage, stopped in the driveway, and rolled down the window, as she watched Leslie, Katie's best friend, walk up to the front door.

"Good morning," Leslie said to Rainey and then waved goodbye to her girlfriend standing by the unfathomably expensive sports car in the driveway. "Bye, honey, see you later. Please leave Durham before the snow comes."

Rainey grinned at the once elusive and now obviously caught Molly Kincaid, who answered, "Don't worry. I don't plan on

27

having this car on the road with snow-challenged southern drivers."

Often employed as an investigator or expert witness for the Kincaid Law Firm, Rainey and Molly had become very good friends. It worked out well that Katie gained a friend too, when Molly brought Leslie home a few years back. Leslie was coming over to help with a project for Katie's foundation and they were all supposed to have a chili dinner and wait for the forecasted snowstorm.

Rainey teased Molly from the window of the minivan, "Aren't you two just precious?"

Molly's wit was one of the many reasons Rainey liked her. She shot back, "That minivan does nothing for your Agent Sexy mystique."

"I'm going undercover as a soccer mom," Rainey said, laughing at Molly's use of the tag name a stalker/blogger had assigned her. Rainey could laugh now that it was behind her, but not long ago "Agent Sexy" wasn't funny at all. "My car is in the shop for an upgrade."

"Are you installing a machine gun turret?"

Molly thought Rainey was incredibly paranoid and pointed it out often. Rainey liked to fuel that belief by not answering any of Molly's questions with yes or no answers, which drove the defense attorney nuts.

"I'm installing a drone launcher, so I can spy on people through their windows," Rainey said, trying desperately to sound sincere.

Molly laughed. "I would have believed the machine gun." The levity left her voice when she asked, "Are you still driving to the funeral with this storm coming?"

Rainey looked at the gray sky and sniffed the rapidly cooling air. "I think I'll be back before it gets here. You know how it is. They swear it will be a blizzard and then nothing happens." She felt the cold wind bluster in through the open window. "I can't miss this funeral."

"I understand. Be careful. I'm looking forward to taking some more of your money at poker tonight."

Molly slipped into her sports car and rolled down the driveway. Rainey was about to follow when her cell phone rang through the car speaker system. She hit a button on the steering wheel and answered.

"What did I forget?" Rainey knew it was Katie, without making the verification on the dashboard touch screen.

"Are you still in the driveway?" Katie asked.

"Yes."

"Good, then you don't have to come back. Wait there."

Rainey looked up to see Katie coming down the front steps toward her, carrying a canvas grocery bag, with her cell phone tucked under her chin.

"Since you will not listen to reason," Katie said, her voice coming through the speakers and the window Rainey had yet to close, "open the side door."

Rainey hit a button and the side door opened automatically. With triplets to wrangle, hands-free operation was a selling point when they bought the van just before Christmas. The fact that three child safety seats would fit on the second row was another.

"If you should get stuck or, God forbid, wreck during this snowstorm that you don't believe is coming"—Katie set the bag down behind the driver's seat, hung up her phone, stuffed it in her jeans pocket, and continued talking without the stereo effect of the car speakers—"even though every weather source within the United States borders says it is"—she opened one of the compartments in the floor—"here are some warmer clothes in case you need them and there are snacks, juice, and water in this middle compartment. Your tactical boots are in the bottom of the bag under your clothes, because flats and snow do not mix."

Rainey marveled at Katie's ability to multitask and stay focused enough to remain on point, even if she was working herself into a lather. She released the seatbelt latch and got out of the van. She turned Katie to her, pulled her tightly into her arms, and kissed her thoroughly. Rainey used the same philosophy Rhett Butler did with his little firecracker. Katie Meyers should be kissed, and often, but only by the woman who knew how. There had not been enough time and effort put into making that happen lately. Rainey intended to rectify that. She did not relinquish her grip until she felt Katie give into the kiss and the tension leave her body.

Katie sighed against Rainey's chest. "Damn, I needed that."

"There's more where that came from. Valentine's Day is two days away and you and I have a hotel and spa reservation. No kids, no phones, just us."

Rainey had planned the whole romantic evening. She hoped they actually took advantage of the night alone. Not like their last anniversary, when Katie's mother took the kids for twenty-four hours, most of which Rainey and Katie spent catching up on lost sleep. She had Katie's gift in her coat pocket, a diamond necklace to replace the one Weather made off with. She forgot to take it out yesterday when she came home from picking it up. It was best to just keep it with her. Rainey feared one of her girls with a passion for sparkly things might find it. In her mind, it was safer keeping it close.

"Are you planning to get me drunk and take advantage of me?" Katie asked, playfully.

"You betcha," Rainey answered, and then pecked Katie on the lips again, before releasing her embrace. "I'll be back around noon, one at the latest. If this storm does come, I will be careful and make good decisions. Remember, I've lived where it actually snowed all winter. I can handle this. I promise I will not wreck your new van."

Katie popped Rainey on the shoulder. "I am not worried about the van. I'm worried about you caught in a blizzard. This man must have been important to your father for you to do this."

"He was. The fact that I missed his call and then he was killed—" She hesitated just a bit, as the emotion scratched at her throat. She missed another call once. This one felt too much like the first. "I need to tell his wife what he meant to my dad and me, Katie. I can't miss this funeral."

"Okay, okay, I know you have to do this," Katie said, conceding, but under protest. After standing on her tiptoes to kiss Rainey one more time, she added, "We love you, Rainey Blue Bell. You be careful."

Rainey kissed the wife she loved beyond measure on the top of her head and replied, "Always."

#

8:30 a.m., Overcast, 26°F, Windchill 17°F

An hour later, heading south toward Smithfield, Rainey made a call, reciting the number to the hands-free Bluetooth system from memory.

After only one ring, the booming voice of her business partner, Miles Cecil "Mackie" McKinney, filled the car, "I just talked to your wife."

"I bet you got an earful," Rainey said. "I get one every time yours calls to bitch about the remnants of fried food she found in your truck. You know some handy wipes and a trash bag could save you a lot of trouble."

"I'd need a change of clothes too. Thelma can smell deep fried a mile away."

"It would be simpler to just do what she says."

"Simpler, but not as much fun." Mackie found himself amusing. The bass notes of his laughter vibrated the speakers in the van violently.

Rainey turned down the volume, before she continued talking. "So, how was the flight to DC? Are you ready for the big fraternity reunion?"

"We got in last night. All is well. I'm ready to dance until dawn," Mackie said with a chuckle.

"I guess that means your doctor's appointment went well yesterday."

Since his open-heart surgery last spring, Mackie had lost over a hundred pounds. He looked more like the professional football player he once was. For the first time in his life, he was eating the right kinds of food. He slipped occasionally, but it was rare. His knees were shot from years of being overweight, not to mention his time as an NFL defensive end and the wounds he suffered in Vietnam. Rainey watched Mackie 'suck it up' with the same determination that saved him and Billy Bell from certain death in the jungle. He and Rainey walked the trails at the old place on the lake three times a week, when the weather permitted. Junior trained with him at the gym twice a week. Mackie was working

31

toward a set of new knees when he reached his weight loss goal. Rainey was glad to see him taking control of his health.

"I'm cleared for full resumption of all activities, no restrictions," Mackie replied.

Rainey could hear his smile through the phone. "That's fantastic. Junior will probably be glad to hear that."

"I don't know, Rainey. Maybe we ought to leave him running the skip board. He's done a good job."

"Are you going to retire on me too?" Rainey teased. "First Ernie's only working two days a week and now you're going to bail out, aren't you?"

Junior was doing a great job. Rainey just needed this decision to be Mackie's. She wasn't about to force him into an office job unless he was ready. With Rainey's time consumed amid consulting and investigation jobs and Ernie cutting back hours, Mackie had been gradually taking over Rainey's duties in the day-to-day operations of the bail business while he recovered. Ernie still did the books, but was training Junior's new wife to take over. Billy Bell's Bail and Bait had morphed into Bell's Bail and Investigations, and the younger generations were assuming their places in the business.

"Rainey, I'm getting too old and slow to be chasing these young thugs. I think I've earned the right to sit out a few."

"I know you have. I just want you to make that call. I don't have a problem with giving Junior more responsibility, but we should also give him a bigger cut. You figure up what you think is fair and I'll sign off on it."

"I'll do that," Mackie answered, and then changed the subject. "Have you heard from Ernie?"

"Not since they left port," Rainey answered.

"She talked about that Alaska cruise for years. I'm glad she finally went."

Rainey agreed, "Me too. I don't think I've ever seen Ernie so giddy. I'm glad Henry gave in. I was afraid Katie was going to go with her and leave me with the kids."

Mackie's laughter rumbled through the van. "That might have been worth paying to see."

"I would have made you help me," Rainey said, returning his laughter.

The laughter died out and Mackie asked, "So, are you heading to Captain Wise's funeral?"

"Yes, I thought I should. He left that message about a cold case. I still have no idea what he was talking about. His phone signal was weak, so I only got a piece of it. I had that court case with Molly to wrap up and when I called back yesterday, his wife told me about the hunting accident and the funeral today. I should have called him last week."

"That's a shitty way to go for a survivor like the Captain. He and Billy lived through all that hell to get back home, only to die for no reason. It's a fucked up world."

"No kidding. I'm again reminded that life is not fair. Anyway, Katie's freaked about the weather. How bad can it get really? It never snows more than a few inches. This van is all-wheel drive. I shouldn't have any problems, even if the snow comes earlier than they predicted."

"Captain Wellman Wise was a stand-up guy. He came to pay his respects to your father. I expect Billy would want you to return the sentiment. I told Katie as much."

"Thank you, Mackie. I suppose, the next time Thelma calls I'm to tell her a little fried food now and again will not kill you, at least not instantly. I'll see you Monday at the office. Ernie has been griping about cash flow. This cold weather will have the skips hunkered down. We should be able to find a few and make her happy."

"I'll text Junior to start looking for likely targets. He'll be busy writing bonds on the Valentine's Day-gone-bad domestics this weekend and it's a full moon too. I probably shouldn't have left him on his own."

"What? And let Thelma down? She's been talking about showing off your sexy new physique to those old belles from your college stud days."

Mackie's belly laugh filled the van. "She has been eyeing me some. Romance is in the air."

"Don't tax yourself. And stay away from the fried stuff. Grease is not an aphrodisiac."

"You and Katie enjoy your Valentine's getaway. See you Monday. And you be careful in that snow, baby girl."

"Always."

#

Hominy Junction Town Cemetery
9:30 a.m., Overcast, 28°F, Windchill 18°F

Rainey couldn't concentrate on the chaplain's words. Her mind was occupied with reliving the morning her father drove her to Hominy Junction fourteen years ago, nearly to the day. She played it over in her mind on the drive down, and still she ran through it again. Captain Wise had discussed a possible school shooter threat with her. Then she and Billy drove home and ran into those punks outside the old store. Nothing else stood out about that day. Rainey had mailed the school shooter report to the Captain after she returned to Quantico and never heard from him again, until her father's memorial service. Now, she was attending his burial in a quaint little cemetery on the outskirts of the hometown Wellman Wise had loved enough to return to, after serving his country. His country was thanking him today.

Rainey's body jerked with the sound of the first rifle volley from the military honor guard. The memories flooded back of another military funeral, almost five years ago. Two more volleys followed the first; each sending remembered shock waves of heartbreak through her soul. Rainey recalled that she held it together at her father's service, until the first notes of "Taps" began to reverberate across the surface of Jordan Lake and did her in. She lost it and Mackie put his huge arm around her and pulled her under his shoulder, as if he could shield her from the pain.

Her mother was there. Rainey recalled being surprised at how Billy's death had seemed to deeply touch Constance. She had never thought about her parents caring for one another, even though she knew the story of their elopement. She saw real pain in her mother's eyes as the last notes of "Taps" echoed on the water and faded away. Looking back, Rainey thought that was probably the first time she realized her mother was human.

A soldier had approached Rainey, bearing the folded American flag that accompanied her father's ashes during the memorial service.

"This flag is presented on behalf of a grateful nation and the United States Army as a token of appreciation for your loved one's honorable and faithful service. God bless you and this family, and God bless the United States of America."

Rainey remembered hesitating to take the flag from the soldier's hands. It was Ernie who actually thanked the man, took it, and placed it in Rainey's lap. She kissed her on the forehead and whispered, "He loved you more than life itself."

The rest of that day was a blur, except for a conversation with Captain Wellman Wise. It was the reason she felt compelled to come and show her respects to a man she met three times in her life. Rainey remembered it as clearly as the day it happened. It played out before her mind's eye, as Captain Wise's wife received her own flag and the thanks of a grateful nation.

He had found her standing on the end of the dock alone. "I'm going to miss fishing with your father," he said upon his approach. "He loved this place."

Rainey wiped the tears from her cheeks and replied, "Yes, he did." She gathered herself a bit more and added, "Thank you for coming, Captain."

"I needed to pay my respects to the man to whom I owe my life, at least all that came after he dragged me out of the jungle nearly dead. Your father was a real hero, Rainey Bell. You should know that."

"A hero that died the victim of a senseless drive-by shooting," Rainey said, some of the anger she had been suppressing rising to the surface.

"You're angry and you should be. Nothing I can say will take that away, but I need to tell you about my last mission in Vietnam. It concerns you. You see, I knew who you were before you knew Billy Bell existed."

He handed Rainey a handkerchief and began his tale.

"I was on a special mission. Your father and six other soldiers were my escorts. The mission was highly classified due to the fact we were crossing into a country we had no legal right to be in. The facts don't matter now, other than you have to know we were not going to be rescued if something went wrong."

"Something went wrong, I'm assuming," Rainey commented.

"Yes, very wrong. I'm pretty sure it was a trap from the get go, that our information was compromised, but that wasn't my main concern after getting shot in an ambush. Four out of the seven of us survived the initial assault. We managed to lay down enough fire to escape into the jungle, but I was shot up pretty good. I figured I was going to die there and my wife would never know where or how, but your father wasn't about to let that happen."

Rainey smiled for the first time in days, when she said, "He used to tell me, 'As long as you're breathing, there is always hope.'"

Captain Wise nodded. "He said that to me that day. He patched my wounds and, although the other two guys wanted him to leave me, thinking I was dead already and going to slow them down, he refused to give up on me. I'll never forget what he did. He looked those men in the eye and smiled. I kid you not, we are about to die, me especially, and he's grinning like the Cheshire cat."

Rainey chuckled. Her father's laughing face appeared in her memory. "He always did that. He'd survive something that would kill another man and he'd laugh, like it was just a twist in the game of life he was playing."

"He did have that air about him," Wise said. "He told those boys, 'Y'all go on, if you need to. Me and the Captain, we'll be right along. If you get to base before me, explain how you left us here to the brass, 'cause I'm sure I'm gonna want a beer rather than deal with that shit.' "

"Did they stay?"

"Yes, but only because I think they truly believed he really would make it out alive without their help, but they weren't so sure they could make it out without his. For two days, they carried me, until we reached a point we could be air lifted out. For those two days, when we would stop, your father would show me a picture of a baby with a mass of thick dark curls on her head. He told me stories of where he wanted to take her and the things he wanted to teach her, how special she was, and how he knew he was still alive because of her, because she needed him to be."

Rainey choked on the emotion welling inside.

Captain Wise put his hand on her shoulder. "That was you, Rainey. When I saw him again, many years later, the first thing we talked about was you, how proud he was, and how it had been true—he survived because of you."

The voice at her side snapped her back to the present.

"Are you Agent Bell?"

Rainey looked up to see a tall man who looked a lot like Wellman Wise. "Yes, well, I was. I'm just Rainey Bell, now."

"I'm Bill Wise. My mother wanted me to ask you to be sure to come by the house. I know with the weather coming you'll want to get on the road, but it seems important to her."

Rainey stood up. "I'm so very sorry for your loss. Please tell you mother I'll be happy to stop by."

The man smiled, reminding Rainey of his father. "Just follow the processional back to the house. I'll make sure Mom knows you're coming and we'll get you back on the road as soon as possible."

Bill Wise walked away and as the crowd of mourners thinned, Rainey stepped up to the coffin. On her way to the tent covering the site, she had been handed a long stemmed white rose. She placed it on the top of the coffin with all the others.

"Say hello to Billy for me," Rainey said. "Godspeed, Captain Wellman Wise."

#

10:30 a.m., Overcast, 28°F, Windchill 18.6°F

"Katie, I was at a funeral. I had my phone turned off."

Rainey called home on the way to the Captain's house. Katie had become an amateur weatherman and was reporting all the reasons Rainey should already be on her way home, and scolding her for not answering the phone. The state of North Carolina was in a panic, stirred up sufficiently enough by the snowfall predictions to cancel school before the storm arrived. Katie, in her fatigued and emotional state of late, had gotten caught up in the constant weather bulletins and dire warnings of a historic blizzard. Calling home, Rainey thought, may have been a mistake.

"Nobody turns the phone off. They put it on vibrate so they know someone is trying to reach them."

"*They* should tell someone *they* are attending a funeral so that someone will leave a message and wait for a return call, like this one."

"Whatever, Rainey, just come home."

"I will, but first I have to stop at the house. Captain Wise's wife asked to see me."

"She didn't see you at the service? Doesn't she know the weather is going to get bad?"

"Katie, chill out. I'm sure Mrs. Wise had other things on her mind while putting her husband in the ground."

The phone went silent for a few seconds. Rainey could hear the kids in the background, loudly banging pots and pans, a favorite nerve-racking pastime. As patient as Katie had been with the triplets and their demanding needs, rarely appearing overwhelmed, the first months of age two had begun to challenge her limits. Rainey waited to see what sort of reaction her "chill out" comment would bring. She was pleasantly surprised when Katie spoke again.

"I am so sorry. My whining must be getting on your nerves. Of course, do what you have to do. Please be careful and call me before you leave."

"I will. Is Molly back yet?"

"No, but she's on her way. She went home to change cars. She's bringing Joey and his friend, Theodore. Leslie didn't want Joey to have to stay at Molly's alone, if she can't get home tonight. You might be missing a slumber party, if you can't make it back."

"Who's Theodore?" Rainey asked, not liking strangers in her home if she wasn't there.

"You remember him. He worked on the computers at the women's center with Joey."

"Oh yeah. Man that kid's weird. Who actually goes by the name Theodore? You'd think he would have given himself a nickname, if no one else did."

"Rainey, you're terrible. Theodore is eccentric, not weird. I thought you liked him. You talked about computers for an hour."

"I talked about computers. He wanted to talk about the BAU. He's a "Criminal Minds" junkie."

"So are a lot of people. Does that make them all weird?"

"No, just naïve if they think that's how it is, jetting from one crime scene to another. And the dress code is not quite that sexy."

"How would you know if you haven't seen it?"

"Sometimes there isn't much on the tube when a baby is teething. It was either Shaun T or Derrick Morgan. I mostly just marveled at the team's ability to be so many places at once."

The car in front of Rainey braked and then pulled to the curb. A steady stream of people exited cars and formed a line walking up to a small, restored Victorian home.

"Well, it looks like I'm here," she said to Katie, and pulled the van over to park.

Katie's end of the call went silent again. Rainey assumed she was preoccupied with a toddler, but that wasn't the case at all. When she spoke, Katie's voice was soft and loving. This was the Katie that knew all Rainey's secrets, the wife and lover, not the mother of their children. This was the woman who knew the losses of Rainey's life and loved her through the recovery.

"Rainey, I know that service was hard on you. I'm sorry you had to do it alone. I wish I could have been there for you. If we had more notice, I could have come with you."

"I know, honey. Thank you. I'm okay. Besides," Rainey laughed to lighten the conversation, "we wouldn't want us both stuck in the snow."

"It's a good thing you're cute," Katie said. "Hurry up and get home. It's supposed to start snowing after noon. You just might make it before it gets bad."

"I will do my best," Rainey promised.

"Be careful. I love you." Katie's voice grew fainter and Rainey realized she was now on speakerphone. "Tell Nee Nee bye bye."

A chorus of bye byes rained down on her from the speakers. "Bye, bye," Rainey replied. "I love you, too."

Chapter Three

The Home of Captain and Mrs. Wellman Wise
10:58 a.m.
Overcast, 28°F, Windchill 17.5°F

Rainey flipped the collar up on her full-length, black wool coat and pulled the white silk muffler a little tighter. This was her first winter without long hair and she had yet to grow accustomed to the cold on her neck and ears. She looked up at what had been a clear but crisp day to see menacing gray clouds closing in. The further south she had driven from home, the more blue sky she had seen and thought maybe she had been correct about the weather prognosticators exaggerating again. These clouds suggested that Katie's forecast was closer to the truth than Rainey's doubts.

She joined the mourners walking quietly toward the Wise home, hands jammed in their pockets, shoulders hunched against the cold. There were whispered words between a few, but for the most part the processional into the house was somber. As she moved with what appeared to be the bulk of the town's population, Rainey noticed that the Mayor's prediction of the suburbs catching up to Hominy Junction had been correct. The once dying town had rejuvenated with the influx of new blood. Fresh coats of paint and a bit of remodeling replaced the decrepit and falling down. A glance over her shoulder toward Main Street showed vibrant village shops now surrounding the still operating drug store in the middle of the block. Hominy Junction was reborn, but today it laid one of its native sons to rest.

"The circle of life," Rainey whispered to herself.

Nearing the porch, she began to hear music. When the front door opened, Creedence Clearwater Revival's "Run Through the Jungle" poured out to the street. Rainey didn't know what she expected, but this wasn't it. Upon entering the Wise home, Rainey saw wall-to-wall people, most holding paper plates with little white-bread ham sandwich squares and a pickle slice. She smiled, remembering the Captain saying he snuck off to the diner for white bread so his wife would not know. It was sweet that she was serving his favorite at what Rainey now understood was a celebration of his life and not meant as a memorial for his loss.

Rainey handed her coat and scarf to a vaguely familiar looking man in the foyer. She checked to make sure her concealed holster was still clipped securely to the back of her slacks and covered by her suit jacket. Funeral or not, life good or not, Rainey Bell went nowhere unarmed. Yes, maybe she was a little paranoid, as Molly liked to point out, but so far it had served her well. The thing about criminals was they did not wear signs stating their intentions. If they did, it would be so much easier to see them coming.

Rainey's recent history proved she was no better at picking the murderer in the room than anyone else, at least not until they gave her a hint. The fading scar on her cheek and the permanent one on her chest and torso were daily reminders of how close evil could get, before tipping its hand. It was a common misconception that behavioral analysts could "read" people a la Sherlock Holmes, but even Sherlock had his Miss Adler, who outwitted the great detective.

After the cheek scar-causing incident last spring, Rainey had to explain to Katie why she did not see the danger coming until it was almost too late.

"I'm an analyst, not a psychic. What I did for the BAU was an after-the-crime activity, based on developing a criminal profile from crime scene analysis and other evidence. It takes a different skill set to interpret the behavior of a known person as opposed to that of an unknown subject. I wasn't looking for a psychopath, and even if I was, I saw only what I was allowed to see. I can see more at a crime scene of a criminal's true personality than I can across the dinner table from them. Hence, the reason I am always armed. You just never know."

Weapon secured, Rainey went in search of Mrs. Wise. One of the first things Rainey learned, as a behavioral analyst, was she never really knew a person until she saw where they lived and what they held sacred. As she wandered from room to room in Captain Wise's home, she saw that family, God, and country were his sacred things. He and his wife lived in an uncluttered, restored Victorian. Pictures of the family were placed tastefully around the rooms. A few pieces of art depicting old farmhouses hung on the walls. The furniture appeared soft and inviting, meant to be lived in. This was a family home, nothing showy, or frilly.

Making her way to the food table, Rainey recognized the woman serving. She was fourteen years older, but definitely the girl named Leda from the diner. She was smiling now, her head held high, shoulders back and proud. Rainey could only guess what had turned a sad, browbeaten teenager into a blossoming young woman, but she imagined it had something to do with not seeing her hostile mother anywhere around. She took a plate and exchanged smiles with Leda, while thinking, *"Good for you."*

Rainey found a corner to stand in, hoping to spot Mrs. Wise or her son in the still growing crowd. Creedence was now singing about being born on the bayou, while she ate her sandwich and people watched. She noticed the guy that took her coat standing with a tall ginger-haired man and then it dawned on her where she had seen them both before. These were two of the basketball players she had seen at the diner. She wondered if the one named Skylar set the record that night. He and the ginger-haired man, she thought they had called him G, were coming toward her and the opportunity to ask him was about to present itself, when a very pretty blonde stopped them just a few feet from where Rainey stood. She listened to their conversation, because there was nothing else to do but wait for Mrs. Wise to appear.

"Hey, Sky," the blonde said, a bit of flirtatiousness in her voice.

Skylar smiled, still possessing perfect teeth, only now bleached unnaturally white. "Ellie," he said, and hugged her, "How's life on the farm?"

She winked at him, "You'll have to come out and visit again, now that the work is done on the house."

G took his turn at hugging Ellie, bending down to the shorter blonde. "You look good enough to eat."

"Thank you, Gordon. Always the ladies' man," Ellie said, quite coquettishly Rainey thought.

She had also learned that G stood for Gordon, and apparently an initial for a name is only cool if you're a rapper or a teenage baller.

"I'm sorry I haven't been out to see you, yet. I heard about Burgess," Gordon said. "What a freak thing to happen."

The freak thing that happened to Burgess did not appear to distress Ellie at all. The explanation for her lack of concern came with her comment. "Burgess and I split up a year before it happened. Our divorce would have been finalized five days after it happened. I tell people I was one week short of being a divorcee instead of a widow. Timing is everything." She punctuated her punch line with a little giggle.

The men chuckled uneasily at Ellie's dark sense of humor.

Ellie seemed to realize how callous she sounded and attempted to recover with, "Of course, I was completely devastated. I still can't understand how he ingested peanuts. He was always so careful. And the EpiPen not working has always been a mystery." Her attempt to fake some emotion with her follow-up statement of, "I loved him a long time. I really miss him," amused Rainey enough to force her to turn away to hide a smile.

Ellie, Rainey recalled, had witnessed her parents' murder and the shooting of her brother. She had also pulled the trigger on another human being. Bad guy or not, shooting someone was traumatic to the average person. A certain amount of emotional disconnect could be expected from trauma like that. Rainey thought it might explain Ellie's apparent lack of emotion concerning the death of a man to whom she was married, or she was simply a cold-hearted bitch.

Skylar spoke next. "Yeah, Burgess was a good guy. So was your brother. Ely and I might have butted heads in high school over Cassie, but after he was shot, we became good friends. I couldn't believe it when I heard he was dead."

Gordon may have taken on an adult name, but his tact was still that of a clueless teenager. He proceeded to stick his foot firmly in his mouth. "How in the hell do you drown putting in a boat? I heard he was drunk as a skunk."

Skylar looked up at his old friend and shook his head. "You know, you are never going to change. You are still a dumb jock. I'm going to get a beer. Ellie, you want one?"

Ellie said, "Sure," but hung back long enough to pat Gordon's chest and reassure him. "It's okay, G. I wondered the same thing when Ely died. Come on, Skylar will get over it. Let's have a beer for old time sake."

So, Ellie wasn't a total bitch, Rainey noted and looked for someone else to watch as they moved away. Leda had come from behind the table and was moving about the room, picking up empty plastic cups and plates. Rainey finished the last bite of her sandwich just as Leda approached.

"I'll take that," she said, smiling at Rainey and pointing at her empty plate.

"Thank you. It was delicious," Rainey replied, handing it over.

"Mr. Wise loved those sandwiches, bless his soul. Were you a close friend? I don't remember seeing you around here. I'm Leda, by the way, Leda Mann Janson."

Rainey wasn't the only person checking people out it seemed.

"It's nice to meet you, Leda. My name is Rainey Bell. My father served with Captain Wise."

"Well, you look lonely over here by yourself. If you need company, you can come chat with me over at the food table. I have some brownies I haven't put out yet. Make sure you get one. It's momma's recipe. Mr. Wise loved them. I suppose she can cook them in heaven for him now."

Ah, so that explained the transformation Leda had undergone. The mother that terrorized her died. Rainey never wished her mother dead, during the turbulent times of their relationship, but gone far away. A place with no phones would have been good. They got along now, since the babies came, but they still had moments. Rainey found herself reminding Constance that saving her life last spring did not equate permission to stick her nose in it.

A teenaged boy stepped up to Leda. "Mom, I put the last bags of ice in the cooler on the back porch. Anything else?"

Rainey saw it and she was sure everyone else in town saw it too. Leda's son looked just like Skylar. From her observation of Leda and Skylar fourteen years ago, she would never have put the two of them together in a million years. Yet, there was no denying that kid was related to the handsome former basketball star. Body language proved it when Skylar crossed close by and Leda saw him. She instinctually moved between her son and the man that was probably his father.

Just when Rainey was finding this little nonverbal communication interesting, another complication was added to the story when the teenager saw someone across the room and said, "Dad's here."

He wasn't looking at Skylar, but at a man that looked nothing like him.

"Go see if he'll take you to the gym, honey. I don't think I should leave while all these people are still here."

"Okay, Mom."

"If it starts to snow, don't walk home. One of us will pick you up at the gym."

Leda watched him cross the room to the man he called Dad. Dad looked over, smiled and waved at Leda, as she returned the gesture. Genuine affection there, Rainey thought. She followed Leda's eyes to Skylar and saw indisputable contempt. There was definitely animosity and a story between those two.

"How old is your son?" Rainey asked, curious now, and it was an innocent question, almost.

Leda turned back to her, "He'll be fourteen in the fall. They grow so fast. Do you have any children?"

"Two year old triplets, a girl and two boys," Rainey said, with some pride and a wide smile.

"Oh, bless your heart. You must be exhausted, but how wonderful for you. I hear people say horrible things to multiples' mothers, like 'I'm glad it's you, not me', and I always think, 'I'm glad it's not you either'. You are lucky to have all that love in your house, I say."

"Thank you, we think so," Rainey said.

"Does your husband help you? Benjy was great with Taylor. Both the men in my life are just as sweet as they can be."

"I don't have a husband," Rainey answered, leaving just enough time for the reaction, and then said, "but I do have a wife." She reached in her jacket pocket, pulled out her phone, woke up the screen, and turned it toward Leda. "We took this at Christmas," she said, beaming.

Leda took the phone and examined the picture. "What a beautiful family you have. Your wife is simply gorgeous."

"Yes, she is," Rainey said, receiving the phone back from Leda.

"Well, it's been very nice meeting you, Rainey Bell. I need to get back to the table. Don't forget to get a brownie."

"I will, but don't tell my wife. She's limiting my sugar."

Leda laughed. "Shame on her, but I promise your secret is safe with me."

Rainey turned her attention back to the room and was just about to take another turn through the house to look for Bill Wise, when a voice spoke at her elbow.

"Rainey?"

She turned to see Mrs. Wise looking up at her.

"Yes, Mrs. Wise, I'm Rainey Bell. I'm so sorry for your loss. Your husband was a great friend of my father's."

"Your father was very important to us. I almost didn't recognize you with the short hair. It's very attractive, by the way."

"I'm sorry, have we met before?"

"Yes, I met you at your father's memorial service, but I doubt you will remember me. You were so devastated."

"I'm sorry, I don't recall much from that day, but I do remember your husband and what he said to me. I will cherish his words, always."

"Would you come with me?" Mrs. Wise asked, beckoning with her hand for Rainey to follow. "Wellman left some things on his desk I think he meant you to see."

Rainey followed the shorter woman, stopping with her when people wanted to offer condolences, until they reached a closed door at the end of the main hall.

"This is Wellman's study. His sanctuary, as he called it." Her eyes filled with tears, but she gathered herself and opened the door.

Rainey followed her into the study. The walls were lined with military memorabilia and the bookshelves with military history books, except one small section. Rainey recognized those books, written by former profilers and criminal psychologist, as the same ones she had in her office at home. A laptop was open on the desk.

"Captain Wise had a laptop? I'm impressed," Rainey commented.

"After he took that class with the FBI, he set about teaching himself to be computer literate. It kept him busy. It also gave him and Bill something to do together, even long distance."

"Good for him. I'm glad he found the class inspiring. That's where I met him first, but I did not know who he was or that he was a friend of my father's. In fact, I knew nothing of their experience in Vietnam until Captain Wise told me at Dad's service."

"Our son, Bill, is named after your father."

"I'm sure he was honored," Rainey said, realizing the full scope of her father's importance to this family. "What can I do for you, Mrs. Wise?"

"Please, call me Harriet." She moved over to the desk. "I wouldn't let Bill touch this file until I could show it to you. Look here."

Rainey stepped around the desk and looked at the legal pad where Harriet pointed. On the top of the page she saw her name and the phone number for the office.

"He left a message, but I called back too late," Rainey said. "The message was garbled, a bad connection, so I'm not sure what he wanted. He said something about a cold case, but I have no idea what that meant."

"Maybe he meant the Colde case, Graham Dean Colde, with an e."

Ding, ding, ding, the bell went off in Rainey's head. "Oh, the kid who shot his neighbors. We talked about that when my dad brought me to see the captain, fourteen years ago this week as a matter of fact. Did he wake up from the coma?"

"Oh yes, he woke up. Could not remember a thing. The doctors at the state hospital kept him there five years. He had to learn how to do everything again, just like a baby. When he turned twenty-one, they saw no need to keep him anymore. A judge agreed that it was cruel and unusual punishment to keep a man in prison for something he did not know he had done. They said he was not a danger to himself or others; so the judge let him go, even let him change his name to avoid the stigma of what he had done as a child. Wellman supported that decision."

"He supported letting a double murderer out of prison?" Rainey asked, just to verify she heard Harriet correctly.

"Yes, he did. Of course, he never believed the whole story was ever told. He was sure someone else was involved or put the Colde boy up to it. He was obsessed with that list. Especially when the people on it started dropping like flies." She moved some papers and produced a thick file. She handed it to Rainey. "I think he wanted you to see this. I can't imagine what else it could be. I don't know what he found, but he was desperate to talk to you about something. He called you that morning and then—"

Harriet started to cry, but reeled it back in and took a deep breath. Strong woman, Rainey thought.

"I'm sorry. It's just that I don't believe a hunter shot Wellman accidently. No one came forward, not that I expect someone to admit to firing wildly in the woods, but it just makes no sense. Wellman did not hunt. He fished, but he still wore a bright orange vest whenever he was out in the woods. People hunt with rifles that are too powerful and have no idea where their bullets end up, he would say. He was very cautious about that."

Rainey was taken aback. "Are you saying you think he was murdered?"

Harriet looked Rainey in the eyes and said, "I do, and I think the answer to who did it is in this folder or on that computer. The last thing he said to me about it was, 'If I'm right, more people are going to die,' and then he did."

"He didn't tell you what he thought he was right about?"

"No, he did not share that information with me." She touched the desk, trailing her fingertips over her husband's things, "I would like to leave you with his notes to see if you can figure out what he meant. I need to go back out and see to the guests. It keeps me from being so damn angry." Harriet looked up at Rainey. "Find out if my husband was murdered because of what is on this desk."

Rainey knew the snow was coming. She knew Katie would be pissed if she dallied around and got stuck here, but what else could she do? Billy would have expected, no demanded, that she stay and figure this out, if she could. If there were any question Harriet or her son was in danger, Billy would have been there for them. Since he could not be, the duty fell to Rainey.

"Let me call home and tell Katie I'll be later than expected," Rainey said. "I can't promise anything, but I'll be glad to take a look and see what I can see."

Harriet spontaneously hugged her. "Thank you, Rainey." She released her from the hug and took Rainey's hands in hers. "Billy used to come down to fish with Wellman. He always spoke of you with such pride. I can see it was not without merit."

Rainey smiled. "Well then, I shall try to live up to my father's billing."

#

11:35a.m., Overcast, 28.9°F, Windchill 20°F

"Are you leaving now?" Katie asked without saying hello.

"No, I need to stay. There's something I need to do for Mrs. Wise."

"Can't you go back another day? If you don't leave now, you'll never make it home tonight. I'm not whining, I just want you home safe so I can stop worrying."

"Don't worry about me. I'll be fine, and you've got plenty of help there." Rainey sighed. She'd really rather be home too. "They named their son after my dad, Katie. I really can't ignore this request."

"What does she want you to do?"

"Find out if someone killed her husband. She could just be trying to make sense of a tragedy, but she's convinced this case he wanted to talk to me about caused his death."

"How do you mean 'caused'?" Katie asked, a bit of concern in her voice.

"Like this wasn't a hunting accident and if that is true, the murderer is probably in this house right now."

"Oh, now that's comforting. You won't be driving in a blizzard, but you may be stuck in it with a killer on the loose. Rainey, life with you is never boring."

"I know, honey, but at least this time I'm not the one in danger."

"Not yet," Katie said, "but if you find out what Captain Wise discovered you're going to be, or had that not crossed your mind."

"Let's not go there. Look, I'll go over this information, and if I can still get home tonight, I will. If not, I'll find a place to stay and come home in the morning."

"All right. I'm sure nothing I can say would change your mind. I love you. Call me later and please be careful."

"Always," Rainey replied, adding, "I love you, too. Kiss the babies for me."

"No. I'm telling them you abandoned us in a blizzard."

Rainey laughed. "You be nice. Talk to you soon."

After hanging up with Katie, Rainey pulled off her jacket and hung it on the back of the desk chair. She took her holster off and set the weapon on the desk. This was going to take a while and sitting with a nine millimeter poking in her back was not comfortable. She unbuttoned the cuffs of her white silk blouse and rolled up her sleeves before opening the thick file.

She said aloud, "Okay, Captain Wise, what did you want to show me?"

On the inside cover of the file, Wise had taped down a copy of the hate rant and the list of names from fourteen years ago. The first page of the stack of papers had a title at the top: "The List" and contained the same list of names with a notation beside each.

> Skylar Sweet – Went to college, played basketball, got a degree, and came home to run the family farm. Still a ladies' man. Cheats on his wife.

> Gordon Terrell – Never left town. Has worked in construction, farming, but mostly works as a hunting guide, when he isn't high on weed. Does a lot of work for Skylar.

> Adam Goodwin – Went to college, graduated, started his own insurance business. Missing as of April 2013. Went to the beach with fraternity friends. Said he was going to meet someone from high school for a drink and never returned to the cottage. Body never found.

> Burgess Read – Married Ellie Paxton after college and moved to Wilmington to work for one of the studios. In February 2013, died from allergic reaction, accidental ingestion of peanut oil. Found homemade cake, partially eaten. After testing, peanut oil found in the cake. No info on how he got the cake or who made it. EpiPen found near body had been used. Possible malfunction of EpiPen. Possible

product tampering? Possible intentional poisoning. Ellie and Burgess were divorcing and she had not lived at the home in twelve months. She was living in Raleigh when contacted about the death.

Benjy Janson – Married Leda Mann. Lives in town. They took over the diner after Doris died in 2001. Son Taylor is obviously Skylar Sweet's kid. Rumors of Leda's rape by members of the basketball team January 2000 – Skylar & Gordon raped her, Adam and Ely witnesses, never confirmed by Leda publicly, but it happened, no doubt.

Ely Paxton – May 2005 Killed in an accident while putting his boat in at the sandpit. Trailer hitch came loose while he was standing on the ramp behind the boat, which was still on the trailer. Trailer was not chained to truck???? Pinned underwater. No witnesses. Toxicology report said .18 blood-alcohol content. Never known to be a big drinker???

Cassie Gillian – June 2001 after graduation, dead of apparent suicide or accidental drug overdose of sleeping pills. No clues as to where she obtained the drugs and no evidence of prior drug use.

Ellie Paxton Read – Married Burgess Read and moved to Wilmington. Worked as an extra in some movies.

Returned to town January 2014, after
Burgess's estate settled.

"Damn," Rainey said to herself. "If my name was on that list, I'd be worried."

She flipped the page out of the way. The next thing in the folder was a copy of the case file for the Paxton murders. Rainey read through it, paying close attention to the autopsy reports for the deceased, medical information on Ely Paxton and Graham Colde's wounds, and the statement Ellie Paxton gave that morning. Nothing jumped out at Rainey as unusual or unnoticed by the investigators. Their reports were well documented and thorough. Without the anomaly of the transcript of the Eric Harris rant in the shooter's pocket, it looked very much like Graham Dean Colde was a suicidal, depressed, love sick juvenile with access to weapons.

Graham Colde apparently walked into his neighbor's unlocked back door to retrieve his father's M1 Garand rifle that had been placed in Mr. Paxton's care. Elbert Paxton, who had slept on the couch, confronted the intruder at the base of the stairs to the second floor. Mr. Paxton died instantly of a rifle shot to the face. His wife, Jane, was next, dying much the same way. She came down the stairs in her nightgown, probably after hearing the shot that killed her husband, and caught a bullet in the brain. Ely was awake by this time and dove down the stairs onto Graham. He wrestled with the much smaller boy, dislodging the rifle from his grasp. Graham then pulled a knife and began to swing wildly. Ellie followed Ely down the stairs, picked up the rifle, and shot Graham Colde twice, once in the head and once in the upper chest, narrowly missing vital organs. The chest shot went through Colde and into Ely's shoulder.

No one had any reason to doubt that was exactly what happened on February 1, 2000. The evidence lined up and the stories matched. Graham Colde was placed in custody of the State Mental Hospital until such time as he either awoke from his coma or died of natural causes. His case was to be adjudicated when and if he was ever fit to stand trial. After five years, in April of 2005, Colde was freed on the recommendation of the state's psychiatrist and the prosecutor, with the stipulation that he not move back to Hominy Junction. His name was changed and there was no further record in the folder of what happened to him.

Rainey looked up from the file upon a knock at the study door.

"Come in," she said, after closing the file.

Bill Wise opened the door carrying a tray containing a cup of coffee and a brownie on a small paper plate.

"Mom didn't want you to miss the brownies. Dad loved them."

"Thank you," Rainey answered, as Bill sat the tray down on the front of the desk. "I heard they were delicious."

"Best I've ever eaten," Bill said.

Rainey watched his eyes trail around the study.

"I'm going to miss that old man," he said, his voice a bit shaky.

"He was very kind. My father thought a lot of him and so did I."

"Your father was Billy Bell. I'm named after him, you know. Did you see this picture?"

He crossed the room to the far wall. Rainey stood and followed him. He pointed at a picture of three variously bandaged, smiling soldiers standing around a hospital bed with a young Captain Wise, looking a lot like Bill Wise did today. The man at the Captain's right shoulder was a grinning young twenty-something Billy Bell.

"They came to see him, after they carried him out of the jungle. Your father was my father's hero. He could never say enough about how much he owed Master Sergeant Bell. I met him, your father. You look like him, the same eyes and hair."

"He certainly couldn't deny I was his, now could he?" Rainey said with a chuckle. "I'm pretty sure your dad couldn't deny you either. You look a lot like he did in this picture."

"They were brave, weren't they?" Bill commented, gazing at a photo he'd seen a thousand times, but today saw with the eyes a mourning child.

Rainey looked into her father's smiling face. "My dad used to say he wasn't brave, just terrified of getting killed. He said it was highly motivating."

"Well I, for one, am glad he was motivated." Bill took another look at the picture and sighed, before turning back to Rainey. "Is there anything I can help you with? I have his passwords, if you need them." He smiled, as Rainey saw a memory pass before him. "Dad could never remember his passwords, but he wouldn't write them down for 'security reasons,' he would say."

Rainey winked at Bill. "We taught him that at Quantico."

Bill chuckled. "Yeah, that class lit a fire under him. He wanted to know how to do it all after that. I am a programmer, so I helped when he got stuck, but he mostly taught himself. He even signed up for a Facebook account about two years ago."

"Now, that, we would have not advised at Quantico."

Bill moved over to the desk. "He said he wanted to be able to talk to his old military buddies. I also think he was using it to collect information for his ongoing investigation."

Rainey had her own anonymous account for that same purpose. Skips were not always conscious of privacy settings and sometimes stupid enough to post pictures and check into locations, identifying exactly where Bell's Bail could find them. She had accounts for all the most popular social media sites. It was a good investigative tool.

Rainey remarked, "In that case, it wasn't a bad idea. Can you open his Facebook page? I'd like to see his friends list, who he may have been following."

Bill sat down at the desk, noticed Rainey's weapon, and shot her a questioning look.

She shrugged her shoulders and answered his unspoken question, "Trouble seems to find me. I just like to be prepared when it does."

"I live in Chapel Hill. I've seen quite a bit of your trouble play out on the evening news. You sure have Billy Bell's survival instincts."

"I think we have that 'terrified of being killed' motivation in common."

Rainey smiled to ease the tension. People never knew what to say to her. The world had been treated to a meticulous account of the most horrific times of her life. It made for pitiful looks and anxious moments when strangers learned who she was and remembered the story of her rape and torture plastered all over the news. She preferred the tongue-tied and shoe-top gazing types to the ones who asked rude questions about details, or tried to get a peek at the scar. That always amazed her, and at times, she was less than tactful in her response. It was best to just move on and let it pass.

She asked, "Did he sign on as himself?"

Taking the cue, Bill replied, "Yes," and redirected his attention to the laptop, hitting the spacebar to wake the screen. "I was checking his email earlier, so we don't have to wait for it to power up."

He typed in the password to open the desktop. A few more keystrokes and Wellman Wise's Facebook page appeared. Bill clicked on the page to reveal his father's list of friends.

"Anyone in particular jump out at you, Bill?"

"Well, I see Skylar Sweet, Ellie Paxton Read, Benjy and Leda—huh," he paused for a second, "Adam Goodwin's page is still active. I guess his family is hoping he'll show back up."

"Did you know Adam?" Rainey asked.

"He was about five years younger than me. He was some kid running around the gym when I still lived here, but he joined my fraternity at State, so I would see him at alumni social functions."

"Did you know the fraternity brothers he went to the beach with that weekend?"

"How do you know about—," he glanced at the folder, "Oh, yeah, Dad's theory. Yes, I knew those guys. No one has a clue what happened. They've been back weekend after weekend, walking the beach, looking for any sign. Adam simply vanished, no car, no body, just gone."

"What can you tell me about your Dad's theory?"

"Not much. Just that he thought someone was killing off the people on that list they found on Graham Colde the morning he shot the Paxtons."

"Do you know if he mentioned his theory to anyone else, maybe spooked someone?"

Bill pushed back from the desk. "My mom told you she thinks he was murdered, didn't she?"

There was no use trying to dodge the question. Rainey answered, "She did say she was concerned that it may not have been a hunting accident. What do you think?"

"I think he went fishing and some kid out hunting with his father accidently shot him, and they both ran away scared shitless. It would have made no difference if they stayed or got help. He died almost instantly."

"A kid? What makes you say that?"

"The forensics guys determined the direction the shot came from. They walked that line. They found two sets of footprints. One was probably an adult male. The others were small, like a kid. The small footprints came closest to where my dad was and then went back to the adult prints."

"That's a plausible scenario. I take it ballistic tests were of no help?"

"We know it was a 30-06 caliber bullet shot from an M1 Garand."

"That's an interesting coincidence. That same model of rifle was used in the Paxton murders."

"My dad has one in the gun safe. It's a soldier's rifle. Lots of hunters use them too."

"And they did not find any brass?" Rainey's mind was churning.

"No, they didn't—even used metal detectors—but it's pretty thick in there."

"But they could see the footprints?"

Bill's brain was turning, too. "Yes, and that's weird, now that you mention it."

"What's in season right now? I know it's not deer." Rainey was fighting the presumption that Bill's father had been murdered, but with every answer, she felt more ill at ease.

"Squirrel, rabbit, and you can always shoot feral hogs."

"I doubt seriously a man of your father's stature could be mistaken for any of those animals."

"No, a safe hunter would never fire at anything he could not completely identify. That's why I think it was an inexperienced and untrained kid with a gun. What kind of idiot puts a weapon in a kid's hands and says fire away at anything that moves? It was hammered into me to know exactly what I was shooting at and where the bullet might go if I missed."

"Your mother said your father did not hunt, but he taught you?"

"No, he was not a hunter. He said he had done his share of bloodletting. Hunting a good fishing hole was the only game he found interesting, and most of the time he released what he caught. Papa Martin, Mom's dad, he took me hunting. He was a real Davy Crockett type."

Rainey looked out the study window. The clouds were hanging lower and thicker than before. It was almost noon. Her window of opportunity was closing fast. Not for the drive home, but a chance to see the crime scene before it disappeared under the snow she now had to admit was actually going to happen.

"Bill, I know this is a tough thing to ask of you, but if there is any way at all I could see where your father was shot, I might be able to answer a few of my questions and maybe put your mother at ease."

Rainey hoped she wasn't lying to this man. It would be better for everyone if it were simply a horrible accident of fate. In her experience with victim's families, if they could tell themselves nothing could have stopped it from happening, it was much easier to accept the death. Murder was a leap with what she knew so far, but seeing the actual scene of the shooting might answer that little prickle of doubt on the back of her neck.

Bill looked a bit surprised, but he said, "Sure. It's just on the other side of town about ten miles. I'll need to borrow a truck. My car won't go back there in this weather and Dad's truck is at the Sheriff's department. I haven't picked it up yet. They took it because it had blood—"

Rainey knew the pain of this loss. She put a hand on Bill's shoulder. "People will tell you in time this too shall pass. It will not. It will get easier to handle in about a year, maybe two.

Eventually, you focus on the good memories, the life of the man, and not his death."

A tear slowly rolled off Bill's cheek. "I knew I'd bury my father one day, just not this soon. There was so much left to say."

"He knew you loved him, right? What else was there he really needed to know?"

Bill stood up, went to the door, and waited for Rainey, who gathered her things and followed. He was in control now and had lost the tremble in his voice when he spoke.

He gave her time to tuck the holster back in her waistband, as he explained, "This weekend, my wife and I were going to tell Dad he was going to be a grandfather. I haven't told Mom, yet. I didn't think I should taint the joy of her finding out with the memory of my father's death."

Rainey reached for Bill's arm to stop him from turning the doorknob. "Tell her. New memories and purpose, that's what she needs right now. She was obviously devoted to your father. She needs somewhere to put that focus. Trust me, grandbabies can work miracles."

#

12:15 p.m.
Light Snow, 28.9°F, Windchill 17.3°F

While Bill made arrangements for transportation, Rainey went out to the van, very glad now that Katie had given her a change of clothes. Back at the house for a quick change into the jeans, a mock turtleneck, a UVA sweatshirt, and her black tactical boots—she smiled because she had married a woman that would include thick socks, two pair. Warm clothes donned, Rainey was ready to trek through the woods in freezing temperatures to view a crime scene. She had not brought a more appropriate coat, so the long wool one would have to do. She had thin leather gloves in her coat pocket, some comfort against the biting wind, but not the protection she needed for an extended stay in the worsening winter storm. Retrieving the gloves, Rainey fingered the small box containing Katie's necklace and thought about locking it in the van, but Bill was waiting out front.

Harriet offered a "toboggan," a word used only in the southern states to refer to not a sled, but a knit hat. "Here, you'll need this. I just heard someone say the wind-chill was down to seventeen degrees. Y'all don't stay out in this too long."

Rainey gladly accepted the hat. Hair smashed into a mass of matted curls was worth the risk with the falling temperatures outside. "Thank you. This shouldn't take too long."

Bill borrowed Skylar's pickup truck with the Sweet Farms logo on the door. Once inside, Rainey couldn't help but think what passed for a farm truck these days was a far cry from the old beater in which she made her last trip through Hominy Junction.

"Farming must be more lucrative than I thought," she commented.

"I guess if your tractors have Wi-Fi and air conditioning, why not drive a forty-five thousand dollar truck into a field?" Bill turned on the wipers, as what had been a few blowing flurries became light snow. "Gordon said he sits in the cab of one of Skylar's tractors, smokes weed, and does what a computer screen tells him to do. Easiest job he's ever had, he said. Of course, Gordon's had plenty of jobs. He's one of those good ol' boys found in every little town. He just can't quite keep it all together. You know the type."

"I basically make a living off of guys like Gordon. They are often in need of bail money."

"So, that's what you do now? You took over your father's business."

"It was never my intention to leave the bureau when he died, but the circumstances changed and it was the right thing to do."

"Leda told me all about your beautiful family. Are your triplets the grandbabies that worked miracles?"

Rainey smiled over at Bill. "Yes, they are. They healed a lot of scars." She was curious and Bill had been very forthcoming with information about Gordon without prompting, so she asked, "What can you tell me about Leda's son, Taylor?"

Bill glanced over at her. "Well, I guess you'd have to blind not to see it. He's Skylar's child, but nobody talks about it. It's a shame, really. That boy is going to figure it out on his own and that just doesn't seem fair to me."

"What exactly is he going to figure out? How he was conceived?"

"I keep forgetting you were looking at Dad's file. Yes, the basic rumor—because you know they morph a lot in a small town—the basic story was that some of the basketball team spent the evening getting drunk down at Skylar's father's hunting cabin. Skylar, Alex, Ely, and Gordon came into the diner for some takeout, as Leda was closing up alone."

"She was alone. That teenaged girl was alone closing down the diner? Where was her mother?"

"Doris finally ran her last husband off the year Leda started high school. She opened every morning and ran the place pretty much alone until Leda got there at lunch. Leda went back to school after the lunch rush and Doris worked with a night cook, until Leda got off from school. Then Leda closed with the night cook. It was like that for Leda all through school. My dad felt sorry for her. Anyway, that night the cook's baby was ill and Leda sent her home early."

Bill and Rainey drove out of town, taking a road that veered off to the left, just past the diner. The houses thinned and then there were none, just fields and forest lining both sides of the road. The snow was not exactly falling in flakes, but rather windblown gusts of tiny white pellets, enough to wet the roads and dust the ditches. Rainey shuddered against the cold and the subject matter.

"I am assuming from Leda's body language around Skylar that her kindness to the cook led to a sexual assault."

"No one believed a handsome boy like Skylar would need to rape a girl like Leda. Most people thought she was a willing participant, came up pregnant, and then cried rape."

"The blame and shame game," Rainey said, shaking her head. "A predictable reaction when it's the all American boy's word against the victim's. I mean, why would a good-looking boy like that need to rape someone, right? I like to remind people of Ted Bundy when they say crap like that."

"Dad was livid and spoke to Doris, who as it turned out knew about the rape and planned to cash in on that grandbaby when it was born. The Sweets have money, quite a bit, and Doris saw her pot of gold in the rape of her daughter."

"That poor girl," Rainey commented, as she felt the heat of anger rise to her neck.

Looking out the window again, she gathered her anger and pity, shoving it in to the appropriate mental box. Emotion clouded her mind. She had learned in training at Quantico to set it aside and focus on the task at hand. After the mental check, she went back to investigating.

"What part does the rumor say the other boys played in the rape?" Rainey asked.

"I heard some of it from Adam, myself. I don't know whether to believe him or not, but he said Skylar started harassing Leda and one thing led to another. He swore it just got out of hand and by the time he and Ely realized what was about to happen, Gordon was cutting off the lights and locking the door."

"And of course he and Ely couldn't go against Skylar, right?" Rainey said sarcastically, still angry but in control of it.

"Adam swore he and Ely just took the food, went back to a booth, and stuffed their faces. He said they heard noises from the bathroom, but they did not go in."

"I suppose he thought that made them innocent of any crime?"

"Yep, Adam was a dick," Bill said, nodding his head. "I never talked with Ely. He was just some kid from town. Like I said, these guys are younger and I was gone to college before they hit high school."

"Do you know if Skylar's family ever paid off Doris?"

"No, I never heard one way or the other. Doris died not long after Taylor was born, heart attack, I think."

Fifteen minutes outside of town, Bill turned off the paved road to a sandy lane that split two large barren winter fields covered in a thin layer of white. Rainey was starting to wonder if the last minute attempt to see the crime scene intact was going to be a wasted effort. They passed several "No Trespassing" and "Posted No Hunting" signs, as they progressed toward a thick, evergreen forest up ahead.

"I think this storm might really turn into the blizzard they've been calling for," Bill said. "You are welcome to stay at the house. You probably won't make it back home if this keeps up."

"Thank you for the offer. I might just have to take you up on that if it gets any worse," Rainey said, thinking how she dreaded that call home.

Rainey felt a little twinge of guilt at not leaving for home sooner. It wasn't just Harriet's request she couldn't ignore. Rainey could have told her she'd come back when the weather cleared, but something akin to the adrenaline rush of her old life as a behavioral analyst had taken over in the moment. It was possible a serial killer was among these townspeople. That presented an opportunity to use the skills she honed for years, but rarely used anymore. Her investigations, even her consulting work with law enforcement, seldom presented the chance to profile an UNSUB of this nature. If the prickly feeling on the back of her neck hinted at the truth, a cold, calculating, patient, and completely invisible killer was probably standing in Harriet's living room right now, eating brownies and sipping coffee with the next victim on the list.

Bill had grown quiet. Rainey surmised they must be near the site and let the silence persist. She remembered trying to comprehend the senseless murder of her father. She gave Bill the time to prepare for the return to the spot where his father took his last breath. She did not envy him the grieving process he was about to endure. She felt the familiar pain in her chest. On May tenth, Rainey would mark the fifth anniversary of the day her father was taken from her. It still felt like yesterday.

After a big bend, the lane entered a woody patch and deteriorated to a series of deep dips and ice-covered puddles. Several old vehicles sat back from the road under the trees, rusting to dust amid the vines and fallen branches that left the headlights to look like eyes peeking from the shadows. Bill slowed the truck to a crawl and then came to a stop, just feet from a fairly large sand quarry filled with water, commonly called a sandpit around these parts. The surface of the water was the only area Rainey could see not covered in thick trees and undergrowth, except for the small clearing where they were parked. She heard Bill take a deep breath and exhale slowly.

"I will not keep you here long. Just talk me through what you know. Don't tell me what the police told you. Tell me what *you* know. You know your father's behavior. You know what he would have been doing. Tell me only that for now."

Bill nodded and began. "He always parked right here, under this tree. See that stump just above the water line. That's his spot. There's a good sandy bottom there. Good place to catch Bream. Shad run through the creek too."

"This doesn't look like a creek. It looks more like a pond, a big pond" Rainey remarked.

Bill pointed out the windshield at what appeared to be a finger-shaped peninsula about seventy-five yards offshore, pointing directly at them. "The creek is actually about three hundred yards north of here. See those trees out there. We call it Track Island. A mining company built a track in the twenties and brought train cars in to take out the sand dug up from about sixty yards out on both sides of that strip of land. The quarry formed an elongated horseshoe-shaped sandpit. When they were finished, the rails were pulled up and the creek was allowed to flood the pit. Eventually, the creek changed its natural course to run through the north end."

Rainey could talk fishing and fishing holes. She was Billy Bell's daughter of Bell's Bail and Bait. "I bet this is a great fishing spot then, kind of a natural Shad holding pond, isn't it? Did a lot of people know your father came here?"

"Oh, pretty much everybody, I guess. It's private property. You have to have permission to fish here, but lots of people do. It's not a secret hole, if that's what you're asking. We used to sneak down here and swim, as kids. The owner would run us off most of the time. It's really not a place for non-swimmers to be hanging out. It's shallow, maybe three feet at the most, here close to shore. It may not look like it, but it's a rock ledge covered in a few inches of sand. About five yards out, the ledge stops and then it drops off into a sharp slope to the bottom. It gets to a depth of about forty feet out by Track Island. I saw a guy messing around one night in a four-wheel drive in the shallows. He went too close to the edge of the ledge and his truck went right over the side. They finally sent divers out there to find it. It had rolled all the way to the deepest point. A couple of kids have drowned in there too. An old hobo guy floated up once."

"I suppose that's why I saw all those 'No Trespassing' signs we passed on the way in."

"Yeah, Mr. Read would shoot a shotgun over our heads if he caught us down here. Scared us shitless when those birdshot pellets rained down on the water, but we kept coming back. It was kind of a game and certainly a rite of passage to get chased by old man Read."

"Read? Any kin to Ellie Paxton's husband?"

"Yes, Mr. Read was Burgess's grandfather. Burgess's parents died when he and his sister were young and his grandparents raised them. I think it was a car accident, but I don't really remember. I do remember when his sister was killed in an accident right after he graduated from high school—ran off the Tarr River bridge over by Old Sparta. Since all the Reads are dead now, Ellie inherited the farm and six or seven sandpits. Dad said she is sitting on a gold mine of mineral rights. She can just sit back and collect the checks from the mining company. I had no idea sand was such a lucrative business."

"There are an awful lot of deaths around Ellie Paxton, don't you think?"

"You're right and not the only person that has noticed. People joke that Ellie Paxton Read is a black cat; it's bad luck if you cross her path, but none of the deaths were anything but accidents, except her parents, and she didn't cause that. She seems to take it all in stride, though. I guess when you've been through what she's been through; a little town gossip is a blip on her radar."

"The world is a comedy to those that think; a tragedy to those that feel," Rainey recited a Horace Walpole quote she used to have tacked above her desk at Quantico.

The quote came in a note from a serial killer she interviewed her first year with the BAU. She kept it as a daily reminder to think more and feel less. It had been tough those first few years of not necessarily hardening to the depravity she saw, but learning to think through it. But to the killer that gave Rainey the quote, it was his way of explaining why not feeling the least bit of remorse while chopping off a woman's head made him happy.

Rainey wasn't through mining information on Ellie Paxton. She was a victim of the precipitating event that led up to Rainey being in the truck with Bill at that moment. "Ellie is a farmer, now? She doesn't look the type. Collecting mineral rights checks—that I don't think she would have a problem with, but running a farm? That seems a stretch."

"She rents the land to the Sweets. Lots of people do. Their operation is large enough to stay afloat and buy the equipment to handle multiple farms. One man on modern machinery can do the work of ten, or so Skylar says."

"I guess that payroll savings buys a truck like this."

Rainey kept the mood light to this point. It was imperative to keep Bill's emotions in check. His information would be more accurate without the fog of mourning. Now, she refocused him on the shooting, and would follow this pattern of light banter and return to the shooting until she had extracted what she could from this grieving son.

"Your father always parked his truck under that tree?"

"Yes, always. He was very much a creature of habit. If the sun was shining, he was down here for a couple of hours at least. My mom always knew where to find him between noon and six."

Rainey tried to remember back four days. "It got up to fifty, if I remember right. It was warm the day before but really windy."

"I talked to Dad on the seventh. He said the wind was blowing so hard he couldn't get a good cast in." He let a second or two pass, before saying, "I wish the wind had been blowing the next day too."

Don't let him think, Rainey thought to herself. She said, quickly, "So, you talked to your father often?"

"Yes, he really was my best friend. He was a great dad. I'm just sorry my kid won't have the chance to know him. He would have been a great grandfather too."

"I'm sure he would have," Rainey granted. She was losing him. It was better to get what she could now, before he became too emotional to be of any use. Harsh as it sounded to play him like a piano, she had to keep him in key for just a few minutes more. "Can we walk to where forensics indicated the shooter might have been?"

"Sure, it's right up on that ridge over there."

The snowflakes were becoming larger as they exited the truck. They landed on her black wool coat displaying tiny ice crystal works of art. Rainey pulled the knit hat a little further down over the exposed parts of her ears and neck. She followed Bill into the thickening brush on the other side of the clearing, blinking away the snowflakes as they landed on her lashes.

"It's really starting to come down," Bill called over his shoulder.

Rainey jabbed her hands in her coat pockets and pulled the wool closer to her body. "Yes, it is. My body isn't used to this kind of weather anymore. I lived up North for a while. This would be an average day up there."

The climb became steeper, as they followed a recently worn path to just below the top of the ridge. Rainey could see there had been lots of traffic, probably the crime scene techs, but there were older signs of traffic too, farther up. Someone had been coming down that ridge recently and rather frequently.

She asked Bill, "The 'No Hunting' signs, does that mean no hunting, or is that just for out-of-towners?"

"No, Mr. Read never allowed hunting on his land. He said he didn't want some yahoo shooting him in that back trying to bag a deer. The Read house is back that way; a couple of miles, but there are also trails all through these woods. People have hiked and camped in here for years with Read's permission, but no hunting allowed. There are a couple of sand ridges where he allowed target shooting, but they are farther up the road."

"So, whoever shot your father was poaching."

"Yes, it would seem so. Ellie told the investigators that she'd been hearing shots back in here, but she can't see who comes and goes from her house, and assumed people were just target shooting down at the sand ridges."

"Had your father mentioned hearing shots?"

"If he noticed them, he didn't say anything to me."

Bill reached a level spot in the climb, a natural ledge. In front of Rainey stood a manmade formation of vines and twigs that to her thinking was a sniper's nest. It may have been meant as a hunting blind, but looking down on the clearing at what exactly?

"You're a hunter, Bill. Would this be where you would hunt on this land?"

"With all the open fields just through those woods? No, this would not be my choice. If I were hunting here, I'd put my blind at the edge of the woods in the corner of that west field we passed coming in. Plus, if I were poaching, I wouldn't be in the one place on this vast property that I know people come often."

Bill moved to stand exactly in the middle of the area Rainey supposed was a sniper nest.

"They said the shot came from here." He pointed at the ground. "The footprints went from this spot to the top of the ridge, joined the larger steps, and vanished into the swamp on the other side.

Bill stepped aside, so Rainey could stand where he indicated the shot was fired. She blinked the snow from her eyelashes again, and imagined Wellman Wise innocently sitting on his favorite stump on a sunny February day.

"Is the grill of his truck chrome?"

"Yes. It's a bright red truck with chrome trim."

Rainey turned to Bill. "Do you see what I see?"

"No, not really," Bill said, confused.

"The sun was bright that day. I remember it because we took the kids to the park. What time was he shot?"

"Sometime between two and three pm."

Rainey looked for a sign of the sun, but she wasn't going to see one. The clouds were low and thick above her, their snow production increasing rapidly.

"I'm turned around. Which way did you say was west?" She asked while brushing snow from her face.

"That way," Bill said, pointing over Rainey's shoulder, up the ridge.

"If your Dad's truck was parked where we are, there is no way a person up here could not at least see the rays bouncing off all that glass and chrome, and his truck was red, especially, if they were standing to take a shot. Plus, he was wearing an orange safety vest."

Bill studied the scene and then the color left his face. "He was murdered, wasn't he?"

"You say it was one shot and he died almost instantly," Rainey said, unwilling to spare Bill's feelings anymore.

She crouched down inside a hollowed out thicket, shaped almost like a gun turret. The brambles made good cover, but she could see the clearing through several small openings. The back of the turret was open, allowing egress unseen from below, up and over the ridge behind a natural hedge of blackberry vines and tangled undergrowth. "Where did the bullet hit him?"

"Dad must have heard something. He walked back toward the truck and stopped in front of it. He was standing, facing this direction when the bullet entered here," Bill put his finger on his upper chest, "about mid-sternum."

Rainey picked up a stick and gently turned some forest debris on the ground, toward the front of the suspected sniper's nest. The wet leaves stuck together like pancakes covered in a thin white icing of snow. Under the debris was a seemingly innocent mound of sand. The forest floor around and under the pile was made up of several inches of undisturbed decaying vegetation, brown wet leaves interspersed with sticks and stems. Sand, although easily accessed by simply moving the vegetation, had been scooped into place and purposely covered with another layer of leaves. Someone had created a natural shooter's ridge out of what was available, rather than carry a bean or sand filled bag to the spot.

Rainey did not disturb the sand. She gently placed leaves over it and backed out the way she came in.

Bill demanded an answer, "Was he murdered?"

"Bill, I can't conclusively answer that question, not yet, not to any standard I would feel comfortable with. What I will tell you is what I see. That sand shouldn't be there. It's a makeshift sand bag for a shooter. If a shooter needs to raise or lower the aim, they nudge the sand under the weapon. The bullet penetrated in the sniper's triangle, an area formed from nipple to nipple and up to the center of the throat. Snipers aim there because if the round lands within the triangle the target will be either killed instantly, paralyzed, or incapacitated and dying rapidly. There was no brass left behind. This is obviously a well-traveled trail. Someone has been to this spot a lot and recently. This shooting position is concealed and too well maintained to be naturally occurring, but painstakingly meant to appear that way. I'm just having a hard time believing the person who shot from this position was an amateur making a deadly mistake."

"Who would want to kill my father? He was just an old retired military guy. He had no enemies."

Rainey looked down the ridge to the clearing. The wet snow was becoming heavier and stuck to the dried old stump, which now appeared a cold and lonely shrine to the man that kept company with it most afternoons. The snow infused fog created by cold air contacting the warmer water swirled on the surface of the pond.

She turned to Bill and spoke the blunt truth, "He had at least one."

Chapter Four

1:16 p.m.
Fog and Snow, 26.1°F, Windchill 14.5°F

By the time they arrived back at the Wise residence, fog had settled on the land and the snow fell steadily, increasing in volume by the minute. Rainey asked to be dropped at the van, so she could move it closer to the house now that most of the mourners had gone in the wake of the coming blizzard. Katie was right. Rainey would not make it home tonight.

Before she exited the truck, Rainey turned to Bill. "Don't say anything to anybody about what we've discussed. If your father was murdered, then there is a killer somewhere in this town. Alerting that person could prove dangerous."

She left the truck and climbed in the van. A shudder went thru her body, as the wind whipped the icy air under her coat. Inside the van was not much warmer, but at least she was sheltered from the wind chill. Rainey hit the Bluetooth button on the steering wheel and waited for the "Ready" from the automated voice system.

"Call Katie," Rainey said, and took a deep breath.

"Hey honey," Katie's cheery voice answered.

About to spoil her wife's good mood, Rainey replied, "You sound chipper."

"I have to show you this. I'll put you on Facetime."

"Hang on, I'm in the van on the hands-free system. Let me get the phone out of my pocket."

Katie voiced concern, "Oh, are you driving in this? Don't answer then. Concentrate."

"No, I'm not driving. That's why I called. I don't think I could make it to the Interstate on these two-lane roads back here."

"Good," Katie said, surprising Rainey. "Stay there and stay safe."

Relieved at hearing no disappointment in Katie's voice, Rainey said, "I'm glad you aren't upset that I stayed."

"No, I'm fine. I'm glad you're safe and warm. I was just a little bitchy this morning. I'm ready for a break and I can't wait to go away with you for an evening of quiet, just the two of us."

"Hang in there. Relief is coming. I have my phone out now. What did you want to show me?"

"Okay, I'm hitting the button."

Rainey's phone sounded a notification and Katie's face appeared on the screen. Rainey touched the "Accept" button.

"Well, hey there, good-looking," Katie said, smiling brightly. "I see you've changed into the clothing I sent with you. The hat is a nice touch."

"My ears were cold. Thank you very much for the change of clothes, particularly for the extra socks and boots."

Katie's image bounced on the screen as she moved from the kitchen to the dining room. "You are welcome. Now, look at your children. They have never been so still in their lives. They are mesmerized."

The image on the screen changed from viewing Katie to the interior of the room. Rainey could see Leslie seated at the dining table. She smiled and waved at Rainey through the camera and then looked down to her right. The camera moved closer to the big window that looked out onto what was now a snow covered backyard, with huge flakes falling from the sky. The backs of three little heads were poised just inches from the glass, hands pressing little steam prints onto the panes.

Katie's voice said, "They have been standing there for ten minutes. Not saying a word."

On cue, Weather, started talking and pointing outside. "Go, go, go."

"No, honey, it's too cold."

Weather went to her recent default position when faced with a response that did not please her. She plopped onto her diaper-cushioned rear end, face reddening, and began to wail loudly. Her brothers were confused, but in solidarity began to fuss as well.

Rainey glanced at the clock on the radio. "It's nap time."

The sound of Rainey's voice stopped Weather's antics, and turned off the boys' half-hearted cries. They looked up at Katie, who put the phone closer so she they see Rainey.

"Rugrats," Rainey said, and the triplets giggled.

Timothy came and took the phone from Katie and carried Rainey to the window.

"Snow," he whispered.

"Yes, snow," Rainey said in support of her children's expanding vocabulary.

This set all three off on a chorus of "Snow, snow, snow."

"They learned a new word," Katie offered from somewhere behind the kids. "Tell Nee Nee bye bye."

Rainey could tell Katie was trying to wrestle the phone back from Timothy, by the erratic movement of the screen. His face appeared on the screen, very close, and then he open-mouth kissed the phone.

Rainey heard Leslie's voice. "Aw, that is so cute."

"Bye, bye, rugrats," Rainey said, which again elicited giggles from the three.

Katie's face returned to the phone. "I love you. Call me later. I'm going to take them upstairs for their nap, before she gets going again."

"She" was Weather, whom they spoke of in pronouns when she was present. Using her name, when she was in a mood, only meant they were paying attention to her and a prime time to display her newly forming manipulation skills. Weather had learned at an earlier age than her brothers that being obstinate sometimes got her what she wanted.

"I love you too. I'll call you before I go to sleep."

"Bye," Katie blew a kiss at the phone and was gone.

She didn't ask what Rainey had found out. She had her hands full at home. Rainey was glad Leslie was there to help. The triplets were almost more than one person could handle, now that they were extremely mobile. Taking care of them was a full-time, never-take-your-eyes-away, job. Still, Rainey and Katie wouldn't trade one minute of it.

Rainey cranked the van and moved it closer to the Wise house. Before leaving it for the night, she opened all the various storage compartments looking for the extra shirts Katie carried for both of them. With three babies, the chances were high that the adults in the family could be in need of clean laundry at any given moment. Katie reasoned that being prepared for anything lessened the stress when things did go horribly wrong; as it did the time all three babies had a stomach virus. Rainey winced at the memory. She'd seen countless crime scenes, but that virus weekend tested her gag reflex even now. It was one of the reasons they had a new van. They could never get the smell out of the seats of the old one.

Rainey had rarely driven the new van, usually only with Katie and the triplets in it. She was unaware of the extent to which Katie had turned the entire van into a giant diaper bag. The first compartment contained a diaper changing station; complete with diaper rash treatments, Vaseline, powder, baby wipes, and hand sanitizer for when the deed was done. The next storage bin was a food source. Crackers, juice, peanut butter, cookies, and more wipes—a person could live out of there for a month and have clean hands doing it. Rainey closed that bin and moved on to the third, finally locating a tee shirt under the box of thirty-gallon trash bags. She laughed at the thought of needing a thirty gallon trash bag for the garbage in the van, but then the memory of the trip back from the beach last summer, which coincided with the stomach virus onset, reminded her it was possible.

Tee shirt in hand, Rainey walked back into the Wise residence. She stopped to shake the snow from her coat and hat, and hung them on the almost-empty coat tree in the foyer. Skylar and Gordon stood with a few people in the living room, coats on, finishing last minute conversations before braving the cold outside. Rainey moved down the hall and saw Benjy and Leda in the dining room, clearing away the catering table. Rainey did not see Bill, but she could hear voices from the back of the house.

She followed the sound and arrived just in time to hear Harriet demand of her son, "William Wellman Wise, I know when you are lying. I have since you started talking. Tell me the truth. Your father was intentionally murdered, wasn't he?"

Rainey took in the room quickly. Ellie and another young woman were washing dishes at the sink but had stopped to stare at the confrontation. An older woman stood behind Harriet, a worried look on her face. Harriet was burning holes in her son with her eyes, and poor Bill was in the center of it all. His shoulders deflated and Rainey could tell he was melting under his mother's glare.

Rainey had to say something, "Mrs. Wise, Harriet, may I speak with you in the study?"

"Go on, Mrs. Wise," Ellie said. "We'll take care of everything."

The other young woman at the sink walked over to Bill and kissed his cheek. "Go on, honey, take care of your mother. I'll see to the guests and get the house back in order."

He smiled down at her and brushed a bang from her brow, "Don't do too much. I'll help when we're done."

Rainey led the way to the study, but did not step behind the desk. Instead she went to the couch and asked Harriet to sit with her. Bill moved a chair close and slumped down in it, the weight of the world on his shoulders. Rainey didn't have a mother to take care of when her father died. Well, she did have a mother, but Rainey's experience with her father's death was much different from Bill's. He could not fully manage his grief with his mother to worry about. On the other hand, Harriet appeared to have her grief well in hand. That was until about thirty seconds after entering the study. She burst into tears, prompting Bill to reach for a box of tissue from the desk, before he buried his head in his hands and wept softly, while his mother vented her frustration.

"I knew it. I told him all that poking around in other people's business was going to get him killed. What did he know? What did he find out that would make someone shoot him like an animal? How could he have survived all he did and die like this? All those nights as a soldier's wife not knowing where he was or if he was alive—" She gasped for air before her anger forced more of the broken-woman rant from her lips. "I thought we'd gotten past that. I thought we would grow old together, away from war and killing, but he just had to go looking for trouble. It's just so goddamned senseless."

His mother's use of profanity brought Bill's head up. Rainey took a tissue from the box he had placed on Harriet's lap and offered it to him. He took it and wiped his tears away.

"Mom, Dad's death will not be senseless. We'll find out what he knew and who that information scared into killing him. If he did uncover some crime, it's on that desk and I'll find it. He will not have died in vain."

Harriet turned to Rainey. "What did you find out there?"

Rainey did not want to tell too much. What she knew should be in the hands of trained investigators, not a grieving widow. Bill might tell her later, but she hoped he wouldn't.

"I believe the person who shot your husband was a trained marksman. That tends to discredit the amateur hunter theory currently under investigation. I'll call an acquaintance in the Dobbs County Sheriff's department. I'll tell him what I know and what the detectives should look for when they return to the scene. The snow may actually preserve much of the evidence the first assessment of the scene missed. Please know it wasn't sloppy crime scene work. I had more information than they did. That gives me a little different perspective on what I saw. They saw a hunting blind, because that is what they expected to see."

"I didn't know I should have told them," Harriet whispered apologetically.

"You couldn't know what they needed until they asked. Did anyone ask you about enemies or reasons someone might want your husband dead?"

"No, they just came to the house and told me a hunter shot him by accident. I didn't think about this stuff in here until later. By then, they had made up their minds it was a scared kid that ran off after he shot Wellman."

"They will probably reopen the investigation when they have all the pieces we have. Bill can show them where to look. But please, it is imperative that none of this information leaves this room. If Bill chooses to share what he knows with you, I can't stop him, but it would be best if you wait until he has spoken with the police, and even then, you must not discuss this with anyone else."

The reality of the situation suddenly hit Bill. "If this person killed Dad because he knew too much, they might try to kill me or Mom if they think we know it too. That's what you're saying, isn't it?"

"Yes, I'm afraid so."

"My soul, what has Wellman gotten us into?" Harriet asked.

Rainey laid it out for them. "Granted, this is just a theory and I have only scratched the surface in that folder; I believe at least one of the deaths your husband was investigating was not an accident, but a murder. The person who committed that murder discovered that Captain Wise was poking around. He spooked somebody, spooked them bad. That means he was close to naming them or they at least thought he was. He called me and left a message saying he wanted to talk about a cold case, or I thought that was what he said. I know now it was the Colde case I had discussed with him back in 2000, when Graham Colde killed his neighbors."

Bill shifted uneasily in his chair. Rainey noted his body language. He knew something. His mother was right. Bill was easy to read.

Rainey concluded her comments with, "I believe your father connected the dots and it all goes back to that list from Colde's pocket. Only four people remain alive from the original list. There are several scenarios that answer a lot of questions. One, Colde did have a silent partner who has spent the last fourteen years collecting on injustices from high school. Or one of the people on the list is actually a murderer. I can't begin to guess at a motive at this point. Or the list has nothing to do with his death and he was simply a target of opportunity, highly doubtful, in my opinion. Of course, it could be that Graham Dean Colde has been out there finishing what he started, after convincing the state's psychiatrists that he was not a risk to society. That happens more often than you think."

Bill leaned forward, his elbows on his knees, chin resting on his folded hands. He was processing the information and, Rainey suspected, about to tell her what he knew. He had the confessional posture she recognized from hours of interrogating suspects and witnesses. She waited for him to come to his own conclusions, ready to prompt or prod if necessary. Something Rainey said had made him very uncomfortable.

"I think I can eliminate the Colde scenario," he began. "He really doesn't exist anymore. His name wasn't all that changed. His memory of that time has never returned. The personality in his body today, as it was explained to me, is essentially a brand new person. He was a complete clean slate when he woke up. He had to relearn everything, like a newborn. I really don't think Colde returned to finish the job. He can't remember any of these people anyway."

"That's right." Harriet confirmed Bill's statement and added, "He doesn't even remember his own mother."

"So, you know where Colde is now?"

"Yes," Bill said. "I work with him. I've been helping him with a game design. I sent it to Dad to verify the gunplay is authentic. He was disturbed by it, though. He said he wanted to talk to me about the game when we came down this weekend. I'm sure it was just the graphic nature he objected to. I warned him about it, but really, it's tame compared to games in this genre."

"What genre?" Rainey was curious, now.

"Well, it's kind of funny that you ask. The female protagonist is a profiler gone rogue, looking for the man that scarred her for—"

The light that came on in Bill's brain could have lit New York City.

"Oh my God, it is you," he said, going pale.

Rainey stood up. "Show me this game."

"What does that game have to do with Wellman's murder?" Harriet asked.

"I don't know, maybe nothing, but your husband called me for a reason. He could have wanted to talk to me about the list or this game. Either way, I think it's something I should take a look at."

Bill walked to the desk and sat down. Rainey moved in behind him, while he woke the laptop and clicked a few keys. Harriet came to stand beside him.

He turned to his mother. "Mom, you probably don't want to watch this. The violence is pretty extreme."

"Bill, I thought you designed programs for the military. I didn't know you worked on video games you wouldn't want your mother to see."

"Mom, you would not want to see half of what I do, including the stuff for the military." Harriet hesitated. "Really, Mom. I can't show this to you."

"Good Lord, Bill, what is it."

"At least part of it, now that I've met her, is what happened to Rainey." He turned to focus on Rainey. "I had forgotten about reading that story in the paper until I met you today. I kept thinking the game's storyboard sounded vaguely familiar, but all these types of games have an element of truth in them. Especially the serial killer profiles."

"People play games about serial killers?" Harriet said in disbelief.

Rainey knew all about these kinds of games. "Perverse, but true. Some of them are just crime genre fare, a little bloody, but the emphasis is on finding clues and solving a murder. Others are more graphic versions of the same thing."

"This game is different," Bill said. "In this one, you can be the killer, while outwitting the profiler on your heels. It's really quite technically brilliant as a game. I have some problems with the content, but that isn't my call. Not even close."

"And you can't say no?" Harriet asked.

"No, Mom, I can't. Extreme gaming is a big business and this game is going to be about as extreme as this type of game gets. My name will not be on it. No one will know I had anything to do with it. Plus, it's still in development. It might not get all the way to production. I just sent Dad a working edition, because I had some questions about how certain weapons impact the human body."

Harriet appeared conflicted. Rainey wanted to see the game, so she moved things along. "Bill is going to show me the game, and then I'm going to look through this file. I'll need some time alone to really concentrate, so I don't miss anything."

Harriet took the hint. "Okay then, I'll go, but if you need anything just come find me. I'll probably be in the kitchen. There is so much food to put away. The storm sent everyone home before they could eat it all."

"I'll be there in a few minutes, Mom. Just sit down and let us take care of you."

She bent and kissed her son on the top of his head. "You have always been the perfect child. Your father and I spoke of it often. He loved you very much."

"I know, Mom." Bill stood and hugged his mother. "Go rest. I'll be out soon."

Once Harriet cleared the room, Bill opened the game folder he'd sent his father with a few clicks of the mouse. The title screen appeared, touting "Come For Me" in letters dripping blood. Written beneath was the tag line, "Be the hunter or the hunted." The artistic style reminded Rainey of the "Sin City" graphic novels with a nod to film noir. Dark, foreboding music, with a bass line mimicking a heartbeat quickening, vibrated the small laptop speakers and mixed with a raging storm soundtrack. Brush strokes indicating pouring rain sliced across the screen, almost obscuring a small house in the background.

The narrator's deep, ominous voice began, as the point of view moved in closer to the house, "The hunter becomes the hunted."

Bill hit the pause button. "Rainey, I'm not sure you really want to see this."

"Play it," Rainey said in a tone that left him no room for argument.

The video began again with the camera view instantly switching to the interior the house, which looked familiar to Rainey. Crime scene photos popped into her head. The images from her memory matched the home on the screen, as the camera moved down a hall toward a lighted room at the end. Rainey had only fleeting memories from the night she was abducted, but she had reviewed the file often enough to recognize the creator of this game had seen the crime scene photos too. When the camera view finally entered the bedroom at the end of the hall, any doubts she may have had disappeared.

Bill moved around nervously in his seat. Rainey stood silently still as she observed a naked female game character tied down to a bed, with a black-masked man straddling her, and carving an "S" into her chest. Flashes of the night a serial killer carved a shallow Y-incision into her skin crowded into Rainey's mind. The part of her brain not sickened by what it was seeing had already begun to question how someone outside of the FBI would have access to this much detail.

Sirens began to wail over the speakers. The killer ran away. A cast of law enforcement crashed into the room. A tall, redheaded man in an FBI windbreaker, who was a spot on representation of Rainey's old partner and her children's godfather, Danny McNally, cut the woman on the bed from her bonds, and kissed her passionately.

"Well, that never happened," Rainey commented, as the camera zoomed in for a close-up of the female's rage-filled eyes.

The narrator spoke, "Saved from the clutches of a madman, Special Agent Stormy Weathers turns her back on the job and the man she loved," the screen changed to a dark office and a close up of Stormy Weathers in the glow of a computer monitor, looking rather deranged, "to hunt the man that scarred her for life."

Rainey wasn't really interested in the story line or what the narrator had to say. The hair on her body had started to prickle to attention. She leaned closer to the screen, taking in the dark office details.

"Oh my God," she whispered. "He's been in my house."

Rainey was no longer looking at the screen. She was focused on Bill. Her expression must have frightened him. His eyes grew wide and he reflexively sat as far back in the chair as he could, creating distance between them.

"Who is he?" Rainey demanded. "That fucker has been in my house—where my kids sleep. Tell me now, where is Graham Dean Colde."

"His name is Theodore Suzanne and he lives in Chapel Hill."

#

2:05 p.m.
Heavy Snow, 25°F, Windchill 12.6°F

"Well, hey there. I wasn't expecting your call for a bit. What is it? Do you miss me that much?" Katie was laughing on the other end of the call, while Rainey tried to make her voice sound normal.

"Yes, I miss you. What are you doing?"

Rainey stared out the window of the Captain's study. The snow was falling heavy, whiting out the sky. There was no way she could get home, not without a tank. She had watched the rest of the video opening to the game, understanding only then the extent to which Colde had penetrated the security she had worked so hard to maintain. A simple name change and he walked right into her life, but why? What had she done to attract his attention? He certainly spent hours watching her. He knew her house, her friends, her car—her life was all right there on the screen. The only difference was his perception of who she was. His Stormy Weather character was dark and brooding, bent on vengeance, and willing to break laws and kill without mercy in order to "rid the world of evil," as the narration said. It was "Dexter" on steroids, with a bit of "Criminal Minds" mixed in.

The twist in the game was the other main character, the Letter Man, who carved the alphabet in his victims' torsos. He was on letter "S" when he got to Stormy. The game offered the player an option to finish the alphabet before getting caught, or hunt the killer as Stormy Weather, the broken and scarred former FBI agent who gave up love and her career to find the Letter Man.

Katie's voice sounded in Rainey's ear. "We put the kids down for a nap and now the adults are drinking coffee and watching the snow and the news coverage of stranded vehicles. The interstate is closing soon. They have so many cars stuck, no one can move. The snow is coming down hard now. I can barely see the back gate."

"Did Molly make it okay?" No need to panic Katie, if Molly didn't make it back with Joey and his friend.

"Yes, she's here. She showed up right after I talked to you. She said the roads were really becoming difficult to travel. I'm glad you're staying put."

"So, Joey and Theodore are there too?"

"Joey is, but Theodore changed his mind and went home, Molly said."

"Oh, thank God," Rainey said relieved.

"Come on, Rainey. He's not that bad."

"Listen to me carefully," Rainey dropped all pretense of joviality. "Do not under any circumstances let Theodore Suzanne into our house, again."

"What are you talking about? He's never been to our house." Katie grew concerned. "What's the matter, Rainey?"

The possibilities ran through Rainey's head rapidly.

"Do not alert to anyone that there is something wrong. Hand the phone to Molly."

"Rai—," Katie started to say.

"Katie, smile. Do not look upset. I need you to listen to me carefully. Someone may be watching you. You are not in danger at the moment, at least I don't think you are or I'd call the police."

"They couldn't get here either, Rainey. I'm telling you nothing is moving."

"That's good, honey. You are safe, but I need to talk to Molly and, Katie, give her access to her weapon."

"Okay, I love you. Don't worry. I can take care of us."

"I know you can, sweetheart. I love you too. Everything is going to be fine. I'll be home in the morning to sort all this out. Just keep the alarm on and do what Molly tells you. I'm going to ask her to handle a few things for me until I get there."

Katie did as she was asked, "Hey, Molly. Rainey wants to talk to you."

Katie would focus on the kids if things went crazy, but Molly would focus on living through it. Molly was a survivor and Rainey needed her to be that right now.

"Well, I hear you're going to miss the snow cream party later, or are you living it up down there in Dobbs County? Glad it's you and not me," Molly's voice said from the phone. She came from Dobbs County, but her childhood was devoid of many fond remembrances.

"Molly, put on that lawyer face. There is nothing wrong, got it?"

The tone in Rainey's voice must have alerted Molly to danger. She answered, "Sure, enjoy your time as a single woman."

"Good, now listen. Theodore Suzanne is not Joey's friend's real name. He was held but never tried on a double murder in 2000, brain injury, no memory, released from a mental hospital after five years. He has either been in my house, put a camera on Joey, or has tapped into my video surveillance somehow. Either way, he can see and hear you most likely."

Rainey had skimmed the details, but in Molly's line of work she understood facts needed no embellishment.

"Really, we're fine here. All tucked in tight and secure. Don't worry about a thing. Leslie and I are staying the night. Katie will have plenty of help with the kids."

"Do you have your weapon?" Molly carried a small pistol for protection. She was a criminal attorney with some shady characters in her past.

"I certainly do."

"When we hang up, have Katie email the security company. Alert them to a possible threat and give them Colde's, I mean, Theodore Suzanne's description." Rainey wanted so desperately to be home now. She tried not to let the frustration cloud her brain. "I'll leave as soon as I can in the morning. Can you stay until I get home?"

"No problem. Do I need to call Sheila?" Molly was adeptly playing the game. She referred to their mutual acquaintance, Detective Sheila Robertson of the Durham County Sheriff's office.

"No, I got nothing right now except a video game based on my life, but the detail indicates that he has been in my house and in the files I left out at the lake. Katie gave him access to the women's shelter computers. I have my old cases stored in a locked room out there. My own crime scene pictures are in a box in that room. He's seen them. There is no doubt in my mind."

"Well, aren't you the popular one," Molly said.

"Tell me about it. Just take care of my family for me. I feel helpless stuck down here."

"Well, don't do anything stupid, like try to drive home before the roads are clear. We'll stay with Katie and help out with the kids as long as it takes."

"Thank you, Molly. I owe you."

"I'll collect, I'm sure. Here's your wife."

The phone changed hands and Katie came back on the line. "Listen to Molly. Don't drive if it isn't safe. It's supposed to snow all night long. It's not going to thaw anytime soon, so do what you have to do, but be safe."

"Always. I love you. Hug the babies. I'll call you before I go to bed."

"Please do and I love you too."

Rainey hung up and returned to the desk. She sat there for a few minutes trying to comprehend how and why someone like Graham Dean Colde, or Theodore Suzanne, whatever he called himself, latched onto her. Creeps continued to be fascinated by her. Despite her best efforts to live a quieter, safer life, the threats just kept coming.

A knock at the door broke her from her thoughts. She called out, "Come in."

Harriet poked her head in. "May I come in?"

"Please," Rainey said, inviting her in with a sweep of her arm.

"I'm sorry you can't get to your family. I can see how worried you are. Bill told me what Theodore has done. I know now why Wellman seemed so alarmed and desperate to speak with you."

"My family is safe. Someone is staying with them and the security company is being alerted. I'll have to prove Theodore has broken a law before I can have him pulled in."

"Do you really think he'd hurt your family, or you?"

Rainey thought about what she saw on the game video, the flashes of sadism. "His mind is rife with violence and sadistic fantasies. For that reason alone, I do not want him near my family. It is possible that he has a vivid imagination and a fascination with serial killers. Many people do and don't turn into murderers. But this guy has already invaded my privacy, which tells me he disregards boundaries. What other boundary might he be willing to cross?" She locked eyes with Harriet. "I want him stopped before the answer to that question is another murder."

"Do you think he killed Wellman?"

"I really don't know. My training is in identifying the type of person who could commit a crime of a specified nature. Colde certainly fits within the parameters of the profile I'm leaning toward in your husband's shooting, but so could others. I've hardly scratched the surface here, and we still don't know if any of these 'accidents' were really murders. If these deaths were not accidental and can be connected, that's a very intelligent and dangerous criminal mind at work." Rainey indicated all the paperwork on the desk. "It would take hundreds of man hours reevaluating each one of these deaths, before any definitive answers or a profile could be offered."

"It is far more complicated than they make it look on television, isn't it?"

"Yes, ma'am, it is, and it never replaces good investigation techniques. Behavioral analysis is a tool, not a solution."

Harriet smiled at Rainey. "Billy had good reason to be proud of you. Well, he wasn't just proud, he bragged about his FBI Special Agent daughter and her meteoric rise to the elite BAU."

Rainey felt the rush of embarrassment flush her cheeks. "Meteoric, huh?" She laughed. "I wouldn't call it that. It felt painfully slow while it was happening."

"You have his air about you."

Rainey's face automatically formed the smile she had borrowed from Billy Bell, along with his hair, eyes, lanky body, and if her mother was correct, much of his personality as well.

"He could not deny I was his, that's for sure."

Harriet shook her head. "It's more than looks. You have his ability to think under enormous pressure. Wellman said it was the damnedest thing he'd ever seen. While everyone else was preparing to die, Billy was working on a way out. He never stopped to think about dying. He told Wellman and me, with that same cocksure smile you have now, 'In the midst of chaos, there is also opportunity.'"

"Sun Tzu, *The Art of War*, he quoted it all the time."

Another gentle knock at the door turned Harriet's head. She stood to go. "I'm sure they are looking for me. Let me leave you to your reading. Would you like some food, coffee, tea? Ellie said you didn't eat your brownie earlier. She found it when she picked up in here."

Bill opened the door and peeked in. "Sorry to interrupt. Mom, the snow is tapering off, Mrs. Colde is leaving."

"Colde? Is that Graham's mother by any chance?"

"Yes, she was Graham's mother. Theodore knows who she is, because he's met her, but he does not remember her as his mother. As far as she's concerned, her son never woke up from that coma. Theodore is a complete stranger."

Rainey wasn't about to let this opportunity pass, even if she had to follow the woman home in the snow. "Do you think she would talk to me? I'll try not to keep her long, so she can get home."

"Bill, would you ask Susie to step in here for a moment?" Harriet requested, and then turned back to Rainey. "I'm sure she'll talk with you."

The older woman Rainey saw in the kitchen entered the study.

"Susie," Harriet said, as she ushered her friend over to Rainey, who had come from behind the desk to meet her, "this is Rainey Bell, a friend of the family. In fact, Bill is named after her father. Rainey, Susie Colde."

"It's a pleasure to meet you ma'am," Rainey said, extending her hand in greeting.

Susie smiled and took Rainey's hand softly. "I thought you looked familiar. You're Billy Bell's daughter, the spitting image of him too. My husband knew your father, a veteran kind of thing. It's so nice to meet you."

"I had forgotten Billy knew Teddy. Anyway, Rainey has some questions she needs to ask you. It won't take long and we'll get you home straight away."

"What kind of questions?" Susie asked, while being escorted to the couch by Harriet.

"She needs to know about Graham, dear. It's rather important. It could help us find out who shot Wellman."

"Graham? What in the world could Graham have to do with Wellman's death?"

Rainey sat down in the chair Bill had pulled up to the couch earlier and began her questions. "When was the last time you saw your son, Mrs. Colde?"

Harriet answered for Susie, because the other woman appeared stunned by the question. "Oh, she hasn't had any contact with him since he was let out of the hospital. Isn't that right, Susie?"

Susie became very sheepish. Rainey didn't have time to play games. This woman was hiding something and could leave at any time. "You've seen him. Theodore. He's been here, hasn't he?"

After a moment, Susie sighed loudly. "Yes, he's been here. I haven't spoken with him, but I did see him. I called Wellman and told him I thought Graham, or Theodore—it's so hard for me to call him that—I thought he was watching my house. He's filled out a little and grown up now. He has a smaller frame, but looks like his father did at that age. I'd know that profile anywhere."

Harriet appeared stunned now. "Wellman never mentioned that."

Susie turned to her friend. "He said I shouldn't say anything and he would not either. Graham was in violation of his release by being here."

Rainey took control again, asking, "Has your son approached you at all?"

"No, but Wellman spoke to him. I called him like he told me to the next time I saw that white van outside my house. He came over and they talked thru the driver's side window for a moment, and then the van drove away."

"When was that?"

"About two weeks ago. I started seeing the van in early January, but I'm pretty sure he's been coming back here all along. I thought I saw him at Teddy's funeral. I would think I saw him and then convince myself it wasn't him. But these recent visits, it's like he wanted me to see him."

"Do you think he's remembering his old life?"

"He told Wellman he got our home address from his medical records, and that he was just trying to figure out what had happened to him. He promised to stop sitting in front of the house and drove away. He hasn't been back to my knowledge."

"Are you afraid of your son, Mrs. Colde?"

Susie answered without hesitation. "I was never afraid of Graham and to this day I have no idea why he shot those people. He was depressed, but we were getting treatment, all of us. Teddy's injury and PTSD affected our entire family, but Graham was a good boy. He was very smart, too smart it seems. He had a hard time relating to his peers, but he wasn't angry, not that we saw anyway. It just made no sense."

"Mrs. Colde, it is rare to find a parent who saw it coming. You are not alone in trying to make sense of a tragedy." Rainey asked the most important question next. "Could you tell me what kind of experience Graham had with the rifle used in the shooting? Did he hunt?"

"Oh, no. Graham didn't like guns. He never even played those first-person shooter games all the boys liked. He would faint at the site of blood, always did, so it never made sense that he would shoot someone, and it certainly never made sense that he shot a second person after the blood from the first. I guess we'll never know. I lost my son fourteen years ago. I suppose he just snapped."

"It made no sense." "He just snapped." Rainey heard those words often enough. People were always shocked at finding out the person they thought they knew had unfathomable secrets. "I never saw it coming," another frequent comment, one Rainey had made herself. Life, like any good mystery novel, contained all the clues in the beginning. Sudden personality changes were rare. Rainey knew, when a person did something seemingly out of character, she should go back a few chapters, or even to the beginning. The clues were always there, just so much easier to see in hindsight.

"What can you tell me about your son's relationship with the Paxtons?"

"Oh, he loved them. He stayed over there as much as he was home. Ellie and Ely were always good to him. Graham was small and a target for bullies, but the twins protected him. He loved Ellie beyond reason. I've often wondered if her beginning to date was the trigger."

Rainey delved deeper. "Beyond reason. What makes you say that?"

"Well, I told you he didn't like guns, but he joined the shooting club, just to spend Saturday afternoons with the Paxtons at the range."

"Shooting club?"

"Yes, Mr. Paxton was a world class marksman. He started a competition-shooting club for the kids that fall before—" Susie paused to gather her emotions.

Rainey gave her the moment she needed and then asked, "Do you remember who was in the club?"

"There was a whole group of them: the twins of course; Skylar, who had started dating Ellie at the beginning of the school year; Gordon, who is still Skylar's shadow; Cassie, she was Ellie's best friend and dated Ely; and I think Benjy Janson was out there too—most of the neighborhood was involved. Graham wanted to belong so badly. He went probably three times and then just stopped. He said the noise bothered him, even with ear protection."

"Then he did know how to fire a rifle." Rainey said, confirming that Susie was contradicting her earlier statement about Graham's dislike of guns.

Susie seemed to realize this as well. "Well, yes, he knew how to use a rifle. He just wasn't gun crazy like so many boys his age were."

"How did he gain access to the rifle he used?" Rainey was testing how readily available firearms were in the Colde household.

"Well, that's the thing. That awful note they found in Graham's pocket, it led the police to believe he may have been planning to go to school that morning and kill those kids on his list. That was Teddy's rifle. He loaned it to Graham for the shooting club. Mr. Paxton kept it at his house because he transported the weapons for the shooters in his truck to and from the range. He said it eliminated the poor judgment young men were prone to and saved the road signs on the way back to town. The police believe Graham went to the Paxtons with the intention of retrieving the rifle and was surprised by Ellie's father. The rest is just a tragedy."

"And his obsession with Ellie, did that ever give you pause?"

"Yes, I worried that he was too invested in her, but she was always so sweet about it. She told him he was her best guy friend, but he wanted more than that, I'm sure. I'm so sorry he ruined her life, after the kindness she had shown him. You know, Ellie was the first person in this town to come to the house after Graham shot her parents. She wanted us to know she didn't blame us. I was one of the first people she came to see when she moved back to town in January."

"One last question, Mrs. Colde. Did Graham ever talk to you about being bullied?"

"He didn't complain. He said he was chastised in class sometimes for knowing all the answers, and the bigger boys used to pick him up, jostle him around, which embarrassed him. He was one of the youngest in his class, but he was too smart to hold back. He was sensitive about his stature, but the bullying never seemed malicious. We did what all parents do. We told him to toughen up and ignore them. In hindsight, that probably was not the advice he needed."

"Thank you, Mrs. Colde. I appreciate your candor."

Rainey stood with the other women and stepped aside so they could exit. She had started for the desk, when she turned for one last inquiry. "Mrs. Colde, did Graham know Burgess Read and Adam Goodwin?" These were the only remaining names Colde's mother had not mentioned from the list.

Susie stopped at the door. "Why, yes. Burgess was the closest thing Graham had to a real friend, other than the twins. I'm quite sure it was their mutual grief that brought Ellie and Burgess together after the deaths."

"And Adam?" Rainey reminded her.

"Adam he knew, but they were not close. Adam was one of the bigger boys that liked to give Graham a hard time. He was in that shooting club too, now that you mention it." She shrugged her shoulders. "That's the whole list of names, isn't it—everyone my son intended to kill? I've looked at that list a thousand times. I'll never know why he hated them so much and I can't live my life dwelling on it. My son is dead, Ms. Bell. This Theodore Suzanne, if he had something to do with Wellman's death, I hope you catch him and put him away forever, this time."

As Susie and Harriet exited, Benjy Janson poked his head in the door holding a plate covered in plastic wrap in one hand and a white foam cup filled with something steaming in the other. "My wife insisted that I bring you a plate. She was afraid you were locked in here with no food or water." He laughed easily. "Her mission in life is to feed the world."

"Thank her for me. I am hungry and whatever is steaming in that cup looks fantastic."

Benjy brought the gifts from Leda to the desk and put them down. He extended his hand. "Hi, I'm Benjy Janson, and you are the woman with the beautiful family my wife keeps going on about."

Rainey offered her hand and her name. "Rainey Bell. Nice to meet you. Your wife is very sweet."

"I think so too." He looked around, saw a cup on the table beside the couch, and walked over to pick it up. "I thought I got everything out of this room earlier."

"Were there people in here?" Rainey started scanning the desk, trying to remember how she had left it before they went to the crime scene.

"I caught Skylar and his latest bed bunny in here earlier. This one is the new preacher's wife. Christians do some of the most unchristian things, don't they?"

Rainey picked up the coffee Benjy brought. "Yes, they do. I actually caught a serial killer in a church parking lot once. He was a youth minister."

Benjy laughed, probably because of the irreverence Rainey had voiced in agreement with his statement. "Now that is one of the reasons you won't catch me in the pew on Sunday. I talk to my God outside. I'd rather be in the woods on Sunday morning, than sitting with hypocrites like Skylar Sweet."

"I take it you don't care for Skylar," Rainey egged him on.

"No, he's a poor excuse for a human being. And that goon he hangs with, Gordon, what a dick. I ran into him poaching on the Read property. I told Leda I wouldn't be surprised if he's the one that shot Mr. Wise. He's always high. He probably doesn't know what he's shooting at half the time. He's also coward enough to run away instead of get help."

"Did you tell the police you saw him poaching out there?" Rumors were easier to spread than making an official statement. Most people willing to say something in a diner would back down the rhetoric when talking to a badge. Rainey was testing Benjy's voracity.

"I sure as hell did," he answered immediately.

"Do you know if they questioned him?"

"The guy laughed at me. Said Gordon Terrell was the best shot in the county. That's a small town for you. Good ol' boys win every time."

"You really think he did it, don't you?" Rainey was pushing Benjy. She wanted to see if he angered beyond the mild display so far.

"Whether he did or not, I don't want him poaching in those woods. My son and I hike in there all the time. I don't want to be the next victim of an accidental shooting. If you ask me, there is nothing accidental about pulling the trigger. You either know your target and see it clearly or you do not shoot. It is as simple as that."

"Do you hunt, Benjy?"

"No, but I used to shoot some at the range. I was in the shooting club with most of the people I can't stand now. At one time, we were friends, but then the shooting happened and a bunch of other stuff and we all went our own way. Well, except Skylar and Gordon, they have been inseparable since grade school, which is probably the reason no one has ever just kicked either one of their asses. There are always two of them, three when Adam was around."

"Did you ever see anyone bully Graham Colde?"

"Yes, all the time. The jocks were relentless."

Rainey needed clarification. "By jocks, do you mean Skylar and those guys?"

"Yes, especially Skylar. I'm telling you, Skylar Sweet is a prick. He always has been. I don't hate many people, but that son of a bitch is at the top of my list."

Rainey stopped the smile that tried to creep to her lips. Skylar was on the top of everyone's list. "Do you know about the list found in Graham's pocket the morning of the shooting?"

"Yes, everybody does."

"Do you have any idea why your name was on it?"

Benjy's body language changed. He deflated from his moral superiority somewhat. "I wasn't always a grown up. I did my share of stupid things. You wouldn't know it by looking at me now, but I was Goth back in high school, long dyed black hair, painted nails, piercings sticking out of me everywhere. I was even in a death metal band with Burgess Read. We were such dorks."

"How did that get you on Graham's list?"

"The Halloween before the shooting, we took Graham into the woods and scared him so bad he fainted. Then, of course, we told everyone."

"What exactly did you do?" Rainey needed to know how traumatizing the event might have been.

"We went out to this old graveyard. It's up in the woods on the Read property. Burgess and Graham had been friends forever, but as we got older, Graham just—well, now that I have my own kid, I realize he was just maturing at a slower rate than we were. He was still reading graphic novels and talking about superheroes. We were after chicks and weed. Graham was always trying to hang around."

"He was cramping your style."

"Yes, but nobody meant to really hurt him. We just wanted him to go away. So we took him out there to the old graveyard. There used to be an old crumbling mausoleum back there. It's gone now and the bodies have been moved, but back then the caskets were still inside. We pried the door open and Cassie Gillian dressed up in a costume to look like a dead girl that had been hit by a car. She had pig's blood all over her. We start telling this ghost story about a girl killed on prom night and then she pops out. Graham fell over instantly. He woke up and fell over again. Finally, Burgess got worried and we took Graham home, but he never forgave us for that."

"Did Burgess know Graham fainted at the sight of blood?"

Benjy looked surprised. "No, I don't think so. None of us did. Even being the dicks we were, I don't think we would have done that if we knew."

"He couldn't control it. Fifteen percent of the population faints at the sight of blood. It's actually thought to be an innate phenomenon left over from our caveman days," Rainey explained.

"Wow, that throws a whole new slant on his reaction. Damn, kids can be so cruel."

"Yes, they can," Rainey agreed.

Benjy was ready to move on. "Well, if you're ever in town again, bring your beautiful family by the diner. Leda would love that."

"Thank you, Benjy. It was a pleasure to meet you and your lovely family, as well."

He smiled back at her on the way out the door. "Watch for a Janson in the sports pages. I think that boy of ours is going to be a star."

"I'll do that," Rainey replied, while thinking about genetic prodigies.

With Benjy gone, and the door closed behind him, Rainey sat down at the desk again. She reopened the file and looked at Graham's list.

She spoke aloud, quoting one of the Columbine shooters, Dylan Klebold, "The lonely man strikes with absolute rage." She focused on the drawing at the bottom of the page, where the stickman assassin took aim, bloody bodies at his feet. "Were you a lonely man, Graham Colde?" She looked up from the paper, glancing over her shoulder at the freezing fog and low clouds spitting an occasional snowflake. "Is Theodore Suzanne a lonely man now?"

Chapter Five

Rainey spent three hours reviewing the evidence Wellman Wise collected and still she wasn't sure what he had found. Maybe it was nothing. His phone call to her could have been to warn her about Theodore Suzanne. He may have been killed before he uncovered the clue to the mystery he tried to solve for fourteen years. It was clear from his handwritten notes that Captain Wise believed there were too many dead people on the original list to be a coincidence. He examined the case from every angle, establishing motives for the four living people from the list, although some were a stretch. He scrutinized what he could find about each one's whereabouts when the other's died. Leda wasn't on the list, but she had just as much motive as anyone else, and hers made more sense than some of the others. If the accidents were actually murders, they all could have done it.

The Captain also tracked Theodore. He contacted his doctors at the hospital after seeing him at his mother's, but was given no information directly related to his care, just some hypothetical answers to his questions about recovered memories. He seemed to be leaning toward Theodore remembering his past. Wise had asked the doctors if a patient with an injury like Theodore's could fake the amnesia. They were highly doubtful, but did concede that no one knew how much he might eventually recall.

One note was of the most interest to Rainey. The doctors were forthcoming about Theodore's obsession with his own case and the psychological profiling of Graham Colde. He spent his time trying to understand what made Graham kill. He read copious amounts and asked endless questions. The doctors saw no ill effects and it actually helped him process what had happened in his past. When they learned that he had returned home, the doctors said he was probably still trying to connect the dots. Theodore's behavioral analysis of his former persona became a passion driven by one burning question—what went wrong?

Rainey emerged from the study just after six and sat down with Bill, his wife Morgan, and Harriet for another meal of ham sandwiches and brownies, with sides of potato salad and pickles.

Bill leaned back and patted his stomach. "I may never eat another ham sandwich in my life."

Morgan stuffed the fifth dill pickle into her mouth, while the rest of them had a second round of coffee after the brownies. Rainey counted because she remembered how ravenous Katie was when she was pregnant and how many jars of Ernie's homemade pickles she had eaten. Ernie had to make a second batch just for her.

"Mmm. These pickles are delicious," Morgan said, chomping on number six.

Rainey saw the smile creep onto Harriet's face. "Do you two have something to tell me?"

Morgan nearly choked on the pickle. Bill's face turned red. Rainey felt like an intruder, but she couldn't leave.

Harriet prodded Morgan. "I ate my weight in pickles when I was pregnant with Bill."

Bill gushed, "Well, I guess now is as good a time as ever. Mom, we're having a baby."

Harriet was thrilled and while they were all hugging, Rainey slipped out of the kitchen and went to the foyer where she could look out the large glass panes in the front door. The sky was dark now. The streetlight cast an amber glow on the snow-covered corner, where the Wise home stood. The snow smoothed all the edges, hid all that was unsightly, turning Hominy Junction into a picturesque Christmas card scene. Somewhere out there, a killer may have been lurking, thinking they got away with murder, multiple ones if the Captain was right.

Rainey had done all she could. She would call Brad Dawson at the Dobbs County Sheriff's office and tell him what she knew. It wasn't her place to become involved in an open investigation without being asked. She did as the family requested, reviewed the information. Now, it was someone else's job to investigate.

Rainey had more pressing matters. Though related, her reasons for wanting to find Theodore Suzanne had nothing to do with Wellman Wise's shooting or any supposed murder plots. Her family was of most importance, and being stuck here away from them was frustrating and a bit unnerving. Knowing the security she had in place would probably stop an intruder, she couldn't help but wonder, if Theodore could invade her privacy as much as he had, what was he capable of doing. Could he hack the locks, disable the system, could he get to her wife and kids?

"There you are," Harriet said behind her. She stepped beside Rainey to look out the window. "Isn't it beautiful?"

"Yes, it makes everything look so pure."

"Pure as the driven snow. That must be where that comes from," Harriet surmised. "It's warmed up some." She pointed at a weather station on the wall. "It's nearly thirty degrees now. Maybe we won't get that half-inch of ice they've predicted. I sure hope not."

"There will be massive power outages if that happens," Rainey commented, remembering the last ice storm to come through the Carolinas.

"We have a generator, so if the power goes out, just stay put. Wellma— Bill will have it back on in a few minutes."

Rainey smiled. "Your son is a good man. It's a reflection of his parents. Your husband has left you in good hands."

Harriet patted Rainey's arm and smiled up at her. "He did do that. Would you like to join us in the den for hot chocolate?"

"That sounds fantastic."

Rainey followed Harriet to the den where they joined the giddy Bill and Morgan. Now that their secret was out, the mood of the day had shifted. Rainey had been right in telling Bill to inform his mother of the baby. The whole family was glowing.

Bill stood on their entry and lifted a cup and saucer to Rainey's hand. He smiled and whispered, "Great advice."

She returned the smile and took a seat in the corner armchair.

Morgan looked over at Rainey. "Bill tells me your dad taught him how to break a pair of handcuffs. I don't believe him. If they are that easy to break, then why do the cops even use them, or can you only break the cheap kind? You were in the FBI weren't you? Could someone break the cuffs you used?"

"He's telling the truth, the chain between the two cuffs or the part that holds the chain on the cuff can be snapped fairly easily. The more expensive, the easier they are to break. Strength and size are not necessary either."

"Then why don't the criminals just break them and run," Morgan asked.

Rainey did not crack a smile when she replied, "Because we would shoot them."

"Oh," Morgan said.

Rainey could maintain the straight face no longer and started to laugh, which caused the room to erupt.

When the laughter died down, she said, "They do break cuffs occasionally, but dangerous criminals are transported with more than a single pair of cuffs to contain them."

"See, honey, I wasn't making that up. He also taught me how to pick the lock on the cuffs and how to use a shim to defeat the ratchet part on the cuff itself. He could also break out of zip ties."

Morgan asked Rainey. "Why would your dad know all that stuff?"

"SERE training. He was in Special Forces. Plus, he ran a bail business, so he stayed up on things even after he left the service for good. It's smart to know all the ways someone can escape from custody."

"What is SERE training?" Morgan wanted to know.

Bill answered before Rainey could. "Survive, Evade, Resist, Escape."

"Billy was quite a character and, as Wellman would testify one hell of a soldier, but he had a heart of gold" Harriet said from the rocker by the couch, where Bill and Morgan were seated. "We were out on the porch one night—he'd come down to fish with Wellman—when he says, 'Hey, Captain,'—he always called him Captain—'Hey Captain, I'm going to walk around to Teddy Colde's house and pay him a visit.' We didn't even know he knew the Coldes. It seemed that when he heard about what Graham had done and the trauma Teddy had already been through, he started visiting now and again, taking Teddy for long drives just to talk and get him out of the house. 'Billy Bell is just one of the good guys,' Wellman would say."

Rainey's heart felt heavy and light at the same time. On one hand, she missed him horribly. On the other, the stories of her father's benevolence turned up all the time. Billy, it seemed, spent his spare time helping veterans experiencing PTSD. Even before it was a household word, her father knew these men were damaged and needed help. The 'never leave a man behind' mentality stayed with Billy, even after his uniform was packed away for the last time. He was in the National Guard for years, beyond the time he spent on active duty, retiring at age forty, but Billy Bell was in the Army until the day he died.

"Brothers in arms forever," Rainey said. "He lived by that."

"Well, I'm glad he was around," Morgan commented, patting Bill on the chest. "I'm told I wouldn't have his namesake here, if not for your father. That's an amazing story. Someone should write about it."

Harriet responded to Morgan's suggestion. "I asked Wellman why he didn't write the story down. He said we only knew what he chose to tell us, and without the details it was just another story of ordinary men surviving that hellhole in an extraordinary way. He said they all had stories like that. It was a hell of war."

"And then they were spat on," Bill said, injured by the dishonor to his father.

As a salve to Bill's wound, Harriet offered, "It was a turbulent time in our country. The public is more supportive now of our soldiers coming home from wars they don't necessarily agree with. That pleased Wellman immensely. Duty can have no political agenda for the soldier. I believe the Vietnam vets are to thank for that shift in public perception."

"And yet, there is so much more to be done to help our soldiers recover from the injuries they've suffered, both mentally and physically," Rainey said.

Morgan piped in excitedly, "Bill worked on a program to help soldiers with head injuries recover brain function."

"Did Theodore help you with that program?" The man stalking her family was never far from Rainey's mind. She wanted to know more about him.

Bill sat up, assuming a more professional air. "Actually, it was his idea. This kid is brilliant. His social skills are underdeveloped, but the part of his brain that can write code is incredible. I couldn't believe all the things he knew about the human mind."

"Where do you work?" Might as well interrogate Bill while he was sitting in front of her, Rainey thought.

"Programming by Genius in Research Triangle Park."

"I know someone else that works there: Joey Erickson," Rainey said, putting the puzzle pieces together in her mind.

Bill smiled. "Joey, yeah, he's a cool kid, different, but cool."

"He's kind of a ward to a friend of mine. In fact, he's at my house right now."

Bill's smile vanished. "You know he hangs with Theodore. They share social deficiencies in common, so they sort of ended up together. They are both incredibly talented, just extremely—"

Rainey spoke up, "Joey has Asperger's. I can see how a brain injury like Theodore's could mimic the same effect. And yes, I knew they were friends. Theodore has not been to my house, or at least I'm unaware if he has, but he and Joey were given carte blanche at my wife's women's shelter. They helped her with a program for her computer system."

"Is that how he got all that information for the game?" Harriet asked. Obviously Bill had let her know what he and Rainey found.

"Do you have access to military-grade surveillance equipment?" Rainey asked, knowing that's what it would take to break into her security system.

Bill's face answered the question before he did, as concern wrinkled his brow. "Yes, we do. We have to know how everything works in order to make the virtual training videos."

Morgan was unaware of the undercurrent of the conversation. "They use virtual actors because it's cheaper than real people. Soon, we won't see real people at all in the movies, right honey?"

Bill turned to his wife. "Well, a combination, like the movie "300.""

Rainey's mind was racing through scenarios. Was Theodore in her house? Did he trick Joey into wearing a camera? How safe were the people in her house tonight? If he was watching Rainey, he knew she was not at home. In fact, if he was watching that closely, he knew she was in his old hometown. If he killed Wellman Wise because of what he knew, then he may suppose Rainey knew it now. At least nothing was moving outside. That was some comfort.

Morgan bantered on, changing the subject that apparently did not interest her. "Speaking of actors, do you know what Ellie told me? She said that estate she just inherited was worth over two million dollars. She said she was giving up auditioning forever."

Harriet chimed in, "Well, she sure used as much of Burgess's money as she could trying to be famous."

Rainey snapped out of her thoughts of Theodore. "Benjy told me that he and Burgess were in a death metal band in high school. Ellie doesn't look like the type to hang with the Goths. I pictured her as a cheerleader and homecoming queen."

"I remember her in high school," Harriet said. "In a small town, the school is pretty much our social life. We went to the football games and plays. Ellie was the head cheerleader and starred in all the productions. Everyone was so proud of how she bounced back from the tragedy. Burgess was an excellent musician, even if he did dress rebelliously. He was handsome, artsy, could paint, sing, play most instruments. They hooked up right before they graduated."

"Hooked up?" Morgan laughed. "Mama Wise, when did you become so hip?"

Harriet joined in the laughter. "I watch TV. I'm keeping up with the times."

"I know why Ellie hooked up with Burgess," Bill interjected. "He got that internship to work in Wilmington at one of the studios. He was brilliant with sound. I talked to him that summer. I was home just after I graduated from college. He asked me if he should go to school and I told him he could learn more working in the industry. As it turned out, I was right. He moved right up the food chain. Last I heard, he was running one of the sound studios down there."

"Ellie left because her looks were beginning to fail and she needed to find that rich man to take care of her the rest of her life," Morgan said, with an assurance that turned all heads toward her.

Bill chuckled. "What makes you say that?"

"Oh, I watch "Real Housewives." I know how women like Ellie operate."

"Burgess had all that money coming. Why did she leave him?" Rainey asked.

Harriet answered the question. "Old man Read hung on forever and no one really knew how much money he had. He died after Ellie left Burgess, but before they were divorced. He'd roll over in his grave if he knew Ellie Paxton was living in his house. He always called her a gold digger."

"This is why we aren't living in a small town, Bill," Morgan said. "Everybody knows everybody's business."

"How did he die?" Rainey asked.

"They found him slumped over on his boat, apparent heart attack. Not far from where they found Wellman." Harriet finished the sentence and then went quiet.

"Who found your father?" Rainey's brain was crunching facts. The prickly feeling was returning.

"Ellie. She has a habit of going for a cold dip, even in winter. She says it keeps her skin soft," Morgan answered, because Bill and Harriet were lost in thought. "She said the salt water in California was better, but for now the sandpit would do. Anyway, she usually goes early in the morning, but she went to Raleigh that day. She went for a swim after she got home."

"So, she was gone when the shooting took place?"

Harriet looked up from her shoe gazing. "Oh, you don't think Ellie shot Wellman, do you? She loved him. He spent hours with her after the shooting. She looked at him like a father, said so many times. Ellie would have no reason to kill Wellman. I think he thought someone was killing all the people she cared about. Cassie was her best friend, Ely was her brother, Burgess her husband, Adam had been Ely's best friend, all these people were connected to her."

"I know," Rainey said, leaning forward. "That's what makes this puzzling. She is either the most unlucky person in the world, or these things were done for her benefit in some warped mind."

Bill was putting his own puzzle together. "What if Theodore does remember his old life? What if he's still obsessing over Ellie? That would explain a lot of things."

"Your father warned him to stay away," Rainey said. "In an erotomania personality, someone with attachment issues, the person can sometimes be forced to remove obstacles to their obsessions. If something or someone gets in the way, these types of personalities can become extremely unpredictable."

"Why would this guy still be obsessed with Ellie after all these years?" Morgan asked.

"A person with this personality disorder believes the individual they fixate on is in fact in love with them. A smile from a colleague becomes a declaration of true love. Opening the door for a woman can signal to her a love match. There is no way to convince a person with an erotomania attachment that the person does not return their devotion. Worst case scenarios end up in the murder of the object they desire but can never have."

Morgan looked at Bill. "You are now forbidden to open doors for strange women."

"And you don't smile at coworkers," Bill added.

Harriet spoke next. "You know so much about deviant behavior. I'm sure you've seen the worst of us humans. No wonder you wear a weapon."

"Well, I seem to attract trouble, as my wife says, so I'm prepared should that happen."

"Bill told me about your past. You must have nine lives," Morgan commented. "And you're so normal. I'd never come out of the house, if I'd lived through all that. I'd figure my luck had run out."

"She doesn't need luck." It was Harriet commenting. "She's Billy Bell's child. I suspect her DNA has kept her alive more than providence."

"There is always a way out, until you give up. That's what Dad said Billy kept saying in the jungle. He thought Billy Bell was the bravest man he'd ever known. I told him once that I was going to be a brave soldier just like him and win lots of medals, but you know what Billy said when I told him that?" Bill waited a second, but he really didn't want an answer. "He said, 'Don't confuse courage with pride, Bill—"

Rainey finished her father's oft-repeated warning, "It'll get you killed."

"I've always remembered that," Bill said, reflectively.

"Wellman and Billy, they were a different breed. You don't find too many of those types of men around anymore," Harriet said, adding, "I'm extremely proud to have known them both."

"Me too," Rainey said, toasting with her cocoa cup.

"It's snowing again," Morgan said, looking out the window.

"Snow is better than ice," Bill said. "Hopefully, I won't be getting up in the middle of the night to start the generator."

Morgan patted his knee. "Just wait until you're changing diapers and three a.m. feedings."

Rainey laughed. "Yep, you should sleep as much as possible now. I haven't felt rested in two years."

"May I see your children?" Morgan asked. "Leda said they were precious."

Rainey pulled out her phone and found the picture they took at Christmas. She handed the phone to Morgan. "The biggest boy is Mack. The other boy is Timothy, and the girl is Weather."

"How absolutely beautiful. Look at these babies, Bill."

The Wises passed Rainey's phone around, while she showed them more pictures. It was eight-thirty when they finally ran out of stories to swap. Harriet was exhausted, understandably, and excused herself to her bedroom, after making sure Rainey's sleeping arrangements had been made.

She hugged Rainey, before leaving her in the hallway. "Thank you so much for coming. I do hope you will come and visit me. You remind me so much of your father, and it was always a joy to have him around."

"I'll do that," Rainey said, and she meant it.

Harriet squeezed Rainey's hand. "I know you'll find out who killed Wellman."

"I'll do my absolute best, I promise. I won't let them allow this case to go cold. I'll stay on it."

"I know you will. You're Billy's daughter. You will make things right."

With Harriet's expectations weighing heavy on her, Rainey returned to the study. She reviewed the files one more time. Still, no smoking gun jumped out at her, literally. No one had a motive to kill all of those people. Each individual had a reason to kill one or more, but not all.

Ellie gained financially on the death of her parents, brother, and husband, but the links to the other deaths were thin. Skylar may have killed Adam with Gordon's help, because he was going to tell or blackmail them over the rape. Maybe Leda and Benjy were blackmailing Skylar. Why not just kill them then? Too obvious, maybe. Rainey scanned to the next living soul on the list, Benjy. His reasons, along with his wife's, were compelling, but the two actual perpetrators of the rape remained alive. Why kill Burgess Read? Maybe his death was an accident and it was simply muddying the water. Cassie Gillian's death was never questioned as anything but an accidental overdose. And then there was Theodore, the only person with a reason to kill them all and the means to do it, his mind. If this were a criminal conspiracy, it would take a brain of enormous capacity to pull off. Cunning, ruthless, and patient criminals were the hardest to catch and the most dangerous.

Rainey closed the file and opened the laptop. Bill had written the password down. She typed it in and waited for the computer to wake, before finding the game folder. She started the game and watched the opening movie again, looking for things she may have missed earlier. She paused the video at each scene change, amazed at the details that popped out at her. In the killer's lair, where she had been tortured, she saw her clothes on the floor by the bed, just as she'd seen them in the crime scene photos. Most of her memories came from those photos and were not memories at all, but information her brain used to fill in the gaps in the dreams it sometimes sent to haunt her. It was difficult at times to distinguish between what she actually remembered of that night and what she dreamed had happened. The movie revived the memory of the experience, but with a morbid curiosity she watched.

The sexual assault was handled with quickly changing camera angles, as if the viewer was flipping pages in a graphic novel, showing just enough to let the viewer's imagination fill in the blanks. The close-up slow motion clip of the letter being carved into the flesh of Stormy Weathers was bloody and gruesome.

"What the hell?" Rainey sprang from the chair.

She ran to the door and called out for Bill. He came on a run.

"What is it? What have you found?"

Rainey ushered him to the desk, saying, "Graham Colde would pass out at the sight of blood. How does Theodore react around all this blood on the screen?"

"Uh, well, he doesn't see it. All of his drawings are in black ink. We take his storyboards and turn it into computer-generated images. Theodore actually refuses to watch and Joey does it for him."

"Joey Erickson has seen this game?"

"Yes, he's on the team." Another light bulb moment for Bill lit up the room.

"I think I'll have a talk with Joey when I get home," Rainey said, but was secretly glad it was Joey and not some leak in her security that had invaded her space. "I'm sure he was easily led. Joey is very smart about some things, but socially, he lacks discretion."

Bill defended Joey's actions. "I'm sure he meant nothing more than making it right. He's a stickler for detail. It probably never crossed his mind that it was inappropriate."

Rainey agreed. "I'm sure it was more about the fact that he knows a real profiler and this is what her office looks like.

Accuracy is Joey's thing. He has almost eidetic recall of things he sees."

"It's nice of you to react that way. Most people would be pissed at the breach of trust."

Rainey smiled. "Joey is the last person on earth that would breech a trust. If he's told to keep a secret, good luck getting it out of him. I had hell getting the passwords to the women's shelter's computers after he reset them."

Bill yawned. "Excuse me. It's been a very long day."

Rainey was growing tired too. "Well, I guess we should get some rest," she said.

"What do you think, Rainey? Can you figure out who killed my dad?"

"Bill, there is a lot of information here, but not nearly enough to do a profile. You need someone in law enforcement to buy your father's theory that these accidents were intentional murders. That's what it is going to take to gather enough information to come up with a behavioral analysis of this crime, and I'm still not sure if the Colde case is related or not. We could be dealing with a random assailant and your father a victim of opportunity. If the motive for his murder was the investigation into the Colde case, it presents problems of its own. There are many jurisdictions to approach about autopsies and accident reports, photos to analyze, witnesses to interview. It's just not a call I can make with the little bit of info I have here. While compelling, the file isn't enough to solve the mystery that obsessed your father."

"Well, then we'll have to convince someone Dad wasn't shot accidently by a hunter."

"I think that's a good start, and I'll make that call tomorrow when I get home. I'd like to talk to Joey first. He might be able to give me more about Theodore. I'd like to have all the information I can before I call the Sheriff's department. Dawson is a good man. He'll make sure the ball is not dropped."

"Okay, I know you'll do your best. Thank you for the help. You'll have to let us take you out to dinner sometime, you and your wife."

Rainey shook Bill's hand. "Make sure you have my info before you leave. I'm holding you to the dinner date. Just make sure it's before the baby is born, or you will never find the time."

#

9:15 p.m.
Snow, 33°F, Windchill 23.4°F

Rainey undressed in the guest bedroom and pulled the spare tee shirt she found in the van over her head. The old Victorian's upstairs rooms were a bit chilly, so she shivered upon hitting the cold sheets. She checked the time on her phone. Katie would be putting the kids to bed about now. Rainey decided to wait a bit before calling. This was the earliest she had been in bed for a long time. The house was quiet now, except for the occasional creaking caused by a gust of wind.

Rainey closed her eyes and listened to the silence. It was almost too quiet. Even when the triplets were asleep, she could hear them in the monitor by the bed. The cribs squeaked with their movements, they giggled in their sleep, they snorted and sniffed through the night, and it was comforting to hear them. The room Rainey occupied in the Wise home had no sounds of sleeping babies to lull her to dreamland. She opened her eyes and stared at the ceiling. Rainey missed home and being snuggled up to a beautiful blonde, listening to the familiar sounds of all being right with the world.

The bed began to warm from her body heat and she relaxed into the pillow. It was still too early to call home. Katie would be putting things away from the day, preparing for the next. Rainey began to hear Creedence Clearwater Revival playing in the back of her mind. "Run Through the Jungle" grew louder as she concentrated on the sound.

"Creedence was my dad's favorite band," Bill had explained about the music playing when Rainey first walked up to the house. "He wanted a celebration of his favorite things," he said, on the way back from the crime scene.

"The Captain had a nice send off," a voice said.

Rainey opened her eyes to find she was standing in the jungle, water dripping off the huge green leaves surrounding her. The ground rose up in front of her, and a mound of foliage became a camouflaged soldier, his face painted green and black, with only the whites of his eyes hinting at a human under the Ghillie suit. Rainey jumped instinctively, but then stopped to peer into the green irises looking back at hers.

"Dad, you look scary as hell," she said.

"Rainey? What are you doing here?"

Under all the camo, Billy Bell was the young man he had been in the picture hanging on the wall of the study downstairs.

"I don't know. I think I'm dreaming."

"Roger that." He squatted down, scanning the horizon, realized she was standing, and pulled her down with him. "Keep your head down. Those little shits are out there, you just can't see them. They blend in with the trees. You think you're looking at a tree and then it shoots you."

Rainey noticed Billy was holding an M14 Vietnam-era sniper rifle. "Why are you dressed like that? You weren't a sniper."

Billy looked at himself and seemed surprised at his attire. "I don't know. It's your dream."

Instantly they were transported inside the profiler game, where they stood watching Stormy Weather's virtual assault.

Billy leaned into Rainey's shoulder, still in his Ghillie suit and war paint. "You know, I would have cut his balls off and fed them to him."

"Yes, Dad, I know." The dissociation from the scene struck Rainey as odd. She watched the assault, as if it had nothing to do with her. "You have grandkids now, three of them."

"You, with three kids? I'm sorry I didn't stick around for that. Remember, you reap what you sow."

Flash, they were back in the jungle, standing at the edge of a rice patty, just inside the tree line. This time, the Creedence song filled up the sky overhead, punctuated by helicopter blades.

"That's my ride," Billy shouted over the noise. "It was good to see you, Rainey."

Billy started running toward the landing chopper.

Rainey called after him, "Be safe."

He turned to grin and wave, shouting, "Always, baby girl. Always."

Rainey watched the chopper land. A hand waved at her from the cockpit. She squinted into the windshield to see a young, svelte Wellman Wise at the helm. Without warning the music changed to the children's song "Three Blind Mice." It played as the chopper lifted and flew away, with her Ghillie-suited father standing on a skid, waving a different rifle in the air, an M1 Garand, the type used to kill Wellman Wise.

Billy shouted down at her, but she could not hear him for the noise.

"I can't hear you. Wait. What are you saying? Dad, come back."

The "Three Blind Mice" song started over at the beginning before Rainey realized it was the ringtone for Katie and she had fallen asleep. Shaking off the short trip into dreamland, she reached for her phone.

"Hey, baby, I just had the weirdest dream," she said into the phone upon answering it.

"You fell asleep. I was waiting for you to call and you were sleeping," Katie said, but she wasn't mad. "Good for you. I'm glad one of us is getting some rest."

"I'm sorry. I was waiting for you to get the kids down and I guess I dozed off."

Katie sounded worried when she asked, "It wasn't one of those dreams, was it?"

"Those dreams" were night terrors and Rainey sure as hell was glad it wasn't one of those. "No, I dreamed I was talking to my dad."

"It's probably because of burying his friend. I'm sure you talked about him today."

Rainey rubbed the sleep from her face. "That's it, I suppose. The dream kind of had bits and pieces of today thrown into the jungles of Vietnam. Weird, like I said."

Katie let out a tired sigh. Rainey recognized the sound that came each night when the mother of three finally flopped into the winged back chair in the master bedroom.

Katie said, "It's been a long day and it sounds like you're trying to process a lot of information."

"I guess. Are you headed to bed?"

"No, I'm going to go downstairs and hang out with the adults for a bit. I don't get to do that very often."

"I'm going to have to talk to Joey when I get home, but I don't think anyone has been in the house or hacked the security system. I'm pretty sure Joey unwittingly participated."

"You're being so cryptic. What the hell happened down there?"

Rainey explained about the game and the detail it contained. Katie was shocked that the files at the shelter had been compromised and pledged to change the locks. Rainey knew Katie would do anything to keep those files out of their house. They contained things no mother would want in a home.

"I really don't think Joey would break a trust. I'm sure once he understands, there will be no more trouble, and I'll have Molly shut the game's production down. It shouldn't be hard to do."

"Rainey, do you think Theodore is dangerous?"

"Yes, I do. He crosses boundaries with no thought to consequences. That is scary enough."

"Well, the security company knows what he looks like. Leslie had a picture on her phone and I emailed it to them. The guard at the gatehouse said, 'Another one?' Really, Rainey the neighborhood security guards are going to want a pay raise. Like I said, you attract trouble like a magnet. Have you given any more thought to changing our names and moving to the south of France?"

Katie spoke of the fantasy life they craved of anonymity and escape from the hoard of nutcases that fixated on members of the BAU. Rainey had not written a book. She had not sought appearances beyond speaking on public safety issues to women's groups and at universities. She tried to remain a blip on the radar, but they found her.

"I think about it all the time," Rainey answered, and she was serious.

114

"I see you as a grape farmer, in overalls, no shirt, barefooted—oh my God, we need a night alone. I can't wait for Valentine's. I'm starved for you."

"Just let me get home tomorrow and very soon, I'll take care of that appetite."

"Okay, call me before you leave in the morning. I love you. Sweet dreams. Stay out of the jungle."

"I love you too. And sweet dreams to you as well. Hope the kids stay down."

"Joey and Molly wore them out for me. I owe them one."

"Good, then get some sleep. We're not sleeping through this vacation from the kids, not again."

Katie chuckled. "Not on your life."

The call concluded, Rainey set the alarm on her phone and checked the temperature on the weather app. Thirty-three degrees and light snow, with a wind chill factor making it feel like twenty-one. The hard freeze may miss them yet. Rainey hoped so. She was ready to be home so she could play in the snow with the kids.

Before she fell asleep, she thought back on the short dream earlier. What was her brain chewing on to spit out that particular collection of things? Her dad, Wellman Wise, the video game, she understood those appearances. They had been the center of conversation for most of her day. The sniper rifle, Ghillie suit, and then the switch of the rifle to the M1—her mind was combining the topics of the day into one short snippet. If there were a message, it would have to wait or be explained more clearly in another dream, because the heaviness of her eyelids won the battle, and Rainey Bell fell asleep in frozen little Hominy Junction.

Chapter Six

Thursday, February 13, 2014
6:15 a.m.
Light Rain, 34°F, Windchill 24.6°F

While Rainey slept past six a. m. with no little fingers prying her eyes open or bouncing on her back, the weatherman gave the good news on the television downstairs.

"We braced for a worst-case scenario yesterday and into early this morning, predicting up to a half-inch of ice. But folks, we dodged a bullet with temperatures warming up to about thirty-five degrees through Wednesday night. Expect the roads to remain slick in spots with ice still present in patches, until we get a bit warmer after sunrise. Keep in mind as the temperatures climb into the thirties today, the wind chill factor will still make it feel below freezing. Not a good day to stay outside for long periods, so monitor the time your kids spend outside on this snow day. We'll be back with the complete forecast in two minutes."

The alarm sounded at six-twenty a.m. Rainey rolled over and felt for her phone. Once in her grasp, she slid her finger on the screen to silence the noise. She slipped from under the covers, and stepped lightly through the cool room to the window. It was still dark. The street light glow revealed the predicted ice had not fallen. The trees glistened with the manageable weight of a thin glaze that stiffened them against the occasional gust of arctic wind. Hominy Junction was frozen, but not solidly. Rainey knew the ground was too warm down south for the snow to stay. A few sunny hours and the town would return to its previous state, dirt and flaws exposed. For now, Mother Nature hid the imperfections under a thick blanket of ice covered white snow.

Rainey smelled bacon cooking, an aroma detectable by stomachs around the world. It was the internationally understood call to breakfast. She redressed, made up the bed, grabbed her tee shirt, and went in search of a bathroom. The door was locked on the first one, with a retching Morgan inside. Rainey remembered those days of morning sickness with Katie and moved on. She found the downstairs powder room open. With a freshly washed face and hand smoothed curls, which was somewhat of a lost cause, Rainey emerged a few minutes later hell bent on leaving as soon as possible.

"Good morning, Rainey," Harriet welcomed her with a steaming cup of coffee and a breakfast plate of bacon, eggs, and a homemade biscuit, with a side of ham. "You don't have to eat the ham," she said. "I'm just trying to get rid of it. Leda must have thought we were feeding an army. I'll see if I can get someone to take most of the leftovers to Goldsboro, to the homeless shelter where they feed our lost boys. That's what Wellman would have done."

Rainey sat down at the table. "Thank you very much. It looks delicious. Have you heard anything about the roads?"

"The report on Wellman's scanner was the county roads are probably going to be cleared by eight or nine this morning. They worked all night, once the temperature got up above freezing. You'll be able to get to the highway then. You'll have to watch for patches of ice they say, but," she patted Rainey's hand, "you'll be able to get home this morning. I can see how anxious you are to be with them."

"Yes, ma'am. The triplets saw a little snow last year, but this is the first time I think we'll really get to play with them in it. I don't want to miss that. It probably won't be here long."

"Two is such a challenging age. They are learning as much about you as you them. I remember Bill being very precocious, well, I don't actually remember, but I kept a very detailed account of his childhood. Wellman was gone so much, I didn't want him to miss a thing."

"Katie is making a video diary. She also keeps written notes. I look forward to reading it again when we're rocking on the porch surrounded by grandkids."

"Wellman would have loved to be here for Bill and Morgan's child. I guess we'll just have to tell the baby all about Grandpa Wellman, won't we. I'm sure you'll share your father with your children."

Rainey remembered telling Timothy about the "coo doo." "Yes, ma'am. I started already. They'll know who he was. I'll make sure of that."

"Well, let me let you eat your breakfast. I'm going to check on Bill and Morgan."

"Is Bill sick too?" Rainey asked.

"Morgan has morning sickness and Bill Wise has the gag reflex of a cat. He's in there with her. It's a vicious cycle. Oh, I'm sorry, you're about to eat."

Rainey smiled and picked up her fork. "I have a cat and two years of babies under my belt, I could eat on top of the diaper hamper."

Rainey ate alone in the kitchen. She occasionally heard wisps of voices, but no one came to join her. She finished, rinsed her plate at the sink, and poured a second cup of coffee. The tee shirt she'd worn to bed sat on the counter. She carried it and the coffee to the foyer. The tee shirt went into the pocket of her coat, still hanging on the coat tree. The sky was lighter now, an overcast haze, but the sun was definitely shining somewhere.

"What do you think? You going to give it a try?"

Rainey turned to see Bill coming down the hall toward her. He looked a little pale.

"I think I'll wait a bit longer, give it time to thaw a little. How are you feeling?"

He smiled. "I don't know how long this morning sickness lasts, but I hope not long."

"How is Morgan?"

"Oh, she's fine. She's in there eating breakfast like it's no big deal. I'll be lucky if I'm able to get something down by lunch."

Rainey chuckled. "You'll survive. I think Katie's lasted about three months."

"In three months, I'll be a stick. I've already lost five pounds." Bill said, rubbing his stomach. He looked over at the weather station on the wall. "Thirty-four degrees. Boy, that's cold." He reached for his coat and hat. "Well, standing here isn't getting that snow off the porch and driveway." He looked over his shoulder. "And I'm getting out of here before Morgan's breakfast makes a retreat."

Rainey raised her coffee cup in a thankful toast. "I appreciate the warning."

Bill opened the front door just as Harriet entered the hallway. She called out, "Bill, don't you at least want some coffee before you go out there?"

Bill turned green, hustled out the door, and threw a "No ma'am" over his shoulder.

"Poor thing. He used to throw up if the cat had a hairball," Harriet said with a chuckle.

"It's funny what our bodies are programmed to do. Some faint at the sight of blood, others can't curl their tongues. Our genetic makeup sometimes removes choice from our plate."

Harriet came to stand beside Rainey. "So do you think an evil person is born that way? Susie and I have had this discussion for many years. She's convinced they did nothing wrong as parents." Harriet shrugged. "She is also quite positive that they could not have stopped it from happening."

Rainey answered without hesitation. "She may be right about not doing anything wrong as parents. It's often true the parents were concerned, were active, were attempting to solve the child's issues. It is also true that just as often parents were ill equipped to, or simply did not, recognize the blatant signs of impending violence. Who thinks their child capable of murder? Hindsight is the answer to all the questions no one asked before a tragedy happened."

"Amen to that," Harriet commented.

Rainey continued, "Your question of being born evil is a complicated one. Yes, some people have genetic anomalies that have been found to predicate certain behaviors. But, for example, people born without empathy are not always evil. Deliberate choices are made by all but the most seriously mentally ill. One psychopath becomes a wealthy, non-violent, CEO. Another becomes a mass murderer. DNA contributed, but the choice to commit a crime of violence against another human being, in most cases, was ultimately that of the perpetrator. A lot of behaviorists don't agree with that, but it has been true in my experience. We all have demons, Harriet. Those that choose to let them out have to be held responsible for their actions. I might fantasize about murdering someone. That doesn't make me evil. Choosing to pull the trigger does."

"Whoever shot Wellman was pure evil," Harriet said, eyes focused on her son shoveling the walk out front. "I hope they find him and put him away forever. And I agree with Susie, if it's her son, lock him up and throw away the key. I believe, in this instance, the bad seed was planted and took root, no matter who he claims to be today."

Rainey patted the shorter woman on the shoulder. "You can count on me locating and thoroughly investigating one Theodore Suzanne. If he did this, I'm going to find out."

Harriet reached to touch Rainey's hand on her shoulder. "I know you'll do your best. I can't thank you enough for all you did."

Skylar Sweet's truck coasted to a slow stop in front of the house. Rainey and Harriet watched as Gordon bailed out of the passenger side and grabbed a shovel from the back of the truck. He went straight to work shoveling alongside Bill. Skylar exited the truck, but did not grab a tool to begin working. He exchanged greetings with Bill, which Rainey and Harriet could not hear beyond muffled sounds, and then preceded to the front door. He smiled through the glass at them with his moonbeam teeth and let himself in.

"Good morning, ladies."

"Good morning, to you too," Harriet said, "May I offer you some coffee?"

"No, ma'am. We have some thermoses in the truck. We were headed over to Grandma's to shovel her walk and saw Bill might need a hand."

"How nice of you," Harriet said. "Thank you all so much. And you tell Grandma Sweet hello for me. I'm going to go back and check on Morgan."

"You just call if you need anything, Mrs. Wise. We're glad to help. Mr. Wise was a good man and we plan to do right by him."

"You are very kind, thank you."

Harriet left Rainey and Skylar alone in the foyer. Rainey thought Skylar was a little jumpy, a bit over eager to please, and about to burst to say something to her. He looked around to assure they were alone before he finally spoke.

"I understand you're an FBI agent down here investigating Mr. Wise's death for the CIA, and looking into that damn list he carried around for fourteen years."

Yet again amazed at how rumors could move so fast and be so distorted, Rainey let Skylar's misconception of her status stand for the moment. "So, you know about the list? What else do you know?"

"I know I have no reason to go around eliminating people from Ellie Paxton's life. I mean, Ellie and I had some fun in high school, but she wasn't the love of my life. I was never obsessed with her or anything."

"What do you mean by fun?"

Skylar grinned like a fifteen-year-old boy. "Oh, Miss Ellie isn't as sweet and innocent as she'd like people to believe. She was kinky in high school. She's even more so now."

"How would you know what she's like now? Are you having an affair with her as well?"

Skylar flushed red. "Wow, in town one day and you have my number. Hey, I'm a hound, I'll admit it, but trust me, I've got better things to do than go around killing people, especially Mr. Wise."

Rainey couldn't help herself. She smiled at Skylar. "Why should I trust you, when your wife can't?"

Skylar froze for a second, and then offered sheepishly, "I guess you have a point, but I still didn't shoot Mr. Wise."

Finished with Skylar and suspecting he was actually being honest with her—or one of the best liars feigning earnestness she'd ever seen—she turned her focus on his friend shoveling snow out of the driveway now.

"What about Gordon? He's a hunter. He was reported poaching in the area. He's a known drug user."

Skylar interrupted. "Man, you are good. You found out all that in one day?"

Rainey let a sly smile turn the corner of her lips, playing to Skylar's perception of her investigative powers, though all it took was listening to local gossip for a few minutes.

She asked, "Do you think he could have been high enough to mistake Wellman Wise for a deer or some other game?"

Skylar seemed relieved to have the spotlight off him. He volunteered information on Gordon freely. "Nah, Gordon could be drunk off his ass and still shoot the wings off a fly. I've seen him hit a quarter stuck in the bark of a tree after consuming two six packs. He usually doesn't do much more than smoke a little weed these days, but he used to drink quite a bit. Gordon had nothing to gain by any of those deaths. And if anyone's seen him up in Read's woods, it's because he's filming Ellie on her daily skinny dips. I'm almost inclined to believe she knows he's up there in that little blind he made."

"Did he ever date Ellie?"

"No, but we partied with her some, if you know what I mean."

"Like you partied with Leda?"

Rainey had waited for the right moment, when Skylar thought she had dismissed him as a suspect. His smile faded and his visage became flat, the rage behind his eyes clearly visible.

"I hate this fucking town," he spat.

Rainey pushed him. "That is your son, Skylar. You can't deny you had sex with her. Is her story true? Did you rape her? Did you and Gordon take turns? You don't strike me as the sloppy seconds type, or are you? Did watching him with her turn you on again? Did you have to go back for more after Gordon shot his wad?"

That last part got to his ego and she saw a flash of anger Skylar had heretofore concealed. His voice grew tight, as he tried to control his rage. "I never touched that bitch after he—"

"But you did touch her. You raped her, and you got away with it. Or have you? All the witnesses are dead, except Leda and the obvious walking DNA contribution you made. Is she blackmailing you?"

"I pay goddamn child support, okay. I paid her off. I set up a college fund for that kid. I was drunk, stupid, and out of control. I don't know why I did it. I have never forced a girl to do anything since then. I don't know what happened. I just lost control of it."

There it was, Skylar's remorse. It was a good sign that he was probably not a cold-blooded killer or serial rapist. His philandering was common knowledge, but Rainey had heard no other rumors of Skylar forcing himself on anyone. His restitution, though it would never erase Leda's trauma, was his way of undoing the crime in his mind. Rainey believed he was genuinely regretful for his actions, if not wholly apologetic toward the victim. Skylar's ego would only let him repent so far. Lurking somewhere under that pretty shell was the man who believed the "bitch" deserved it. He made Rainey's skin crawl.

Rainey sneered at him. "The 'it' you can't control is sexual addiction. You need help, Skylar. Your chemistry is off or your brain is wired differently, but you are an addict. Addicts can't be trusted. They will do whatever they must for a fix. Eventually the world crashes down around them, and they find the addiction took everything they cared about away. Keep feeding that monster inside you, Skylar, and it will rear its ugly head again. This time, you probably will not get away with it." Rainey decided to really scare him. "All it would take at this point is an accusation. They'll parade Leda's son in front of jury as proof of the animal you are. Do you think a soul in this county would believe you didn't do it? I'm surprised some gold digger hasn't thought of setting you up. It sure as hell would be easy."

"Look, I just didn't want the FBI to waste time focused on me. I didn't kill Wellman Wise, but I bet Graham Colde did. Gordon and I saw him. This white van had been coming around, sitting on the road, watching the fields. I checked him out through Gordon's rifle sight. I even had Gordon look. We both thought he looked like Graham's dad, Teddy Colde, but he's dead, so it had to be his son."

123

"Thank you for the information. I'm sure the police will want to talk to you."

A look of confusion crossed Skylar's face. "Aren't you the police?"

"No, just a family friend. I'm retired from the FBI."

Seemingly relieved Rainey was not an active agent, Skylar resumed his normal man on the prowl persona. "Gordon said you were too hot to be a cop. He heard you were a lesbian with a MILF wife. I guess you got it when I said Ellie was kinky. She and Cassie were up for anything. I guess all lesbians are like that. If you and your wife ever want to get freaky," he flashed his pearly whites, "give me a call."

Skylar was a fountain of information, but he disgusted Rainey. She wanted him gone. She bore into him with her eyes. "My wife, as you accurately called her, is the mother of my children and someone I love and respect enough to tell you to go fuck yourself, you idiot prick."

"Is everything all right down there?" Harriet called from the other end of the hall.

"Yes, ma'am, I was just leaving," Skylar responded, and gave Rainey a wide berth on his way out the door.

Harriet approached as Rainey said, "I should shoot him now and save some husband the trouble."

"That may be the case one day. I'm afraid his forced vasectomy only gave him license to screw anything that would stand still long enough."

Rainey smiled at Harriet's candor, but asked, "Forced? Who forced him?"

"Oh, his daddy threw a fit over that thing with Leda. He threatened to disown him if he didn't have the operation. Of course, he could have had it reversed after he married, but I suppose he never did. Wellman said Skylar liked the freedom it gave him, and that trophy wife of his was more than happy to forgo ruining her perfect figure."

Rainey started to giggle at first, followed by an all-out laugh. It could have been she was just a little off her game. She was away from home, stressed over some guy being a possible mastermind killer and making a game of her life. Whatever the cause, Rainey could only ride it out. Harriet caught the bug and joined Rainey, chuckling even though she didn't know what for. Rainey thought they both could probably use the release laughter offered the soul.

When she could, Rainey said, "I just keep hearing that old Jeannie C. Riley song, "Harper Valley PTA," playing in my head. I guess little towns everywhere are all the same. Everyone knows your secrets."

#

8:00 a.m.
Overcast, 34°F, Windchill 26°F

Harriet called her friend at the county offices to assure the roads were clear for Rainey's departure. The word was the streets in town were still covered, and the four lane out of town was one lane but passable. Once Rainey made it to the main highway, she would have cleared roads to home. Her neighborhood would probably be thawed by the time she arrived, but she hoped the snow would stick around until she got there. Rainey looked forward to Weather's first snowball. She had quite an arm.

"I do hope you'll bring your lovely family down for a visit," Harriet said, as Rainey pulled on her coat.

Bill returned through the front door, after freeing all the windows of Rainey's van of ice and warming the engine for her.

"All nice and warm for your departure," he said, as he stepped inside.

Rainey turned to Morgan. "He's a keeper."

Morgan smiled and slipped her arm around her husband's waist. "I know."

Rainey hugged Harriet. "I promise to keep you updated and I will stay on the detectives until you have an answer."

Harriet patted Rainey on the back. "Thank you, sweetheart. I know you will. You drive safe now."

"Always," Rainey said.

"Your father used to say that," Harriet said, releasing Rainey from the hug and smiling broadly.

Rainey returned the smile. "Yes, he did."

#

It took Rainey twenty minutes to get out of town and onto the four-lane. The four-lane was really single lane traffic on either side of the median. One lane had clean ruts to follow, but the rest of the road was frozen slush or solid ice. Rainey went slower than some of the brave souls that took to the outside lane to pass, but there was very little traffic. She picked up a black SUV on her tail, following too close, but she had no place to move out of its way. She sped up to a speed with which she was comfortable.

Rainey did not drive the van very often and was not accustomed to how it would react if she hit a patch of black ice. The SUV was going to have to be patient or pass in the snow packed and slushy lane to Rainey's left. That's exactly what it did. At the first opportunity, with no other traffic in sight, the SUV pulled to the left and up onto the snow pack. As the vehicles began to travel side by side, Rainey slowed. Up ahead, in a spot yet to be greeted by the sun, her lane lost its ruts and became an ice covered, snow packed, bend in the road. A strip of evergreen forest shaded the deep sloping ditches and the minute shoulder. This was an accident waiting to happen.

Rainey tapped the brake again, looking for fluffy snow to slow her momentum. Hitting the brakes harder could lead to a skid. The SUV slowed too. Rainey wanted it to pull ahead and give her more wiggle room, but it stayed right beside her. The driver apparently sensed the danger as well, but was causing more staying next to the van. Frustrated, Rainey tapped the brake again, trying to let the SUV pass. Just as they entered the curve, the SUV sped up. Rainey was about to breathe a sigh of relief when the driver in front of her lost control and fishtailed into her lane.

"Oh, shit," Rainey shouted, and began trying to avoid the SUV.

The van went into a slide as soon as Rainey turned the wheel. She turned into the slide even more, trying to regain control. The van began to slow as it spun into the other lane, hit the curb on the median, and bounced off in the direction of the ditch. The ice had the vehicle now and all Rainey could do was brace for impact. It wasn't half bad, actually. Once the van wheels hit the snow on the ditch bank, it slid gently down the slope. Rainey exhaled when the van came to a stop. The whole thing had been so slow and nonviolent, the OnStar sensors did not activate. She did not hear the van hit anything, and once towed from the ditch, Rainey could probably continue her drive home.

She had waited to call Katie, wanting to be up on the highway before giving her an estimated time of arrival. Now, that call was to be two-fold. "Honey, I'm on my way home, but your van is in a ditch." Great, Rainey thought, just fan-fucking-tastic.

After a minute of struggling with the door because of the angle at which the van was leaning, Rainey emerged into ankle deep snow. The biting wind nipped at her cheeks and ears. The wind chill was definitely below freezing. She heard a voice at the lip of the ditch calling down to her.

"Oh, my God. Are you all right? I'm so sorry."

Rainey shielded her eyes against the glare from the snow to see Ellie Paxton Read standing above her.

"I'm fine. I'm going to need a tow truck though," Rainey responded to Ellie's question, and then clawed her way up out of the ditch to face her.

"I am so sorry," Ellie said again. "I shouldn't have tried to pass you there. I don't know what happened. It felt like the ruts just threw me in front of you."

"It's okay. No harm done, at least I don't think so. I'll know when they get it pulled out, but it felt like it just slid to a stop." Rainey pulled the phone from her pocket. "You wouldn't happen to know the closest tow truck number, would you? If I call the service, they'll probably send someone from further away and I'd like to get home this morning."

Ellie grabbed Rainey's arm. "Let's get out of this cold air. Come with me." She led Rainey to the rear of the SUV, now stopped about thirty yards ahead on the tiny shoulder. "Get in," she said, and disappeared on the driver's side of the vehicle. Rainey hesitated. It wasn't fear of Ellie that froze her to the spot, but the appearance of a white van coming toward them. She reached into the back of her jeans and slid her hand around the grip of the Glock concealed there. The van slowed and came to a stop. The driver's window gradually rolled down, revealing an older gentleman.

"Ellie, are you all right?"

Rainey couldn't see Ellie, but she heard her respond, "We're fine, Mr. Bryant. I have Bart on the phone. He's going to pull the van out. Thanks for stopping."

The gentleman waved, rolled up his window, and pulled away. The wind blew up the tails of Rainey's coat, stinging her legs under her now wet jeans. Climbing out of the ditch had soaked her from the knees down. She hustled toward the passenger side of Ellie's SUV and climbed in.

Ellie was on the hands free phone speaking toward the mirror. "—just bring it to my house, Bart, and put the tow on my tab."

A male voice came over the car speakers, "Will do. It'll be about an hour. I got a few before you."

"Get to this one as soon as you can and I'll make it worth your while, handsome," Ellie flirted.

The voice laughed. "I'll have it there lickety-split."

"You do that," Ellie said and put the SUV in drive.

She pulled away from the shoulder, while Rainey was saying, "I could just wait with the van."

"Oh, don't be silly. The least I can do is give you some hot coffee and let you dry your pants. You're soaked."

And with that, Rainey found herself headed to the pretty blonde, kinky girl's house. "Trouble finds you, Rainey Bell," she heard Katie say in her head.

"I need to call home and let them know I'm going to be later than expected," she said, pulling out the phone again.

She touched the screen a few times and put the phone to her ear.

"Hey, good-lookin'. Are you headed this way?" Katie said cheerfully.

"Well, I was, but I got into a bit of an accident."

Ellie shouted at the phone. "It was all my fault. I'm very sorry."

Katie's cheeriness vanished. "Are you okay?"

"Yes, I'm fine, the van is fine, but it's in a ditch. The tow truck guy said he would bring it to me in about an hour."

"Where are you?" Katie asked.

"I'm in a car, going to a place to stay warm until they bring me the van."

Ellie shouted again, "Don't worry. I'll take good care of her."

"Who is that?" Katie wanted to know.

"It's the driver of the other car. We're going to wait at her house for the tow truck."

Katie teased Rainey, "She better be ugly."

Rainey lied. "Oh, she is. She is very nice."

"Oh, my God. She's gorgeous, isn't she?"

"I'm good," Rainey said, non-committal.

Katie became distracted by the loud baby noises somewhere near her. Rainey could tell because she started talking faster. "You behave yourself and call me when you get back on the road. I'm glad you're safe. I have to go. Mack is on the kitchen counter. Love you, bye."

The "Love you too," Rainey offered went unheard. Katie was gone.

Ellie asked, "Was that your wife? I heard you have a beautiful family."

"Wow, that Leda is quite the town crier," Rainey commented.

Ellie laughed. "Town gossip, you mean."

She turned the SUV down a long dirt lane lined with evergreen forest on both sides. An ancient two-story farmhouse stood majestically at the end of the tunnel created by the tall snow-topped pines. The fence that lined the lane looked new. The structures that came into view, though antebellum constructed, appeared freshly painted and squarely built.

"This is a nice spread," Rainey commented.

Ellie seemed to enjoy speaking of her new home. She chattered proudly, "The house was originally built in the early 1850s by Adolphus Read, my late husband Burgess's great-great-great-grandfather. Old man Read, Burgess's grandfather, did a lot of rebuilding and preservation. He kept up the maintenance on all the buildings. When I took it over in November, I had the interior updated, but I left the exterior as it is. A fresh coat of paint and the old girl looks good as new. I moved into the house in January this year. I've still have boxes to unpack up on the second floor."

When she finally took a break to breathe, Rainey said, "It's like an era, frozen in time. You don't see houses like this much anymore. Not in this shape anyway."

"I blew my chance at the National Historic Registry when I remodeled the interior, but I'm going to be here a long time, and I'd rather be warm and comfortable, than historically correct."

"I can understand that," Rainey said, as the SUV came to a stop at the side of the house.

Ellie looked over at Rainey. "Well, sorry it's under these circumstances, but welcome to my home."

Rainey kicked the still clinging bits of snow from her boots and the hem of her jeans before following Ellie through the side door.

"We can take our shoes off in the mud room and I have a pair of Burgess's old sweat pants you can change into. I'll throw your jeans and socks in the dryer. It shouldn't take long."

Rainey sat on a bench in the mudroom untying her boots, across from the brand new washer and dryer. She had only seen this room, but could already tell Ellie sank some money into the old house.

Ellie dug through a box inside a utility closet and reappeared with a pair of gray sweatpants.

"I knew I had a pair left. Here you go. You can change in the powder room there." She pointed at a door in the corner of the room. "I'll go make us some coffee. Just come on through this door and you're in my kitchen," she said and then exited out of sight.

Rainey finished taking off her boots, contemplated not changing out of her jeans, but then decided they were just too wet to sit around in for an hour. Ten minutes in the dryer and they would be much more comfortable, the socks too. Once in the little powder room, Rainey realized she had a dilemma. Without the jeans, she had nowhere to hook her holster. The Glock was too heavy and pulled the waistband down when she tried attaching it to the sweatpants. With the wet jeans and socks in one hand and the Glock and holster in the other, Rainey exited the powder room to find Ellie waiting for her.

Ellie saw the Glock and twisted up her face. "Uh, I don't allow guns in my house."

Rainey was thinking she'd just put her jeans back on, because she never let her weapon out of sight, but Ellie took the jeans from her hand before Rainey could suggest that she would redress and wait on the porch.

"Just stick it in your coat pocket for now. As long as I don't see it, I'll be fine," Ellie said, while throwing Rainey's clothes in the dryer. "I don't know how much you know about me, but since Skylar said you were an FBI agent investigating 'the list,' I'm guessing you know about my parents' murder."

Rainey decided to cooperate, mainly because Ellie had her jeans and socks. She stepped over to the peg on the wall, where she'd hung her coat when they entered, and stuck the weapon in one of the pockets.

"I'm aware of what happened," Rainey answered. "But I'm not an FBI agent anymore. I retired early."

"Good," Ellie said, "I'm glad the FBI isn't wasting time looking into a bunch of accidents. I told Wellman I thought he was crazy. Why would anyone spend time killing people associated with me? Graham was the only one who wanted me to suffer and he's gone, replaced by someone that doesn't have a clue who I am."

Rainey followed Ellie into the kitchen, and asked, "Why do you think Graham Colde came to your house that morning?"

"He needed his dad's rifle to do what he was planning, I guess. The only good thing that came out of that tragedy was my dad. He woke up and tried to stop Graham. People say I'm a hero, because I shot Graham and stopped him from killing the people on his list, but it was my dad that alerted us to trouble. He was the hero and died trying to save us all."

"So, you believe Graham was going to kill the people on the list."

"Yes, he was angry with all of us for one reason or another. I'm just glad I stopped him."

131

She handed Rainey a cup of steaming coffee, retrieving it from the single serve coffee maker on the counter, and dropped another plastic coffee filled cup into the machine. The coffee maker began to gurgle and spit a stream of hot liquid into Ellie's waiting cup. The kitchen was in the corner of an open floor plan. Ellie had knocked out the old walls and created a large room on the first floor. The interior of the old farmhouse resembled a New York loft apartment, with modern appliances and industrial design elements.

"I would have never guessed this was what the interior of the house looked like," Rainey commented.

Ellie smiled. "I loved the old house, but a girl needs her modern amenities. Come on, I'll give you the tour."

Again, Rainey wasn't asked, but told to follow Ellie, which she did. She sipped the coffee and trailed behind her, as Ellie showed her the entire house, ending with pointing through the French doors to the new redwood sauna on the back deck. By the time they were through, Rainey had finished the coffee and Ellie went to the kitchen to make another.

"Sit down at the table there," Ellie said, pointing at an old barn door converted to a tabletop.

Rainey sat down peered through the French doors to the woods beyond. "I'm turned around here. Which way is it to the sandpit where Mr. Wise was shot?"

Ellie came to the table with Rainey's coffee and her own. She pointed through the glass in the doors. "See that path cut in the woods. That will take you there if you know where you're going. I got lost in there for a couple of hours when I first came back. The trails go off in several directions. Now that I know the way, I can make it to the sandpit in about an hour at a leisurely walking pace. It's a nice hike and I do it every morning, unless the weather is bad, like today."

"I was told you've been hearing rifle shots."

Ellie sat across from Rainey. "People use the sand hills in those woods for target practice. It's safer than firing at a can in the backyard."

"And that doesn't bother you?" Rainey asked.

"No, I grew up with guns. I just don't want them in my house. You can understand that, right?"

"Yes, it's perfectly reasonable."

"And those accidents Wellman was convinced were murders meant to hurt me, I just don't believe it. Cassie would eat any kind of pill. Ely was a drunk. Burgess did a stupid thing, eating something he wasn't sure was safe. And Adam probably disappeared on purpose. He was always nuts anyway."

The house was warm, too warm. Rainey stood up. "I need to take off this sweatshirt. I'm overdressed."

"It is hot in here. Make yourself comfortable," Ellie said, and then winked. "We can get real comfortable, if you're so inclined."

Rainey stopped halfway through pulling off the sweatshirt and stared at Ellie. "I'm not inclined," she said. "I'm married."

Ellie openly flirted. "Well, it never hurts to ask."

Rainey removed the sweatshirt and placed it on the next chair over and resumed her seat. "I'm flattered, but committed. I don't sleep around on my wife."

"That's commendable, but boring," Ellie said, punctuated with laughter.

Rainey recognized Ellie's kind, a woman whose self-worth was wrapped up in her sexuality. These women and men confused lust with emotion, sadly chasing the rush found in the beginning of a physical attraction that can never last. A conversation not involving sexual innuendo or outright advances was rare with this type, because they were constantly seeking the next fix. Ellie was as much an addict as Skylar. Rainey found them both boring.

She grinned at the sexy young blonde, fifteen years her junior, and said, "Sport fucking has its place and time in a person's life. Mine has passed."

Ellie leaned forward, exposing cleavage on purpose. She appeared to find Rainey a challenge and it excited her. Rainey could see it in those big blue eyes, while Ellie tried to use them as a weapon to pierce her prey's defenses.

"You're married, you're not dead. I don't see a thing wrong with seeking pleasure from outside a marriage. Suppose your fantasies aren't compatible with your spouse's. As long as no one gets hurt, what's the harm?"

"I suppose if all parties involved are in agreement, then you're right, but it's exceedingly rare when those agreements remain intact. Someone usually upsets the balance and the whole house of cards comes crumbling down." Rainey leaned in, unafraid of the vixen's powers. It was time to stop this conversation. "I am married and not dead, as you say, but my wife fulfills my fantasies, which include a committed relationship and a family I adore. Risk that for a piece of young, pretty, tight, southern ass? Well, I guess you haven't seen my wife."

Ellie was undaunted. "Maybe you have fantasies you haven't even thought of? Variety is the spice of life. I could teach you a few things to do to that wife of yours."

This was how people got in trouble. They listened to the courting coos, fell for the colorful plumage, not to mention the excitement of forbidden fruit. At some point the first small boundary was crossed, which made crossing the next one so much easier. Rainey had no interest in this young woman, or any woman other than the one to which she was married, but she could see how Ellie could get less committed individuals to bite the bait.

"While there are plenty of people who would take you up on that offer, I'm not one of them. So, please, if you would, drop the come on."

Ellie's facial expression flattened for a moment, but then she smiled. "Wouldn't you know the hottest thing to come through Hominy Junction in months is happily married. A mother of three that can hold a spouse's attention—she must be one hell of a woman. How fortunate for you."

The overt sexual come-on had not worked, so apparently Ellie was going for the "you must be so underappreciated because your wife is busy with the kids" angle. This chick was a piece of work. Rainey gave Ellie a thin smile, while thinking of throwing her outside to cool off. She was stuck in this woman's house for at least an hour. She did not want to spend it fending off sexual advances. Rainey was about to attempt a change of subject again, when the doorbell rang.

Ellie stood up. "Well, that was fast. I didn't hear him pull up." She batted her eyelashes at Rainey. "I guess I was distracted. Let me get him to come around to the side door. I know Bart. He's covered in mud, I'm sure."

Ellie headed for the mudroom. Rainey finished her coffee, grabbed her sweatshirt, and followed. Ellie was already outside when she entered the room. Rainey could hear her muffled voice beyond the door. Rainey pulled her still slightly damp jeans and socks out of the dryer and slipped into the powder room to change. She wanted out of this house as soon as possible. This chick gave her the heebie-jeebies. Ellie was one of those vacuous women who chose to use her body as currency, buying affection and opportunities, void of any true connections beyond sexual ones. Rainey was ready to put distance between her and this woman, before she found out how far Ellie Paxton Read was willing to go to get what she wanted.

Rainey heard the side door open and hurried to get her socks on. She folded the sweatpants and left them on the back of the toilet. Her stomach lurched again and she felt the sweat glaze her skin. Damn, it was hot in that house or the kids brought home another virus from the day care at the women's center. She splashed cold water on her face and tried to quell the woozy feeling that was creeping up on her. No way was she getting too sick to drive. Rainey was going home, even if she had to sit with one of Katie's garbage bags in her lap. She was dressed and only needed her coat to get the hell out of that house. Leaving the hot little powder room was a start. She dried her face and opened the door, before noticing she still needed her boots and how odd to have forgotten she wasn't wearing them.

"Hey, Rainey," the male voice said. "Sorry you got involved in all this."

Rainey looked up to see Theodore Suzanne standing right in front of her. Tunnel vision cloaked the room around him in darkness. Too late, Rainey realized she was falling and had no time to cushion her impact with the expensive Italian marble floor, before the room went black.

Chapter Seven

9:53 a.m.
Overcast, 35°F, Windchill 26°F

Rainey surfaced from the effects of the drug to someone trying to shove her foot into a boot.

"Don't fight me, Rainey," Theodore said. "You have to put on your boots."

She tried to push him away. The drug grabbed her again. The blackness returned.

#

10:48 a.m.
Overcast, 36°F, Windchill 28.5°F

"That's right—stick your arm in—good. Well done. Now, the other one. We have to get your coat on. You don't want to freeze to death out there."

Theodore tugged on Rainey's coat, pulling the shoulders into place, as if he were dressing a life-sized doll. She could see him, or a blurred object that sounded like him. He let her slide down onto the bench, where the blackness opened its arms and pulled her down again.

#

11:51 a.m.

"Come on, up you go. Lean on me. You don't have to walk far. We're just going to the van. It's right outside."

"I want to go home." That's what Rainey tried to say. It sounded more like one on the triplets trying to manage a sentence.

"Okay, then, walk with me to the van. That's it, one foot in front of the other."

"Call Katie," she slurred. Rainey wasn't aware of why she felt so out of it, but something told her she needed to call Katie.

Her focus switched to the three steps down to the ground and then the tunnel she could see through filled with the earth rising to meet her. Rainey urged her arms to thrust forward from behind her back, only to find she couldn't move them and face down into the dirt she went.

"Whoa, come on, stand up. Just a few more feet."

It took all the concentration Rainey had to make it to the side door of the van, where she was helped onto the floor between the bench with the babies' car seats and the front passenger area of the vehicle. A blanket was thrown over her, bringing her dark companion for another dance with nothingness.

#

1:13 p.m.
Light Rain, 36°F, Windchill 30°F

The van door slid open again, waking Rainey from a deep disorienting sleep. Theodore pulled her into a seated position and stuck a paper cup to her lips.

"You have to drink this," he said.

She drank because her throat was dry. She felt as if all the liquid had been drained from her body. The cold water cooled her burning mouth, but was bitter. Her brain woke up in time to see what she was doing and choked the last swallow into a cough, spewing the liquid into the air.

"Just rest, now," he said, and pushed her back to the floor.

The van door slid shut. The darkness returned.

137

#

The muffled sound of rain on a tin roof woke her. It took a few minutes to grasp her situation, but eventually Rainey's mind cleared. She was in the van, inside a barn. Through the sliding door window, she could see the wood studs and the cracks between the planking. The OnStar mirror was missing from the windshield, the wires cut. Her last memory was of heading into the mudroom to retrieve her clothes from the dryer. She had done that, Rainey supposed, because she was dressed, even wearing the heavy wool coat and her boots, which was a good thing, because her breath created little puffs of fog in the cold air.

Rainey was on her side, on the floor between the seats, and covered in a blanket. Her hands were handcuffed behind her. She could break handcuffs, true, but had never successfully accomplished that with them locked in place at her back. Rainey could pick the lock without looking, but she needed a shim or a paperclip. There had to be something on the floor in the van she could use as a pick. The more her brain recovered from the drug, the faster it began to look for a way to survive. Rainey didn't have time to wonder what happened to Ellie or who held her prisoner.

Sitting up from her prone position without the use of her arms was proving difficult. She was on top of her coat, which pulled her down each time her shoulder rose from the carpet. Not knowing how much time she had, Rainey needed to decide if the time and energy spent trying to sit up would be better used on setting her hands free. Even if she could get up, what was waiting outside the van? Rainey needed the use of her hands.

"There is always a way out, until you give up." She heard her father's voice in her head, reminding her to think and not panic.

Rainey scoured the floor and realized she could have eaten off the carpet it was so clean. Katie was a neat freak and the van came with a built in vacuum cleaner. She felt around on the handcuffs. Good, they were not the cheap kind. Cheap handcuffs bent under stress, and were harder to break cleanly, and took

138

longer to escape. Expensive cuffs snapped at the weakest point. It sounded absolutely backwards, but the tempered steel on the more expensive cuffs made them brittle. Enough force and the chain or the eye that attached the chain to the cuffs would snap. Rainey would still be in cuffs, but able to move both arms freely. She simply had to get the chain on the cuffs in a bind.

The best way to bind the chain was working it in a circle between her wrists. Each time she thought the bind was taking hold the chain would slip. The thick coat and sweatshirt underneath made the work difficult. Rainey pushed her chest forward, creating more room to work behind her, but still she couldn't get the chain to lock up. Her fingers grazed the cold steel of the seat support. She scooted her body closer to it. Scoring the chain against the support would make the process of binding it easier. Rainey could feel the cuffs biting into her wrist. She had to be careful of cutting too deeply. Blood slicked chains would never bind.

Scrape, scrape, scrape, and twist, twist, twist. Still the chains slipped. Rainey would have already snapped them and left the vehicle if the cuffs were in front. She thought about running with her hands behind her back. The farm was in the middle of nowhere. Rainey had not seen a house within a couple of miles, when they drove in. It was growing dark. The rain fell steadily on the roof. The temperatures would drop back below freezing overnight. Katie was looking for her by now, Rainey was sure, but did she have any clue where to find her. Whoever had drugged and restrained Rainey, and more than likely Ellie too, was counting on no one looking for her at the farm.

Scrape, scrape, scrape, twist, twist, twist. No bind. Flashes from the day started to filter into Rainey's thoughts. It was nine a.m. the last she knew of the time. The sun set around five-thirty p.m. these days. It had to be close to that time, maybe four-thirty. It was hard to tell because of the rain. It could be earlier, if the clouds were thick enough to block the sun. Rainey thought she had been out cold for most of the day.

Who drugged her? Was it Ellie? She drank the coffee too. She said it was hot in the room. Maybe someone was trying to drug Ellie and got them both. Another flash of the mudroom—

someone was tying her boots. Rainey focused on the memory. What could she hear? It was a man's voice. He was talking to her, but she couldn't make out what he was saying. He was looking down at her boots. Rainey couldn't see his face. Someone else was in the room, not moving, behind the man squatted in front of her. She could smell dryer sheets and cologne. Rainey focused again on the man's head. He finished the bow on her boot and looked up.

"I'm sorry, Rainey," Theodore Suzanne said, inches from her face.

Scrape, scrape, scrape; faster now. Knowing who had her only made it more difficult not to panic. To pull off all he had so far, this guy was very clever. He probably did not mean to snag Rainey in his plans, and now that he had, he was unpredictable. Careful planning and plotting was only genius as long as nothing went wrong. Something definitely had gone wrong in this plan. Theodore had no reason to kill Rainey, until now. She believed she was alive only because he was working out how to get away with her murder.

Scrape, scrape—Rainey stopped moving. Light entered the barn. A door had opened somewhere. She heard voices approaching, one male, one female. Ellie was still alive. Rainey heard the sound of breaking glass and scooted a few inches in order to see what was happening. She didn't have to wait long. Theodore Suzanne's face appeared in the sliding door window. He reached for the handle and pulled the door open. He stood there, holding an M1 Garand rifle in his small hands.

Theodore was a little man, five feet four inches tall, maybe one hundred and thirty pounds soaking wet. At twenty-eight, he was already balding, but could still use a haircut and a couple of shampoos. His clothes were ill fitting and rumpled; exactly the guy one would expect to find in an injustice collector with an erotomania obsession. Theodore Suzanne was the poster boy for the disheveled and disorganized. But not, Rainey thought, the mastermind of a long string of crimes that required cunning, patience, and organization. The rifle looked like a large toy in the hands of boy. Rainey didn't feel the least bit afraid of him. In fact, he looked scared to death.

"What in the hell are you doing, Theodore?" Rainey demanded.

He glanced over his shoulder and then looked back at Rainey, saying, "Anything she tells me to."

Ellie stepped from behind Theodore, holding Rainey's Glock at his back. "Bet you wish you'd slept with me now. I would have rocked your world. I still might, just for fun."

"Well, now," Rainey said, feigning apathy. "This is interesting, a female serial killer. Don't run into them every day."

"I came to warn you," Theodore said.

"A little late, weren't you?" Rainey said, analyzing her recently revealed captor. She looked at the rifle. "I suppose that's not loaded."

Ellie laughed. "I'm not new at this, you know."

"So, what now, Ellie?" Rainey asked. "How are you going to kill me and get away with it? I'm sure they're already looking for me. The GPS tracker isn't hooked to the mirror. They know where I am by now."

"Oh, they are looking for you. The police came by to check on me, as this was your last location, before the GPS stopped pinging back. It seems your wife has called out the National Guard—well practically. You do know all you have to do is disable the antenna connected to the OnStar box, don't you? I'm not dumb."

"How did you explain my disappearance?" Rainey said, all the time thinking, *"Good girl, Katie. Keep looking. You're close."*

Ellie answered with mock excitement, "Haven't you heard? Graham Dean Colde has regained his memory and is stalking me, and he may have abducted you after you left my house this morning. No one has seen you for hours. How could they know Colde was hiding with you in my barn? I sure had no idea until I stumbled on him."

Theodore tried to explain to Rainey, "I wasn't stalking her. I was remembering her. I told Mr. Wise that. I told him I didn't shoot those people. I don't know who did, but I know Ellie shot me."

"Like anyone would believe you, you pathetic idiot." Ellie chuckled maniacally.

"Mr. Wise did," Theodore said, his small chest puffing with indignation.

"And Wellman learned it wasn't wise to ask the wrong questions," Ellie countered, and laughed louder. "See what I did there? I'm clever, right? You have to admit that."

"They'll be plenty of questions, if I disappear," Rainey said, while her mind raced, looking for a way out of her predicament.

"You're not going to disappear. You're going to die at the hands of a disturbed young man, just like all the others." The pretty blonde with the big blue eyes put on her best southern charm, thickened her accent, and hid the blackness of her soul. "No one would suspect little ol' Ellie. She's been through so much tragedy. Bless her heart."

Ellie produced a long sliver of thin window glass and slashed at her forearm. At first a dark red line, the wound opened, sending a crimson rivulet down her arm. Theodore saw this and swooned into the van on top of Rainey, still clutching the rifle. Ellie gathered his legs and shoved them into the van.

She looked down at Rainey, who could barely see her through the tangled arms of the man on top of her. "Why, look. He's got Ellie's blood all over him. What a sick, sick boy. How unfortunate that profiler didn't see him coming."

#

5:35 p.m.
Overcast, 35.1°F, Windchill 29.3°F

"That was a mistake, cutting your arm," Rainey said from the floor of the van, as it moved along what she imagined was a rutted out farm path.

Theodore lay motionless at her side, after she squirmed enough to move him off her. The sky was darkening, but Rainey could see trees through the windows. Ellie was driving her deep into the forest.

"I don't make mistakes," Ellie replied.

142

"That's the narcissist talking," Rainey countered. "Arrogant enough to believe you're infallible."

Ellie resumed the innocent southern flower accent from before. "I can't believe he was in the barn the whole time y'all were looking for him, officer. I thought I saw someone and went to check it out. That's when he grabbed me. He must have hidden his van in there while I was gone this morning."

"He got me and not you? Come on, that's a stretch."

Ellie continued, undaunted, "And isn't it lucky that I remembered Graham fainted at the sight of blood. That's why I broke that old blown-glass window in the barn. I put my arm through it and cut myself on purpose. When Graham saw the blood, he fainted, and then I ran out and hid in the woods. I thought they were going to find me out there frozen to death, before he stopped looking for me. I'm so sorry about Rainey. I came back to the house and called as soon as they left in her van. He must have hidden in it, when the tow truck brought it to my house, and surprised her when she was leav—"

Rainey interrupted, "Okay, okay, I get it, an answer for everything. I can't say you haven't thought this through." While they talked, Rainey never stopped scraping and twisting the handcuff chain, the sound of her movements covered by the jostling of the van on the uneven path. "And you're right, no one has suspected you of anything other than being a black cat one shouldn't cross. But do you really think anyone is going to believe this scrawny-ass boy put me in cuffs."

"Now, who's being an arrogant narcissist?" Ellie chuckled. "I'm not much bigger than he is and I put you in cuffs. Keeping handy those little individual coffee servings, with crushed Halcion tablets I got from the sleep dentist, has proved a very effective method of subduing prey of any size. They, like you, became compliant and malleable. Heavy duty scar, by the way. Graham said I should worry. You kill all the people that fuck with you."

Rainey shuddered to think what this woman had done while she was unconscious, but she stayed focused on the cuffs and keeping Ellie talking. "I know him as Theodore, and he is suffering from a vivid fantasy world he's created loosely based on my life, and devoid of many facts pertaining to the reality of my experiences with serial killers such as yourself."

"Oh, you've met someone like me before?"

The narcissist in Ellie believed her to be unique, superior, and capable of unlimited power and success. Rainey had compared her to other serial killers, and still Ellie had to think herself special among them. Killers like Ellie enjoyed one thing immensely, discussing themselves.

"Sure, I've met people like you before. Shall I tell you who you are, Ellie Paxton Read?"

"Please do. I can't wait to hear what you have to say, while you try to buy time to save your ass. Go ahead, enlighten me, before I prove you right about what a cold blooded murderer I am."

"Let's see," Rainey began, "you've committed matricide, patricide, fratricide, killed your husband and several friends, and let's not forget Wellman Wise. You are by definition a serial murderer, killing more than two people with a cooling off period in between each crime."

"You've got me so far," Ellie said, laughing as if Rainey had called her out for dying her hair blond.

"Wait, did you kill Cassie Gillian? I can't see how you gained from that. How was she standing in your way?"

"Does it matter?"

"Yes, it matters. The reason you killed her, if you did, tells me more about you."

"Cassie fell in love with me. I was planning to move to Wilmington with Burgess. She was going to tell everyone about us, and the things we'd done with Skylar and Adam. I couldn't let that happen."

"And Ely, you left out the part about you and Cassie and Ely. The epitome of narcissism, did you fall in love with your reflection, Ellie?"

"Fuck you," came from the front seat.

But it was true. Rainey could tell by the answer. This was a human being with no social boundaries, no empathy, and absolutely no remorse. Who else had Ellie killed that Rainey didn't know about. "Burgess's sister, what about her?"

"Her grandfather was going to send her to medical school. Do you know how much that costs? I couldn't very well let her have that big a piece of my pie, now could I?"

Rainey summarized, "If it stands in your way, it has to go. Ellie wants, Ellie gets. Is that how it goes?"

"I didn't get you," Ellie answered.

"And now you're going to kill me. It kind of makes my point," Rainey said.

A chuckle preceded the, "I guess it does," from the front seat.

"In that case, you have at least one personality disorder, probably more, I'm guessing several more. Narcissism is at the core of psychopathy, and you are definitely a psychopath. We should really give you some tests before I make that call, but seeing as how you are a stone-cold killer, I'll go out on a limb."

"You're funny. I wish I had known you under different circumstances," Ellie said.

Rainey replied, "I don't. I try very hard to stay away from people like you. Whether you kill who you associate with or not, you do damage them. You manipulate and con everyone. You take what you want, and it is always you doing the taking. There is never any quid pro quo. If you do something for someone, it's because you will benefit in some way. You are too caught up in your self-importance to develop empathy, let alone genuine affection."

"That's harsh. I liked Burgess."

"Until what, until he didn't suit your fantasy anymore? You certainly weren't faithful to him. Is that why he threw you out?"

"I left him," Ellie stated, unable to admit defeat.

"After he set boundaries you weren't willing to comply with, right?"

"He wanted me to settle down, have babies, be boring."

"Ah, boring, things can never be boring. That's the histrionic personality. She must have attention, excitement or she'll cause trouble," Rainey said, ticking off another character disorder trait.

Ellie continued to find her own comments amusing, laughing while she explained how status quo murder in cold blood was for her. "Burgess decided we should 'grow up,' his words, not mine. I said, 'Be an adult, just not a boring one.' He was tired of swinging, tired of me swinging without him, so he had to go too. I couldn't just leave him. Sadly, getting half of Burgess's money wasn't enough, but his estate, his insurance policy, and the timely death of his grandfather fixed me up quite nicely."

"I forgot about him. You got to old man Read, didn't you?"

"Old men with bad hearts should not fish alone," was all that Ellie offered on that "natural" death, but Rainey was sure she caused it.

"The Reads paid dearly for knowing you. You couldn't use Burgess or sleep your way onto the silver screen, so he was worth only money to you. How about your brother? I'll bet he had a hefty life insurance policy provided by you, as well."

"Ely was drinking at night, calling me whining, saying he couldn't live with the guilt anymore. What a waste of air he was. He couldn't even pull the trigger on our parents after we had made a deal. I got Graham to come over that morning, I did all the leg work and preplanning. All Ely had to do was pull the trigger and he couldn't even do that."

"Why Ellie? What did your parents do to you?"

"Dad was taking a job in the Middle East and he was going to make us do our senior year in a fucking desert. Our senior year? I was not missing out on homecoming queen and head cheerleader to wear a fucking rag on my head. And Ely would have lost his chance at the scoring record, which he won that next year. Dad would not listen to reason, so we had no choice."

"You mean *you* had no choice. Ely was never really into it, was he? Did he never figure out that when you shot Graham the second time in the chest, you were actually trying to kill him?"

"You're good, I'll give you that. Oh, he wondered, at first, but I told him I tapped twice by accident. He fell for it, but then it was a constant chore to keep him together. He lost his athletic scholarship, flunked out, could never hold a real job. I thought I was in the clear with him when he disappeared down in Mexico for a couple of years, but he didn't stay gone."

"He was a liability, a loose end you had to tie up eventually, right?" Rainey encouraged Ellie to keep talking, pretending to find her reasoning valid.

Ellie loved the spotlight. She continued, "He flew through his part of the money from our parents' insurance and what Graham's parents' insurance had to pay. He was constantly borrowing more from me. I thought, you know I have that big policy on him. Why not make some money and get rid of a problem, before he pulled an Eric Menendez and confessed? That weekend, I told Burgess I was going to hike in the Sierras for few days, which I was known to do. I borrowed, without her knowledge, a friend's identification and flew under her name."

Rainey interjected, "I bet you always have a few friends that could pass for you in a pinch, and vice versa. That wasn't the first time or the last your alibi had you one place, while you were actually at, say the beach, killing an old friend in the insurance business?"

"Oh, Adam. He got too nosey about Burgess's death, because I was stupid enough to buy another policy from him after cashing in on Ely's. Adam had all these questions about both deaths. Okay, yeah, I made that one mistake, but I cleaned it up. No one else ever questioned Ely's drunken mishap, not after Burgess told about his late night drunk dialing. It actually worked in my favor that Ely kept his drinking quiet. It explained his going out on the boat at night, drunk and alone."

"And of course you were sufficiently shocked and devastated upon returning from the retreat to find you brother had been killed in a horrible accident. Really, you're quite cunning. Why didn't some acting agent scoop you up? Was fucking you not all that fantastic, or did they see your flaw?"

Ellie's tone changed. She ignored the sex comment and went right for the narcissistic trigger Rainey pulled. A flaw? She didn't know she had one. "What flaw would that be?"

The chain on the cuffs bound up, finally. Rainey squeezed her wrist together as far as she could, but it wasn't enough. She needed to move and Theodore was in her way.

"I asked you, what flaw?" Ellie demanded.

Rainey answered just as the van came to a stop, "You can't play anyone but yourself. You've paid so little attention to the world around you, you are incapable of an empathetic portrayal of anyone but Ellie Paxton Read. You're a pretty girl, Ellie, but you're not all that interesting."

Ellie put the van in park and sang out cheerfully, "We're here."

Rainey fought the panic, replacing it with a moment of anger and frustration. Was this how she would die, at the hands of a serial killer she hadn't even known existed? All she had done was go to a freakin' funeral. How did this shit keep happening? What load of crap karma brought all these fiends out of the woodwork to fuck with her?

"Dammit," she said aloud in frustration.

"What's that?" Ellie asked, climbing over the center console to stoop in the passenger side foot well facing Rainey.

She began removing the coat, hat, and gloves she'd donned just before they left the farm. Her arm was bandaged now with a piece of cloth torn from the tail of her shirt, fitting her story of surviving in the woods, and she had explained the sound of breaking glass in the barn. This chick was smart, very. She had thought it all out, had an answer for everything anyone could ask. Rainey had been in Ellie's house for a legitimate reason. All the forensic evidence pointing to Rainey's presence would be of no value. The blood in the barn explained away. The motive for the murder, a deranged killer obsessed with the pretty blonde. Rainey and Theodore were the loose ends, and a murder/suicide would tie the bow up nicely.

"I was thinking," Rainey replied, "that after all the crap I have been through, and I die because I came to pay my respects at a funeral. Now that is some shitty karma, right there. You didn't have to kill me, Ellie. I wasn't coming after you. I was going home to watch my children play in the snow. I thought you were a damaged girl who never recovered from a tragedy, but not a murderer. Well, maybe it did cross my mind, but really, I had better things to do, like hunt down this idiot for spying on me."

"Sorry, it's too late to turn back now," Ellie said, continuing to undress, which began to unnerve Rainey even more.

Rainey glanced at Theodore's face, just inches from hers now. His eyes were open, but he was absolutely still. She had no idea how long he'd been awake. The fear in his eyes indicated

148

he'd heard plenty. Ellie was busy unbuttoning her shirt, having already folded her jeans and placed them on the passenger seat. Rainey mouthed the words, "Don't move" to Theodore, and returned to distracting Ellie from her intentions, still working on the handcuff chain behind her back.

"You do know this is going to end badly. I may not be active in the FBI, but you won't be dealing with the locals on this one." She forced a laugh. "I can't wait for the behavioral analyst to get a gander at you, a female killer with no remorse, none, not a drop. So few straight up serial murdering female psychopaths exist, I'm sure they'll enjoy speaking with you on death row."

"They haven't executed anyone in North Carolina since 2006."

Ellie wore only her bra and underwear now. She had a captive audience in Rainey and she milked it removing them. Rainey pretended not to notice, or at the very least be unimpressed. Ego-driven Ellie, she hoped, would lose focus on killing her and try to win even a speck of approval from Rainey.

"You're right about the stay of executions here in North Carolina, but they still have a death row and solitary. Solitary would be like death to an attention craver like you. You're about to kill a former FBI agent because you thought I was about to learn your secret. That's the only motive you have. And the funniest part is I wasn't even looking at you."

Ellie let the bra slip down her arms and smiled. "Do you see me now?"

"Those aren't the first pair of tits I've seen, Ellie. Plus you're about to kill me. That's kind of a turnoff."

Ellie didn't like rejection, evident in her tone when she replied, "Too late now, anyway. I have to get going."

Rainey saw something sparkle at the base of Ellie's neck. "Hey, that's my wife's Valentine's gift. I'm going to want that back."

Ellie laughed again. "She'll never know it's missing, now will she? Your poor family, how dreadful this is all going to be." She threw all of her clothes inside her coat and tied it into a bundle. She picked up the Glock, reached down, and poked Theodore in the back with the barrel. "I know you're awake,

149

Graham. You never stayed out very long when you passed out. Stop playing possum and get up."

A completely naked hot chick with a gun—Rainey thought this was probably some guy's fantasy, but not Theodore's. His hand trembled when he placed it on Rainey's side for leverage and sat up on his knees.

Ellie held her arms out, displaying her body for the scared little man. "Is it all you ever dreamed of, Graham?"

Peeking around the passenger seat, Theodore answered flatly, "No, Ellie. When I dream about you, you always have a rifle pointed at me."

Ellie aimed the Glock at him. "Well," she chuckled, "this will have to do. Get up. Get in the driver's seat." She pointed the Glock at Rainey. "You, don't move."

Rainey stared into the barrel, pointed straight at her head. This was the worst way to die, shot with the weapon meant to keep her safe. Her thoughts ran to Katie and the triplets. Dying wasn't going to be so bad, but the wake of sorrow Rainey would leave behind would devastate the ones she loved. Rainey hoped what they said was true, that she could watch her children grow from the other side. She mostly hoped the ache of loss welling in her chest wouldn't follow her there.

"Fuck," she spat.

"I offered. You refused," Ellie said, her eyes darting from Rainey to Theodore, who was now sitting behind the wheel.

"I wasn't talking to you," Rainey shot back.

"Well, excuse the fuck out of me," Ellie said, waving the gun around for emphasis.

Her personality was darkening with the setting sun. The windshield behind her revealed the last ambient light of day. The dashboard lights brightened in the coming dark, bathing Ellie's naked body in an eerie soft blue light. The last thing Rainey wanted was to die with any image other than her family in her mind. She tried again to break the cuffs.

"I told you not to move," Ellie barked.

With lightening quickness, Ellie bent and backhanded Rainey with the hand holding the weapon, catching the barrel on the bridge of her nose. Beyond the stunning of the blow, Rainey was sure her nose was broken. Blood ran from it and began to pool in the carpet.

"See, this is what happened. You and Graham struggled for the gun."

Ellie wasn't afraid of Graham. Her focus was on Rainey, who was tilting her head to keep from choking on the blood streaming from her nose.

Rainey knew if she was still talking, she wasn't dead yet. In a voice that sounded like she had a severe cold, she tried to buy more time.

"If you shoot us in this van, you won't be able to hear yourself think for days. People will notice and put it together." It was a last effort to get out of van. In Rainey's current position she was at an extreme disadvantage.

She heard Theodore say, "She is correct. The volume of that particular report can be ear shattering in a confined space of this type. You should at least roll down a window to ease the concussion."

The information offered from both of them offended Ellie. "Shut the fuck up. Do you two think I'm retarded, or something? I've been at this a while. I think I can handle it without your input." She turned the weapon on Theodore and said, "Put your foot on the brake and put the van in drive. Do not take your foot off the brake."

Rainey couldn't figure out what the hell this chick was going to do. "Are you going to shoot him in the head while he's driving, with you still in the vehicle? Really, that's your plan?"

Ellie held the weapon in her right hand. She bent down, reaching with her left hand to dip into the pool of Rainey's blood.

While Ellie was bent in the awkward position, Rainey shouted to Theodore, "Hit the gas," hoping to topple the Glock wielding maniac off her feet.

Theodore's reply added a new element of danger. "I can't. The front wheels are in the sandpit."

"Put it in reverse," Rainey bellowed the obvious.

Ellie put the gun in Theodore's ribs, "Touch that gearshift, and I'll shoot you dead." She smiled wickedly at Rainey. "I doubt you'll be able to escape, but should you, know that I'll be on the shore with your weapon, and I'm a very good shot." She backed away, regaining her upright position, and continued to explain her plan. "The van will go off the ledge, float for about a minute, maybe two, and then you'll sink to the bottom. It's too deep to swim up without an air tank. Your ascent rate would be too fast. You probably wouldn't survive the water temperature anyway. It's about forty-five this time of year. I predict they'll find you both, if they ever do, in a pile of bones still in the van."

Rainey didn't care about the water. She wasn't going to be shot. That was what she heard. Her brain was already working out the time she would have and what she needed to do to survive.

"There is always a way, Rainey." The voice in her head urged her to keep hope alive.

"Swimming in those boots and handcuffed, weighted down by that heavy coat, yeah, I want to see your heroine escape this trap, Graham or Theodore, whoever you are. It really doesn't matter anymore. Dead is dead, whatever they put on your tombstone."

Ellie held up the hand with the blood on it. Rainey heard Theodore slump over, as his foot came off the brake pedal, and the van began to roll forward slowly. Ellie grabbed her bundle of clothes and held it in place under the arm holding the Glock on Rainey. With her free hand, she opened the passenger side door, and then climbed onto the step rail. She leaned across the seat so that Rainey could still see her.

"Don't die too quickly, Rainey Bell. I do hope you suffer."

Ellie grabbed a handful of fabric on the thigh of unconscious Theodore's khaki pants, lifted his leg, and gently placed his foot on the accelerator. The van lurched forward, picking up speed on the sand covered rock ledge, as the accelerator moved under the weight of his foot.

"Don't worry, by the time the engine submerges, you'll have toppled over the edge. Trust me, I know what I'm doing. By the way, that little wife of yours is going to need some comforting. I bet she'll have a taste."

Ellie slipped out of sight, followed by a splash, and the door slamming behind her.

Immediately, Rainey started screaming, "Wake up! Wake up!"

She rolled over on her stomach, tangling in the coat more, frantically twisting the chains behind her back. Her nose ached, but that was the least of her problems.

"Wake up! Put your foot on the brake. Wake the fuck up!"

The front wheels fell off the rock ledge separating the shallows from the depths below. The engine sputtered to a stop, as the van tilted forward, lifted, and floated for a moment. The weight of the engine pulled the front end down, leaving the back bobbing in the water like a fishing cork. The electrical system was still working, but would go shortly, leaving no light to find what she needed. Rainey rolled back and forth, trying to loosen the coat's grip on her body, as the water began to fill up the front floorboards.

She tried again. "Theodore, wake up!" No response.

The last roll moved the coat enough to allow Rainey to press her body up against the bench seat. She wedged her knees into the front passenger seat and pushed with all her strength, willing herself to sit up. Once up, she whipped her feet around and got up on her knees. Using the seat in front of her to lean on, Rainey managed to get her feet under her and stand, stooped but standing. She flopped against a baby seat and screamed at Theodore again.

"If you don't wake up you're going to die."

The water covering his feet probably woke him, rather than her frantic cries, but Theodore came to and instantly freaked out. He scampered out of the seat onto the center console, as he looked for higher ground. They were sinking now, the front was filling faster, and Rainey could see the van was halfway under water through the windows.

"Don't look at me. I'm bleeding. Go to the very back and take your shoes off," Rainey shouted, just as the chain she was still working on bound tight. Upright, she was able to get the cuffs in the position she needed. With all her strength, she brought her wrists together quickly. The cuffs snapped apart with a loud pop. She brought her hands around to the front, and with no time to celebrate, started untying her boots. Theodore remained frozen.

153

Rainey did not look up, knowing if he saw the blood, he would pass out. "Get moving. Get to the back. Take your shoes off, now. Strip down to your underwear. Now, Theodore! Now! Move!"

He reacted this time, clambered past her and over the baby seats to the rear of the van, where he started removing his clothes. Rainey hustled, pulling the shoestrings, which were survival cord, out of her boots. Once complete, she threw the boots into one of the baby seats. She looped the cords around one wrist, as her mental time clock counted the seconds. Her eyes kept watch as the water level rose steadily, now just inches from reaching the front seat bottom. Next her coat, jeans, socks, and shirts came off and into the seats, leaving her only in panties.

She still wouldn't look at him, but she could tell Theodore had stopped moving. "This will be the last thing you ever see if you don't get going," she said, already reaching for the compartment where she had seen Katie's trash bags.

"I was looking at the scar," he said, through chattering teeth.

"Stop looking. My nose is bleeding and I'm not carrying your passed-out ass out of here. You'll get yourself out or drown. Keep moving," Rainey said, as she grabbed the box of bags and started pulling them out one after the other. She held one up to Theodore, keeping her head down and out of view. "Come get this bag. Put your clothes and shoes in it and tie it up tight. Leave a little air, but not too much. We have to be able to get it out the window."

"Rainey, look," she heard him say.

She peered over her shoulder, beginning to shiver now, as the water had reached the floor where she stood braced against the back of the center console. Only the rear window remained above the surface, as the frigid liquid began to come through every crack it could find in the van's exterior. They were pointed nearly straight down. The compartments would be under water soon, and what they contained might keep them alive, if they didn't drown first.

"I need you to do what I ask, Theodore," Rainey said, shaking a bag open. "We're going to get out of this, but I need you to focus. Get your clothes in the bag. We have about two minutes.

154

That's a long time, but only if we don't stop to think about where we are."

Theodore listened, fortunately. If he didn't, Rainey was fully prepared to leave him to his own demise. In Rainey's mind, "never leave a man behind" was not applicable in this case. Waiting for him to get his shit together was not an option. She started stuffing her boots, coat, and clothes in a trash bag, adding the extra tee shirts Katie left in the compartment. She closed the bag and tied it tight. Grabbing another, she shook it open and started emptying the other two compartments, throwing whatever she could grab into the bag. She stopped long enough to shove cotton balls in her nose, and then into the bag they went with diapers, hand sanitizer, juice, crackers, baby clothes, a jar of petroleum jelly, and the box with the remaining trash bags. The bag was heavy enough now, more would make it hard to swim with, and Rainey Bell planned on swimming.

With both bags tied tightly, she threw them, along with the empty bags she'd pulled out, over the seat to the back where Theodore stood, shaking visibly. His teeth chattered loudly behind lips starting to turn purple. She retrieved the rifle from under the water at her feet. The cold water shot pain up her legs. It was her body's way of telling her this was a bad, bad thing. "Get out of here," it screamed. Her body trembled, as it tried to create life-sustaining heat on its own. Her brain would take the use of her extremities if necessary to keep her core warm. Rainey had precious little time before she would be unable to function.

She plunged into the icy water to reach for the keys in the ignition. Rainey didn't need the keys. It was the small flashlight on the keychain she was after. The freezing water bit at her skin, as she felt for the silver cylinder they would desperately need when the electrical system finally failed. Once her fingers wrapped around it, Rainey yanked it free, breaking the chain that bound it to the key fob.

She came out of the water holding the light and took a second to wash any remaining blood from her face, and then climbed over the seat to join Theodore. The van came to rest on the bottom for a moment, but it was such a steep angle, it began to roll forward again. All the windows were under water now. The electrical system finally died, plunging them into complete darkness. Rainey turned on the tiny flashlight, illuminating the cabin, careful not to shine it on her face, in case there was any blood dripping from the cotton balls in her nose.

"Fill these empty bags with a little air and tie them off good," she ordered. "Remember, they will expand and they have to fit through the window."

The sliding van bumped into something, jostling its passengers, and then stopped its progression toward the bottom.

"Thank God," she said.

"Wh-wh-what?" Theodore stuttered between his chattering teeth.

"We stopped descending. I don't think we're much more than twenty feet down. Hard to tell, could be a little more."

"C-c-could b-b-be less." Theodore tried to smile, but the cold made his lips vibrate.

"Can you swim?"

He nodded yes.

"You're going into shock. Do not hyperventilate. Your body wants to. Do not let it. Short quick breaths." She demonstrated and resumed instructions, "Focus and determination can go far to overcome this crash. You're going to start feeling slow. Just do as I say. Focus on me. Do not think about anything but surviving."

He nodded again.

Rainey's teeth began to chatter along with his. "W-we'll make it. I'm not d-dying at the hands of that bitch. H-hold this l-light on my h-hands."

"O-o-o-k-k-k-ay."

Theodore took the flashlight. He tried to focus it on Rainey's hands, but it bounced with his shaking body. He was much colder than she was. He was failing faster. Time to move. While Rainey talked she tied one end of a survival cord around an air bag. Theodore's clothing bag went near the other end, with enough line left to tie it to his wrist. It was hard work, with her hands shaking. She did the same thing with the other cord, tying the supplies and the bag with her clothing around one of her wrist.

156

She gave instructions quickly, before the chattering of her jaws made talking too difficult. "H-hold the clothes t-tight to your chest. Let the air b-bag float free. Wedge yourself in here s-so the w-water d-doesn't knock you around. W-w-when I get the w-window open, f-follow the airbag up, after I sh-shove it out the window. L-let the b-b-bag s-surface f-first and d-d-don't c-c-come up r-r-r-right under it. If sh-sh-she's there, hopefully sh-sh-she'll sh-shoot the b-bags and n-n-not us."

Theodore nodded and gripped his clothing bag to his chest. Rainey was shaking uncontrollably now, as the water swirled around her thighs. It was time to go.

"O-k-kay," she stuttered. "I'm g-g-going t-t-o b-break a w-window." The water had reached her waist. The pain was excruciating. "Sh-short b-breaths, n-n-now, un-t-til the l-last b-b-big br-breath b-b-before we g-go. L-let it out on the w-w-way up. D-don't-t g-go un-t-til I s-say. D-d-don't g-g-gasp."

Theodore put his shaking hand on Rainey's arm. "D-d-don't c-c-cut y-y-your-s-s-self." He didn't want to pass out now, and Rainey sure didn't want him to either.

Rainey nodded. "K-k-keep y-y-your h-head a-b-b-bove the w-water as l-long as y-you c-can. W-w-wait f-for it t-t-to s-s-settle. D-d-don't p-p-panic. F-f-follow me."

He nodded again, or he was shaking so bad now his body was convulsing. Either way, they had to leave now.

"H-h-hold on." she stammered.

Rainey placed her back on the rear door of the van and wedged her feet against the seat in front of her. She aimed the barrel of the rifle at the side window closest to her and jabbed it into the glass. The window shattered instantly. The force of the rushing water threatening to knock Rainey out of her wedged position, but she held fast.

Once the water slowed, Rainey cleared the glass with the rifle butt. Their noses were just above the water now, the cold sending shock waves through her body. She dropped the rifle, grabbed the cord on Theodore's wrist, and ran her fingers up to the bag. She dove under, and forced the bag down and out the window. She surfaced, grabbed some air, and then repeated the process with her air bag. Up again for one last breath in the diminishing air pocket, Rainey grabbed Theodore.

"T-t-take a breath. G-go." She shoved him at the window.

For once, he did not hesitate. He dove under and slipped into open water. Rainey was right on his heels. She was too cold to feel any more. Her only concerns now were how far she'd have to swim in the freezing water, and was Ellie still up there? She surfaced quickly, right on the heels of the airbag, but there were no shots. She heard splashing to her right. Theodore was up too, swimming toward shore. They had survived the first part of this frigid nightmare, now to survive the rest.

Chapter Eight

6:41 p.m.
Overcast, 34°F, Windchill 25°F

Five yards felt like fifty. Her limbs were sluggish and dragging two bags, even with the airbag for added support, made the swim even harder. When Rainey finally reached the ledge and felt bottom underneath her, attempting to stand took several tries. She stumbled forward, finding Theodore on his hands and knees, but still in the water. She couldn't talk. Her teeth chattered and the shivering made everything twice as difficult. A hand in his armpit to urge him forward was all she could manage.

When her last foot left the water, Rainey dropped her hand from Theodore and yanked in the bags she towed with her. She got hers up onto dry land and then pulled Theodore's bag to his feet. He was not moving. He stood clinching his wet body, shaking so badly his head bobbed up and down. She couldn't help him until she helped herself. As with emergency oxygen on a plane, the adult should mask up before helping the child. Otherwise, they could both lose consciousness and die. Rainey didn't want to die.

She pulled her clothes bag further from the water and tore it open. She dropped her wet panties on the ground, not sure why she had kept them on. With her hands shaking so badly that she could hardly manage the job, Rainey found her mock turtleneck. It was cotton and absorbent. She did a quick drying of the water from her skin. Wet and cold meant hypothermia would set in faster. With the wind chill below freezing, heat was a premium. She dropped the wet shirt and donned the dry sweatshirt, jeans, and coat. Rainey thanked the universe when she discovered her gloves still in the pocket of the coat. They were difficult to put on, cold and stiff, and her hands were still clammy, but she forced them on. She shoved her socks in the pocket where the gloves had been. She'd have time to put them on later.

Still shivering violently, Rainey had to sit down on the garbage bag to put on her boots, but the dry clothes were helping. The bag kept her from having to sit on the wet ground. The bag was wet, but not covered in wet muck that would cling to her and keep her damp. Dry was the answer to surviving the cold. Boots on, she stood, grabbed the shirt she dried off with, and crossed to Theodore. She moved him away from the shoreline, opened his bag, and then rubbed his skin hard with her shirt, trying to regenerate blood flow to his limbs. He barely registered her presence. One fist was clinched tightly, locked by muscles too cold to function. He appeared to have closed his mind and gone away, leaving behind his body to be handled like a marionette. He never moved when she yanked his wet boxers to the ground. Once mostly dry, Rainey dressed him like a child, and as often was the case with her own brood, she discovered he had lost his socks.

She was warming now. The activity helped speed her recovery. Her skin tingled with the stinging return of feeling to her extremities. Rainey had reached the point where her body no longer felt the need to hoard blood within its vital organs. She still shivered, but the violent shaking had passed. Her jaw began to relax and the teeth chattering slowed and quieted, though her lips continued to tremble. Little white clouds of steam vibrated out of them, as she breathed through her mouth. Her nose was of no use, swollen, and aching. Theodore had not turned the corner yet, but life was returning to his eyes, as she coaxed his damp foot into the shoe.

"C-come on," Rainey said, her power of speech returning. Her stuffed and probably broken nose made her the sound like

Lily Tomlin's character, five and a half year old Edith Ann. "St-Stick your f-foot in. G-Good boy."

She had almost forgotten she was talking to a man. Diminutive and helpless, it was easy to forget Theodore was almost thirty years old. Completely dressed now, Rainey made a turban from the damp shirt for Theodore's head, hoping to help him retain more heat. He was bone thin, with no body fat to speak of, the worst kind of body to have in a hypothermic situation. She turned him toward the lane leading away from the water. She remembered the old cars in the edge of the woods from her trip to the sandpit yesterday, when Bill Wise brought her to see where his father died. Rainey almost met her demise there too, but she had not yet. It was a big yet.

One hundred yards down the lane and away from the water, those were Rainey's goals. She didn't want to give Ellie a second chance to put them back in. She left Theodore for a moment, while she gathered the used trash bags, their underclothes, and recovered the survival line. Rainey flattened the air bags open, rolled everything up together, and tied it all into a bundle with the supply bag. With the bundle in one hand, she tucked the fingers of her other under Theodore's elbow.

"L-let's get out of this w-wind," she said, prodding her nearly frozen companion forward, as a chilling gust swept over them.

He did not respond verbally, but she was happy to see he could walk and follow instructions.

"D-Damn, the fl-flashlight," Rainey lamented, looking back over her shoulder.

Theodore did not say a word, but suddenly there was a beam of light extending from his hand. He unclenched his fist revealing the flashlight. He kept it safe since she gave it to him.

"Th-Theodore, y-you are m-my hero."

"It's Gr-Graham," he said, his speech returning along with his pride.

"W-well, all right, Graham Dean Colde. W-We'll g-get w-warm, w-we'll g-get help, and then—"

He finished her thought, "—w-w-we'll g-g-get ev-v-ven."

"Y-y-yes."

She put him under her shoulder and kept him close. While her shivering was milder now, Rainey knew his shaking wouldn't stop until his core body temperature climbed back nearer to normal. Fatigue was a factor in hypothermia. The more the body shivered, the more energy it used. He would die if he reached the point where exhaustion stopped his shivering. Warm and dry was the only way he would survive a night in the woods in icy conditions. The air temperature hovered around freezing, but anything exposed to the wind was glazed with ice. The rain earlier in the day melted most of the snow and now formed frozen over puddles in the road. Everything was wet, soggy, or frozen. Starting a fire was going to take skill.

"W-We have to b-build a f-fire," Rainey said. "L-look for p-piles of st-sticks in the edge of the w-woods." Her speech began to improve, when she focused her energy on calming her jaw muscles. "S-Some of the ones on the b-bottom could be dry. We m-may n-not have the energy t-to l-look later."

"W-We c-c-can't w-walk out of here. It's f-five m-miles to the n-nearest house, unl-less y-you c-c-count E-Ellie's," Graham pointed out.

"N-not in the d-dark. We're not w-walking out. I r-remember seeing some old c-cars by the lane, just in the edge of the w-woods. I think we can m-make a shelter there."

Rainey took the flashlight from him, because he couldn't hold it steady, and searched the edges of the woods. Someone had cleared a large fallen limb from the road, where it sat rotting and sheltering its collected debris. It had served to keep some of the pine needles and the much-needed kindling dry. Rainey knelt down and swept the wet debris out of the way with her free hand. She gathered dry needles and twigs, stuffing them in both their pockets. Now they needed something else to burn and the more important element, a spark. Rainey had a few ideas about how to make one. Making one with shaking hands in wet conditions, that was going to be the challenge.

"I'm g-glad y-your n-nose st-st-stopped b-bl-bleeding," Graham said, after they'd walked quietly for a few minutes.

"Me too," Rainey said, finally able to speak without the stammer. She pulled him closer to her side. "I'm also glad it's cold as hell, or it would be hurting a lot worse."

"El-Ellie is a b-b-bitch," he stuttered.

Rainey concurred, "Yes, a raging bitch."

"W-will sh-sh-she c-c-come b-b-back?" He asked, looking up at Rainey with terror-filled eyes.

Rainey smiled down at him. "We're fine. She hasn't made it home yet. She said it took an hour to walk here at a leisurely pace. Even jogging, in the dark it will probably take her thirty or forty minutes."

She felt him lean into her like her children did when she read them a story. He was warming. His shivers were no longer rattling his bones quite so violently. His muscles released the contraction that held his body rigid for so long. In Graham's case, this process was fatiguing. Rainey flashed the light into the woods, searching for the old rusting relics that would be their shelter for the night. She kept her voice calm and even, and continued leading the tiring Graham, while she eased his mind.

"Ellie said she was going to call the police. If she does, they will have her tied up with questions, and with a crazed killer on the loose—that's you, by the way—they will not leave her alone. If she gets away from them someway, she probably still will not return until morning, which would match her routine and not draw suspicion. She won't find us. We'll be warm and dry and well-defended by then if she does."

"Y-you're g-going to k-k-kill her, ar-r-ren't y-you?" Graham said.

"We're going to have to talk about your perception of me, but right now, I think we're home."

Rainey shined the flashlight on the rusted front end of 1940s era farm truck, about ten feet inside the edge of the woods. All the glass was missing, along with the doors. There was no chassis, so the floor of the cab sat flush with the ground. The beak-shaped hood gaped open, like the bill of a rust-colored raptor. Thick vines twisted out of it and tangled in the trees above, ancient bonds rooting the old truck in place. Upon Rainey's approach, the yawning mouth revealed an empty engine well, half-filled with leaves, broken limbs, and probably a den of some kind. She cast the beam of the flashlight around at the other vehicle carcasses, all in various states of decay. The truck offered the best shelter for two adults.

Rainey stuck her head under the hood. "Looks like something thought this a good enough spot to den. I guess we need to evict whatever is in here, if it still is," she said.

Leaving Graham standing beside the truck, Rainey found a long solid stick and poked around in the pile of debris inside the engine well. Nothing stirred.

"Okay, I think we're the only ones at the Inn. Hang on a sec and let me take some of this wet stuff off the top of the pile," she said.

Rainey told Graham everything to keep him involved and his mind active. She climbed over the front grill and dropped onto the leaves. It took a few minutes of house cleaning, moving out the soggy top layer of debris, clearing the limbs and sticks, to make the space ready for them. Rainey pushed the pile of remaining leaves and pine needles toward the front of the truck, exposing the hole where the transmission would have been. It formed a perfect little oven under the cab. She kicked at the old rusty metal, opening a hole near the top.

"Look, we have a stove and it comes with a chimney. That will let the smoke go up, but the fire will heat up the metal. A small fire will work very well in here."

She hopped over the grill, recovered the supply bag, and tossed it into their new home. Once she had helped Graham over the grill, Rainey followed him in. Squatting to tear open the plastic holding all they had to survive, she first retrieved the box of trash bags. Pulling one out, she laid it on top of the pile of debris. Out of the wind now, Rainey could feel the difference in the temperature. She wasn't warm yet, but with the shelter, even without a fire, she knew they could survive.

"Okay, sit down here out of the wind. It's going to be tight in here when I join you, but that will help us stay warm. How are you doing? Getting any warmer?"

Graham lowered himself down to sit where she instructed. "I-I th-think s-s-s-o."

164

Rainey dug in the bag again, coming out with a baby diaper, a juice box, and one of Mack's shirts. She knew it was Mack's because his were bigger than Timothy or Weather's. Rainey's mind drifted to home and family. By now, Katie would be frantic. She would have called everyone she knew, including FBI Supervisory Special Agent Danny McNally. Rainey couldn't spend time imagining how they would find her. She simply had to believe they would. She dug in the bag again and found a pack of peanut butter crackers and another baby shirt, this one pink.

"Here, eat these and drink the juice. Your body needs calories to create heat." She reached up and took the damp temporary hat from Graham's head and replaced it with an open diaper, which she held in place by slipping Mack's shirt over it. "Okay, we'll get that head warm so you can help me. I'd like to put that genius brain of yours to work."

Graham fumbled with the cracker package. His energy level was nearly depleted. Rainey slipped the pink shirt over her head, foregoing the diaper until she became more desperate. The shirt served its purpose, covering her freezing ears. The lavender hippopotamus on the front probably went well with the forming blackened-eyes she was sure to have, and the nose she knew must be all shades of deep blues and purples. As she warmed, a distant throb was coming more clearly into focus. Graham continued fumbling with the plastic covering the crackers. Rainey took it from him, opened it, and handed it back. She poked the straw through the juice box for him and placed it in his hand.

"You're going to feel better in a minute, Graham. I know you're tired and cold. Chew slowly and eat at least two crackers before you stop."

Rainey removed the dry kindling from of her pockets and placed it in the proposed stove area, before pulling the socks out.

I would give you my gloves, but these socks will be warmer than leather."

She removed the juice box, covered his pale frozen hand with a sock, and then replaced the juice box, folding his fingers around it for him. He chewed slowly with deliberate jaw motions, crunching tiny pieces one at a time. She removed the cracker from the fingertips of the still uncovered hand. He chewed and stared at his hand as if it were no longer attached to him. On went the sock and the cracker was returned.

"Sorry these have been worn, but I guess you don't care at this point, huh? How's that?" She asked, checking his eyes for signs he was still with her.

Graham nodded, with cracker crumbs on his trembling lips.

"I'm going to put this other pair on your feet. You just eat." She kept the banter up, hoping to keep Graham's mind active, while she pulled his shoes off and put on the socks. He had yet to turn the corner and it was beginning to worry her more by the minute. If his body went into shock, he would need immediate medical care. "I read once that besides your head, more heat escapes from your ankles than any other part of the body. I wonder if it's true. We'll cover yours up anyway, just to be sure."

Cracker crumbs sprayed from Graham's lips, as he said, "M-M-Myth."

Rainey smiled. Graham was thinking and that was good.

"Myth, huh? Which part?"

"H-Heat l-loss p-p-per-c-c-centage e-e-quals ex-p-posed sk-skin ar-rea." he struggled to get it out, but he did.

"Well, okay. Learn something new every day. My mother perpetuated that myth and required I wear a hat. I should have called bullshit. Do you know how bad that bush on my head looked with hat hair?"

He was taking a sip of juice and almost choked when he chuckled.

"Easy there," Rainey said, and patted his knee. "Wouldn't want you to choke to death after all you have survived. You're a hard man to kill, Graham Colde."

"E-E-Ellie tr-tried tw-twice."

Rainey pulled out more trash bags and a juice for herself. Her body needed the calories too.

"Yes, she did, and she will pay for that, Graham. Just eat now. I'm going to work on closing us in a little more and try to start a fire."

"B-Battery," Graham said, pointing at the flashlight.

Rainey smiled at him again. "I should have known a fellow geek would know how to start a fire with a battery."

Graham smiled back this time, thinly, but it was a smile. He began to chew a bit faster, as his condition improved. Rainey relaxed her worry over him and concentrated on preparing for the rest of the night. She hoped it wouldn't be all night.

While she drank the juice, she prayed Katie called Danny in Quantico. When Rainey needed him, he always came through, the bond between them unbreakable. He could be in Hominy Junction already, if Katie called soon enough. If Danny got a chance to talk to Ellie, he would see thorough her lies, the unnecessary embellishments, and the deceptive body language. This was a new crime, a crime of opportunity, one for which Ellie had a good story, but not the time to practice her portrayal of victim.

Ellie was good, Rainey had to give her that. She'd answered Rainey's questions with ease and an appearance of truthfulness. Ellie told those lies often over the years. To her, the lies were second nature to recall with a complete air of sincerity. Ellie fit the profile of a personality that would practice in the mirror, learning the faces of empathy because she had none. The well-rehearsed portrayal of grieving daughter fooled everyone when she killed her parents, even deceiving the brother she tried to kill and finally did. Ellie's latest crime was spontaneous. She knew nothing of Rainey until yesterday. Her crimes were meticulously planned until today. Ellie acting as quickly as she did worked in Rainey's favor, because the serial killer that "did not make mistakes" had gone off script. That was a big mistake.

Finished with the juice, Rainey set about working on the roof or their abode. The hood hinges were frozen into place by years of rot and decay. To cover their heads better, she built a lean-to out of garbage bags, tape torn from the remaining diapers, and the survival cord. Graham ate a second and third cracker, while she worked and only commented when she completed the task.

"We'll b-be dry, if the wind d-doesn't blow hard-der."

Rainey, who had been cleaning away debris in the proposed little fire pit, looked up. A slight smile tugged at one corner of her lips. "Welcome back, Mr. Colde. I take it you are feeling better."

"S-still shaking," he said, but he was visibly better.

"It's okay if you continue to shiver. You're not as cold as you were, so we're making headway. Keep eating if you can. There isn't any need to save it. We won't be here that long."

Rainey dug down to the dirt, removing anything flammable away from the fire area, while trying to keep the kindling dry. The body of the truck acted as a windbreak, but she wasn't comfortable with sitting on a damp stack of dead sticks, dried leaves, and pine needles next to an open fire.

"I need something to contain the fire," she said.

"Wet d-diapers," Graham said.

"What?" Rainey asked.

"I'll show you," he answered, this time with no stuttering. "We need water."

"Water?"

"Fire retardant gel made from the inside of diapers to put down a b-barrier."

A shiver shook Graham, but he was recovering rapidly. The food gave him the much-needed calories to make body heat. Rainey was glad to see his mind working. An active mind also indicated Graham's body temperature was normalizing.

"Okay then," Rainey said, as she reached into the supply bag, "I have three more diapers." She retrieved them and handed them off to Graham. "Are you finished with your juice box?"

"Yes," he said, already beginning to tear the top layer off a diaper.

Rainey found her empty juice box, picked up Graham's, and careful not to disturb the temporary roof she built, started climbing out of their sanctuary.

Graham grabbed her leg. "Don't leave."

She looked down at his fearful expression. "I'll be right back. I'm going to get some water from the puddles in the road. I won't be far. I'll leave you the flashlight."

"Watch for Ellie," he warned.

"She's been gone about forty-five minutes now. If she made it back home, she still has to deal with the investigators she was planning on calling. They'll insist she get medical treatment for that arm wound she manufactured. You're safe, Graham. I won't let her hurt you again."

"Don't let her hurt you," he said. "Be safe."

"Always," she replied.

Graham smiled. "I knew you would say that."

Rainey squatted back down next to him. "Exactly how long have you been stalking me?"

His head dipped, but he didn't answer.

"I'm pretty pissed at you, Theod—," she caught her mistake and changed it to, "Graham, but I'm not going to let you die. I'm just curious how we crossed paths and why you've been obsessively studying my files and my life? You think about that while I go fetch the water. After we build a fire, we will have all night to talk about boundaries and privacy."

"I'm sorry, Rainey."

"I'm sure you are. Make it up to me by helping us not die out here of exposure."

"Okay," Graham said, and then went straight to work on another diaper.

Leaving him to his task and after a somewhat difficult exit through the small opening, which caused a repair she'd need to make on her return, Rainey picked her way from tree to tree in the black darkness. The nearly full moon could not penetrate the low hanging clouds overhead. Five feet into the journey, she tripped over a fallen branch and smacked her tender nose on a low hanging limb. The pain was intense enough to force Rainey to her knees, where she had to wait for her eyes to stop watering before she could see clearly again.

"Fuck, fuck, fuck," she exclaimed.

Graham called out in a panic, "What? What is it?"

Rainey spoke behind the hand holding her throbbing nose on her face. "I hit my freaking nose on a limb. Damn, that hurt."

"Don't be so loud," he reprimanded her. "She might be out there. You don't know."

"By that reasoning, you shouldn't be talking so loud either," Rainey said, finally able to let go of her nose and wipe the tears from her cheeks. "She's not here, Graham. Just relax."

He did not speak again. Once Rainey regained her feet, she moved with one hand shielding her face for the remainder of her slow and careful trek to the edge of the woods. Despite her

169

reassurances to Graham, she hesitated before stepping out into the open. The wind blew through the trees and lifted the tails of her coat. Rainey's body remembered the cold it had endured earlier and rattled her spine with a shiver, encouraging her to hurry back to shelter, but she waited, listening. Ellie had proven herself to be quite the marksman. A night scope would give her all the advantage she needed. Rainey might as well have started waving her arms and shouting shoot me now, as to walk out there and kneel down by the puddle. Her heart quickened with the adrenaline rush of danger.

"Well," she said to herself, "there is only one way to find out."

"Wait."

Rainey heard it clear as day. Her father's voice rang out in her head. She ducked down where she stood behind a tree. Listening intently for further instruction, she waited, peering into the darkness. Very faintly she heard it, a vehicle coming from the main road, moving slowly, but definitely growing louder. A beam of light cut the darkness as the vehicle rounded the bend in the road, bobbing through the series of big dips. Rainey fought the urge to run long enough to get a good look at the front. The height of the vehicle, the spread and shape of the headlights, matched those of a large SUV—Ellie's SUV as a matter of fact.

Rainey remained crouched, but turned toward the shelter and Graham. She could see the glow of the flashlight, which fortuitously silhouetted the trees in her path back to him, but also gave away their position. She stayed low and moved as quickly as she could toward the light, this time remembering to keep her face shielded. She could hear the SUV coming nearer, and risked calling out to Graham before she reached the safety of the shelter.

"Douse the flashlight. Someone is coming."

Graham did not hesitate and plunged the woods into darkness. Rainey stopped moving, just feet from the relative safety of their shelter. She turned toward the road, felt for the nearest tree, stepped behind it, and stood perfectly still. The SUV's headlights lit up the woods in front of her, but did not penetrate where she stood, as it crawled by slowly. It continued down to the water, giving Rainey a chance to feel her way to the old truck. With one swipe, she took out the plastic roof and jumped in beside Graham.

"Stay down," she said, reaching for his shoulder and pushing him down in the corner.

Rainey pulled the plastic away from the front grill just enough to peek through. The SUV stayed down at the water for several excruciating minutes. She risked rising up to peer over the front of the truck and saw a flashlight beam working its way back up the road toward them.

Graham, she realized, was looking too, when he whispered, "She's coming."

"Quiet," Rainey whispered back.

"Our footprints—"

Rainey grabbed his shoulder. She whispered again, this time with more authority, "Shut up, or die, your choice."

The beam grew closer, but then the SUV lights appeared to be moving as well, coming behind the flashlight. Two people were in that vehicle, not one. It couldn't be Ellie, or could it? Rainey's mind wrestled with what to do. If Ellie had a partner in crime, she concealed them very well. Could Rainey take the chance that it was someone looking for her? As the lights grew closer, she caught a silhouetted glimpse of the person walking in front of the vehicle, but not clear enough to get a good look. The shape appeared too tall and broad to be a woman.

The flashlight studied the ground, following the footprints Rainey and Graham left on the road right up to where they turned into the woods. She could see the dark figure stop and turn toward them. Rainey ducked down, pulling Graham with her, just as the powerful beam hit the front of the truck.

"Rainey, are you in there?"

"Danny?"

"Who is it?" Graham said, still terrified.

He grabbed at her as she began to rise from her crouch.

She looked down at him. "It's okay. It's the good guys." The flashlight beam hit her as she stood up. "What took you so long?" Rainey shouted to Danny.

"It's her," he yelled at the person in the SUV.

"Come on, Graham," Rainey said, helping him to his feet. "Looks like we won't have to build that fire after all."

"I could, you know," he said, relief apparent in his voice.

"I'm sure you could," she said, hugging him close to her. "Stay right here. They might still think you are a killer."

Someone was following Danny, as two flashlights came crashing through the woods towards them.

"Is that Colde, with you?" Danny asked.

"Yes, but he didn't abduct me." Graham tensed in her grasp. "You're all right, Graham. No one is going to hurt you. I got you."

"I swear, you are the only person I know that could go to a funeral and end up kidnapped," Danny said, arriving at the truck.

"How did you know to look here?" Rainey asked.

The figure behind him said, "I had a hunch."

It was Bill Wise.

"I guess our families are even now," Rainey said, smiling, ignoring the pain it cause in her nose.

Bill stepped forward and offered his hand to help her out of the truck. "Thank my dad. I read that file all day. So many things happened here that when I told Danny, he said we should just come take a look."

Once Rainey's feet were on the ground outside the truck, she hugged Bill. "I thank you all." She turned to Danny to hug him as well. While she still had him in her grasp, she whispered, "I knew you would come."

Danny pulled back from her and looked at her face. "I had no choice. Those women at your house insisted and Molly sent a chartered jet to speed my arrival. Jesus, what happened to your nose? Damn, I bet that hurts like hell and you sound like a kid with a cold."

"I've had worse," Rainey said, with a little grin.

Danny had witnessed her worst and simply nodded with understanding, but added, "Yeah, but never with a lavender hippopotamus on your head."

Rainey remembered the pink shirt and yanked it off, offering her defense. "My fashion choices were limited."

She threw the shirt at Danny, playfully. Her relief at being rescued improved her humor dramatically and, for the moment, she forgot her face was throbbing.

"Come on, Theodore," Bill said, as he assisted Rainey's fellow survivor out of the truck.

"It's Graham, Bill. My name is Graham Colde and I did not kill those people."

Bill took off his coat and put it over the shoulders of the small, shivering, young man. "Nice to meet you, Graham."

Rainey spoke to Danny. "Supervisory Special Agent Danny McNally, I'd like to introduce you to Graham Dean Colde. He was accused of a double murder fourteen years ago, which I can testify, and, better yet, prove he did not commit."

"Are you going to tell me how you ended up driving off into that sandpit?" Danny asked, ignoring her comment, and eyeing Colde warily.

"Wait, you already know he's innocent, don't you? How? Is Ellie Paxton in custody?"

"No. Should she be?"

Graham and Rainey answered simultaneously with an enthusiastic, "Yes."

Rainey added, "She drove us into sandpit."

Bill asked, "Did she kill my dad?"

Rainey nodded. "He got too close to the truth, I'm afraid."

"I knew she was off," Danny said, as he reached in his pocket, pulled out a phone, and made a call without further prodding.

When someone answered, he said, "Put me through to Undersheriff Dawson." As he waited, Danny said to Rainey. "He's sitting on a murderer and doesn't know it."

Rainey commented, "Serial murderer."

Danny's eyebrows went up, but he waved at her to be quiet. "Dawson, it's McNally. I have Rainey and Colde. They'll be okay when they warm up, but do you still have eyes on Ellie Paxton?" He waited for the answer. "Get some cuffs on her." He must have been asked what charges, because he said, "To start with, two counts of attempted murder."

Rainey held up three fingers. "She's tried to kill Graham twice."

Danny amended his statement, "Make that three attempted murder and," he looked at Rainey to fill in the blanks.

"Nine counts of murder," she said.

"Did you get that?" Danny said into the phone. After a second, he said, "Just cuff her and we'll work out the details after I get these two to a hospital." He paused, and then added, "No, I think we can get to Waitesville faster than waiting for an ambulance."

Rainey watched as Danny nodded while he listened to Brad Dawson, the very acquaintance she was going to call in the Dobbs County Sheriff's office.

He finally responded, "Hold her. We'll be there in a thirty minutes. And you need to send crime scene investigators to—"

"Read's Sandpit," Bill said.

"Read's Sandpit," Danny repeated. "Tell them to block the road at the big bend and don't disturb anything. I'll fill you in on where to direct them, but there are prints and tire tracks that should not be disturbed until you get some light in here." He listened again and then said, "I'll tell her."

Danny hung up the phone and handed it to Rainey. "Brad said he's glad you're safe and for God's sake, call your wife."

Rainey grinned at Danny. "She raised a little hell, did she?"

"I'd say so," Bill commented, as the four of them started out of the woods. "I bet you could see blue flashing lights from the space shuttle."

"You didn't answer Rainey's question," Graham said, holding the little flashlight he still possessed on Danny. "How did you know I wasn't in the woods waiting to shoot you? You just walked right to us and called Rainey's name."

"The footprints," Danny answered. "Even if you had a weapon on her, if you got that close to Rainey standing upright, she would have kicked your ass. She was helping you. Your weight forced her right foot down further into the dirt as you came down the road."

Graham was impressed. "Wow. Did they teach you that a BAU school—how to track people like that? You BAU guys are just total bad-asses."

Danny turned the flashlight on Graham. "I saw that game you are working on. That's a warped sense of what we do and of Rainey's character and mine. We don't track people in the field like bloodhounds, Mr. Colde. We don't hunt them down and exact revenge. We study criminal behavior and that's how we found you. Nothing fancy about it. And to answer your question, I learned how to read track sign from my grandfather."

Graham sounded like a scolded little boy, when he tried to improve his position, saying, "I already told Rainey I was sorry."

Rainey draped her arm over Graham's shoulders. "It's okay, we'll talk about it later." She shot Danny a look that said back off. "Agent McNally and I will explain how the BAU really works to you. Right now, we just need to get warm. Welcome back to the world, Graham Dean Colde. Now, let's go put Ellie Paxton behind bars, shall we?"

He smiled up at her and then went limp under the weight of her arm, collapsing instantly.

"Do we need a helicopter? Is he breathing?" Danny asked, startled by Graham's sudden downturn.

Rainey turned to Danny. "Is my nose bleeding?"

Chapter Nine

7:58 p.m.
Overcast, 36°F, Windchill 28°F

"Danny, have you found her?"

Katie's shaky voice answered the phone. Rainey could tell she'd been crying.

"Baby, I'm okay."

The phone went silent and then all Rainey could hear was her wife sobbing on the other end.

The next voice she heard was Molly's. "Danny?"

"No, it's me. I'm okay. Let me talk to her."

"Glad they found you. And you're okay?" Molly asked.

"Yes, I'm fine. I need to talk to Katie."

Rainey heard Molly say, "Come on, Katie, she's okay. She wants to talk to you."

Molly said into the receiver, "She just needs to catch her breath. She was scared out of her mind. Give her a second."

Rainey said, "Put the phone to her ear."

When Katie's ragged breathing sounded in the receiver, Rainey said softly, "I love you. Catch your breath. It's over, now. I'm fine. I'm so sorry, Katie. I know you were scared. Talk to me. Tell me you're okay."

"Did Theodore do this? Did I let a killer into our lives?" Katie asked through her tears, but she was calming.

"No, honey. He's here with me. He's not a murderer. You didn't do anything wrong. Did you think you caused this? Oh Katie, I'm so sorry."

"I thought I'd gotten you killed," Katie said.

Rainey reassured her, "This wasn't your fault. It wasn't anyone's fault except the bitch that tried to drown me. It was someone neither of us had a clue existed, Ellie Paxton."

"Ellie Paxton? The woman that said Theodore attacked her and abducted you?"

"Yes, and she should be in handcuffs by now. I'm sorry about your van, by the way, but it was under about fifteen feet of water the last time I saw it."

"I don't care about the van," Katie said, sniffling, almost recovered from her shock. "Where are you?"

"I'm on my way to the hospital in Waitesville."

"Are you hurt?" Katie's concern began to rise again.

"Not too bad. I think my nose is broken, but other than that, I'm just cold. I don't think my feet will ever be warm again," Rainey answered as casually as she could, hoping to lower Katie's alarm. "Danny has the heat on full blast, so that's helping. My nose, however, is going to need setting, and I'm afraid I'm going to look pretty horrendous for a few of weeks."

"Is that why you sound so funny?" Katie finally chuckled and said, "You sound like a six year-old with allergies."

Relieved at Katie's returning humor, Rainey laughed. "So I've heard. I'll be home as soon as I can. I promise I'll be there for our Valentine's date."

"My mom already has the kids. Do we need to come get you?"

"Danny's going to bring me home."

"Come as soon as you can. I love you. You honestly have no idea how much."

"The feeling is mutual," Rainey said. "I love you, too. Get some sleep, and tell Molly thank you for arranging Danny's transportation. He found me. You did good, Katie. I knew you would know what to do."

Rainey could imagine Katie's humor and optimism returning when she joked, "Unfortunately, I am well trained in DEFCON 1 operations since I started living with you. I swear you are the only person in the world that can go to a funeral and end up kidnapped."

"Are you and Danny sharing material now? He said the same thing."

"Well, those words may have come out of my mouth a few times today."

"Are you going to be all right, now?" Rainey asked.

A tension release sigh filled the earpiece, before Katie responded. "I'll be better when I can see your face."

Rainey chuckled, peeking into the mirror over Danny's shoulder at her swollen, crooked nose and blackened eyes. "I'm afraid you're not going to see that face for quite a while, maybe never if they don't fix my nose right."

"I'd know those eyes behind a mask. Come home, Rainey."

\#

8:27 p.m.
Overcast, 36°F, Windchill 29°F

Danny pulled the SUV into the emergency entrance at Memorial Hospital in Waitesville. Undersheriff Brad Dawson opened the vehicle door for Rainey, as bystanders gawked and pointed. Evidently, the news of what happened had traveled through the county faster than Danny could drive.

"Good to see you again, Brad," Rainey said, to the buff, handsome Undersheriff.

When she met him two years ago, while working on a case with Molly, he was a deputy. He had moved up the chain of command since then. Rainey occasionally saw Brad at social functions, as he was an old friend of Leslie and Molly's.

"I'm glad Danny found you," Brad said, shaking her outstretched hand. "I would have hated to make another phone call to your house without good news. Molly and Leslie were as bad as Katie. I do believe they would have stopped speaking to me if this hadn't turned out so well."

"Determined women, that lot. Welcome to my world and I'm most happy they are in it," Rainey replied.

Brad looked over her shoulder at Graham, as Bill helped him into a wheelchair held by a waiting nurse. Another nurse covered the patient with a warming blanket.

"Is that Theodore Suzanne?" Brad asked.

Rainey stepped aside and made the introduction. "Undersheriff Brad Dawson, this is Graham Dean Colde. I'm sure you are familiar with his case. We'd both like to make a statement concerning the murders of the Paxtons in 2000. Ellie and Ely Paxton killed their parents and blamed Graham. An injustice was done here and I'd like to see it rectified, right after you arrest her for trying to kill us and the nine other people she already murdered, including Wellman Wise."

Brad extended his hand to Graham. "It's a pleasure to meet you. We'll make sure all this is cleared up."

"Thank you, sir. Could I ask a favor?"

"What can I do for you?" Brad replied.

"Could someone call my mother? I'd like to see her."

Rainey knelt beside the wheelchair. "We'll call her, Graham. Go inside and get checked out." She looked at the nurse. "He faints at the sight of a drop of blood. Can you make sure he isn't exposed to any in there?"

The nurse had a strange look on her face, as she stepped around to the front of the wheelchair and made eye contact with her patient. "Graham, do you recognize me?"

He looked up at her. "No, I'm sorry."

"My name is Lisa. I was in your class in school. You were always so sweet. I never thought you killed Ellie's parents, and I always thought she was a bitch. Come on, let's get you warm. We're going to take very good care of you."

"Thank you, Lisa," Graham said, softly.

He was exhausted from the ordeal and losing energy fast. The nurses took him into the building. Brad nodded at a deputy, who followed Graham closely.

"What was that about?" Rainey asked. "I told you he isn't a criminal."

"It's for his protection," Brad answered.

"Is Ellie Paxton in there?" Rainey said, already moving toward the door.

179

"Rainey, I need to talk to you," Brad said, catching up to her. "Let's go inside, out of this cold."

Danny, Bill, Rainey, and Brad all stepped beyond the automatic doors, and into an unoccupied hallway. When they stopped, Brad's body language told Rainey he did not want to have this conversation.

"I have a feeling I'm not going to be happy with what you have to say," Rainey said.

"No, I'm afraid you will not like what I have to say at all," Brad said, as he shook his head from side to side. "When Danny called me, I kept it very quiet."

Danny interrupted, "But someone squawked that Rainey was alive on the radio, right?"

"Yes, and Ellie must have heard it. The deputy was outside the doors there, talking to me on the phone, when his radio started jabbering about calling off the search. Ellie was in a treatment room near the nurses' station. They have a scanner out there."

Rainey felt the anger start to rise and tried to control it, but she couldn't. "She's gone, isn't she?"

She turned and walked away, without waiting for an answer. She could see it in Brad's eyes. They had not a clue where Ellie Paxton Read had gone.

"Rainey, wait. I need to get a statement from you," Brad called after her.

Rainey wheeled on him. He didn't deserve it, but he got all the frustration of her day thrown right at him. "Ellie Paxton Read drugged me, confessed all her sins, and then tried to leave Graham and me at the bottom of a sandpit. She's already killed nine people. Find her, or the next one is on you. That's my fucking statement. Now, I'm going to get my nose put back in place and go home to my family."

As she turned away and walked toward the nurses' station, Rainey heard Danny say, "It doesn't happen often, but she can cloud up and rain all over you if you're not careful. You better give her a few minutes to calm down."

#

180

Rainey didn't calm down until the pain medication ordered by the emergency room doctor finally kicked in, just before he set her nose and packed it. It still hurt like hell, but she didn't care as much. She had suffered no ill effects from the cold, just an aching for warm feet and a hot drink, preferably a stiff one. Graham was still under warming blankets when she found him in a trauma room.

"Cool mask," he said, referring to the broken nose guard Rainey wore.

"When I told the doctor I had two-year-old triplets, he insisted I wear this," Rainey said, crossing to his bedside. "How are you feeling?"

"I'm better now. My bones don't feel as cold anymore."

"That's good. You'll be staying overnight I hear."

Graham nodded, but didn't answer verbally. Rainey could tell he wanted to say something, but couldn't find the words. He looked so small and helpless. Graham Colde never hurt anyone, but the world sure left its scars on him.

"Graham, do you mind if I sit down?"

He stared at the blanket in his lap, not looking at her when he said, "Okay."

Rainey sat down gently on the edge of his bed. "I really have only one question for you. The list, what was it for?"

Continuing his blanket watching, Graham responded, "I drew the picture, I'm pretty sure. I've never seen the original note, but the evidence copies I did see appear to show the note was printed over my drawing."

"You've spent a great deal of time researching your case, haven't you?" Rainey asked.

"Yes. I just had to know why and the more I dug into it the more I remembered, but then I wasn't sure if those were real memories or wishful thinking. I was never sure until I heard Ellie in the van."

"So you were awake for most of that?" Rainey asked, hoping he was.

181

"Yes, but it won't make a difference. People will always treat me as if I am a murderer. I can never come home."

He had yet to lift his eyes to her. Rainey needed him to understand something.

She leaned closer and said, "I knew a young man who was wrongly accused and convicted of a crime. He spent sixteen years in a maximum-security prison labeled a serial rapist. That's not easy time. After all those years, when he was finally freed and the real rapist sent to prison with definitive DNA evidence, this man stepped into a world foreign to him. He had been told he was guilty for so long, he couldn't remember being innocent. He became a victim of doubting his own self-worth. He didn't know how to look people in the eye anymore, so he couldn't see they were no longer judging him. Look at me, Graham."

He slowly brought his chin up and made eye contact with her.

Rainey grinned and joked, "I know I'm trying to be all serious, but with this nose guard I must look ridiculous doing it. Feel free to laugh."

Graham smiled, but only chuckled slightly.

Rainey began again, "Besides some issues with boundaries concerning my personal and professional life, which I think we can deal with in the future, you have no reason to be ashamed. By the way, how did you copy my office so well?"

"I put a camera on Joey. Don't be mad at him. He thought I was just recording his day for a game simulation. I recorded you when I could to get a good framework for your character's movements."

"That has to stop and the game is going to change. Those files you got into, they represent real murders of innocent people. And my case file—you are most certainly out of bounds using those details. You can't use that stuff for entertainment. You do see how wrong that is, don't you?"

"Yes," Graham said, his chin lowering again. "I never meant any harm."

Rainey patted his leg under the covers. "You know, I really believe that's true, or I'd have you in handcuffs right now."

Graham's eyes darted to hers.

"Don't worry. I think you've learned your lesson. And about the other crimes you were accused of, you need to let go of that guilt. This injustice was done to you, not by you. Your mother never believed you killed the Paxtons. That nurse said she didn't either. People believed in you then. They will believe in you now. Hold your head up, Graham. Look them in the eye so they can see a survivor, not a victim."

"Graham?" A woman's voice said from the doorway.

Rainey turned her head to see Susie Colde, wearing an expression of disbelief on her face. She probably never thought she'd see this day. Susie told Rainey her son died fourteen years ago. A rare second chance had been granted and it was time for Rainey to leave the room.

She patted Graham's leg again, saying, "I think you two have some catching up to do. We'll talk when you're better. I have some ideas about your game and I think you can help me with something. Quid pro quo."

Graham pulled his arm from under the warming blanket and held up his hand for Rainey to shake. He looked her straight in the eyes and said, "It's a deal."

Rainey shook his hand firmly. "I look forward to working with you. Now, say hello to your mother."

She turned to leave the room, but Susie stopped her, placing a gentle hand on her arm. "Thank you, Ms. Bell. Thank you for giving my son back to me."

Rainey patted Susie's hand. "Don't underestimate him. Graham brought himself back. He doesn't remember everything, but he remembers you. That bond was never broken."

"Mom," Graham called out, "I didn't kill the Paxtons."

"I know, honey," his mother replied and crossed the room to her son's side. Rainey took her leave, just as Susie said, "Graham, I've missed you so."

Rainey passed a couple of detectives in the hallway. The badges hanging from the breast pockets of their respective jackets identified them as such. The eyed her closely, but did not attempt to speak to her. She heard them knock on Graham's door.

"Mr. Colde, we'd like to take your statement, if you feel up to it."

Rainey found Danny in the hall by the emergency entrance.

"Can I go home now?" Rainey asked. "I want to get there before the pain meds wear off."

Danny frowned. "You can't just blow the locals off like that. You are a victim and a witness. They need your statement now. You know the drill. Stop throwing a tantrum and write it down."

"Give me your phone," Rainey demanded.

Knowing her the way he did and the mood she was in appeared to leave him no choice but to comply. She knew his password, because he never changed it. Predictable Danny. Rainey opened his voice recorder and began to speak.

"This is Rainey Bell. It's February 13, 2014. Ellie Paxton Read tried to kill me today. She did not succeed. I'm going home now. Details to follow when my face isn't throbbing. Tomorrow begins Valentine's weekend, which I intend to spend with my wife. Don't call me until Monday. That is all."

She turned off the recorder and handed the phone back to Danny.

"Stop being a brat, Rainey."

"Danny, I was drugged. If I signed a lawn care contract right now, it wouldn't hold up in court. Do you think a damn thing I say in an official statement will? Ask me later, when the drugs have cleared my system."

"Will you remember then?"

Rainey narrowed her eyes, "Ask me whatever you want on the way home, but I am leaving, with or without you, McNally."

"You've dealt with witnesses like this. What do you suggest I do?" Danny asked, his hands up in surrender. He shook his right hand slightly, where the keys to the SUV dangled. "Besides, I have the keys."

Rainey stopped being a brat. She knew she was and had let it run its course for a moment. All of the stress of the day had to go somewhere. She remained in control around everyone but Danny. He could take it. He knew how to weather the storm and that it was necessary to blow off bits of steam, before too much bad shit built into a rage. Only Katie knew Rainey better than Danny, and even then, he'd been places with her Katie could never go.

She grinned at her old partner from under her mask. "You don't think I could hotwire that sucker and leave you here holding the keys?"

"You were inches from being a criminal, weren't you?" Danny said, with a chuckle.

"You have to know them to catch them," Rainey replied.

The storm passed, Danny suggested, "You know things that could help them find the woman that tried to kill you."

Rainey shook her head. "She's gone. I guarantee she had a go-bag ready for just this occasion. By now, she's on her way to some out of the way airport, headed for parts unknown, with a new identity, a new look, and plenty of cash."

"That smart, huh?" Danny commented.

"Oh, Ellie is calculating and cunning, but she made a mistake."

"What was that?" Danny asked with an amused expression.

"Ellie didn't kill Graham Colde. He knows what happened. It's coming back to him. He knows this case better than anyone, but he needs help connecting the dots. Talk to him, before she takes another whack at him."

"I thought you were going to say she shouldn't have left you alive."

Rainey started for the door. "Didn't you tell Graham we don't hunt them down and exact revenge?"

Danny's laughter rang through his response. "I was using that 'we' loosely. You will call me when you find her, right Rainey?"

Rainey stopped and turned around. "Yours will be the first number I dial, if you promise I get to watch the cuffs go on her."

Danny's face lit up with a grin. "Absolutely."

Rainey turned back toward the exit and called over her shoulder, "Give my mea culpa to Brad and then let's go see your godchildren. I'm going outside to refreeze my nose."

The doors whooshed open automatically at her approach. Rainey stepped back into the cold night. The chill wasn't so bad with the warmth of the hospital still clinging to her clothes. She noticed Bill standing by the SUV and approached him.

He smiled at her. "The mask does wonders for your mystique."

A nurse had given her an ice pack, which Rainey produced from her pocket. She squeezed it to release the freezing agents and shook the bag hard, while speaking to Bill.

"It's my toddler defense system. Just the thought of one of those little elbows whacking my unprotected nose makes my stomach turn."

Bill winced. "Mine isn't broken and that thought makes *me* feel sick. Good move on the mask, but you might want to get a football helmet for the duration of your recovery."

Rainey leaned back against the SUV and let out a heavy sigh, before tilting her head back and placing the ice bag across her eyes and nose. It had been a long day.

"Did you see Graham's mother?" Bill asked, after a moment of silence passed between them.

"Yes. I assume you called her and filled her in," Rainey said from under the ice bag.

"I did, after I called my mom," Bill explained. "I told her Ellie killed Dad. She couldn't believe it at first, but then I told her she tried to kill you and Graham too, and that Dad was right about all the deaths being connected. It finally sank in."

"Your dad must have asked Ellie the wrong question. He was getting close."

"I studied that file all day. He never made any indication that he thought she did it," Bill countered.

"He knew something or she wouldn't have killed him. She murdered for financial gain or to cover her tracks. There was no passion in her motives. Something in that file points to her, we just have to find it."

"The file is in there," Bill said, indicating the SUV with his shoulder. "You can take it home with you, if you think you can find the answer. I just can't see it. Ellie was smart. She made every accidental death plausible. It's going to be tough to prove otherwise."

"She isn't going to get away with it," Rainey replied, confidently.

"What makes you so sure?"

Rainey peeled up the ice bag and smiled over at the doubting Bill. "A girl-next-door serial killer is international news,

186

especially one that looks like Ellie. She is finally going to be famous. She will have to crow to someone. Her constant need for adoration will override her caution. Pride goeth before the fall is not just an old cliché."

"You saw her spots, as my dad would say. She really did confess her sins to you. I wonder why?"

Back under the ice bag, Rainey answered, "The same reason she'll show herself again. Ellie's narcissism will be her undoing."

"If you find her, I'll name my kid after you. I don't know if Morgan would go for Rainey, though. What's your middle name?"

"It's Blue, as in the color." Rainey pulled off the ice bag and smiled at Bill. "Billy and my mother were hippie wannabes. Don't worry about the name, but you can help me find Ellie."

"I can?" Bill looked surprised.

"You, Graham, and Joey are going to help me. Ellie Paxton Read left a trail and we are going to track it right to her doorstep. Her past will tell us what we need to know about her future. When Ellie killed Ely, she lost her confidant, the one person she could gloat to and impress with her superiority among the mere mortals she was forced to tolerate. Ellie needed an audience. She most certainly leaked—they all do. People know pieces of information that mean nothing individually, but combined with what others know will tell a complete story."

"Should I be worried about her coming after my family?" Bill's concern wrinkled his brow.

Rainey shook her head. "No, she's gone, long gone. There is no advantage to her ever coming here again. That would require a passion for something lost. She's not that type of criminal. Ellie doesn't love or need things like most of us. Ellie loves Ellie and that's where it stops for her. The Ellie identity burned to ashes the moment she knew she was caught. She's a new woman by now, flying to a new life she had planned and waiting in the wings for just such an occasion. Ellie doesn't have regrets, only alibis."

"She was in my father's house, washing dishes, even took time to sit with my grieving mother. Why did not one of us see it? How could she have killed nine people and never batted an eyelash?"

"Remorse, guilt, empathy—Ellie can't express those with any truthfulness. She plays the part required to accomplish her goals. She mimics emotions. A psychopath like Ellie is capable of playing the notes of humanity but not the song. She gunned down her parents, drowned her brother, murdered six more, and played the innocent victim to perfection. Would she feel badly about holding your mother's hand after murdering your father? No, quite the opposite is true. That was duping delight at its zenith. She enjoyed every moment."

"She duped us all," Bill commented, as he shook his head. "No one suspected her."

"Ellie is the ideal friend, lover, business partner, or whatever her victim's desires and needs might be. Psychopaths excel in reading people. The façade of normalcy they work so hard to portray also gives them insight into the weaknesses of others. By the time 'too good to be true' proves once again to be an accurate description, the damage is usually done."

"She fooled a profiler—" Bill started to say, but Rainey interrupted.

"I saw her narcissism, just by observing her behavior around the people in your house, but many people have narcissistic traits, including me. A couple of hours with a file are never enough to offer a profile of any kind."

The emergency room doors whooshed open seconds before Danny came strolling out. Rainey pointed at him.

She said to Bill, "He is a profiler and he would have dated her," she spoke loudly enough for Danny to hear, "at least long enough to enjoy the benefits."

Danny laughed, and added to Rainey's thought, "Psychopaths are great fun in the beginning of the relationship, so willing to please. It's knowing when to get off the ride that can be tricky."

Bill shook his head. "I don't think I've ever been so glad to be happily married."

Rainey agreed, "Me too."

Danny smiled at them. "I'm just doing my part for the dating pool, identifying all the women that should wear "Run Away!" signs on their foreheads."

"He really can pick 'em," Rainey added, with a chuckle.

Danny shook Bill's hand. "It was a pleasure to meet you and thank you for the help finding my wayward friend here. Trouble should be her middle name."

"It was nice to meet you," Bill replied. "Thank you for coming."

Danny smiled over at Rainey. "She's trouble, but she's worth it." He crossed to the driver's side of the SUV. "Bill, do you need a ride?"

"No, Morgan is on her way." He stuck his hand out toward Rainey. "Thank you for believing my mother when I did not. Call me when you feel up to it. We'll get started on finding Ellie."

Rainey shook Bill's hand. "I don't usually promise to bring someone in, but in this case, I can assure you I will find this woman. If it takes years, I will never stop looking."

"Like father, like daughter," Bill said.

Danny rolled the power window down on the passenger side, and called out to Rainey, "Okay, Rain Cloud, let's get you home, before another front comes through or Katie calls me again."

Rainey's big smile caused a twinge of pain, but she couldn't stop it. "She can be relentless."

Danny chuckled. "Yeah, like someone else I know."

Chapter Ten

Friday, February 14, 2014
The Bell-Meyers Home,
12:30 a.m.
Clear, 34°F, Windchill 28°F

"Wake up, Rainey. You have to get us through the gate," Danny said, rousing her from a deep sleep.

On the drive home, they had gone over what she could remember of her interaction with Ellie, until Rainey could hold her eyes open no longer and fell asleep. She blinked awake now, as Danny slowed the SUV to a stop at the security post guarding the entrance to her neighborhood. A guard stepped out to greet them.

"Roll your window down so I can talk to him," Rainey said.

The window came down all the way before the guard spoke. He was very alert and suspicious. Rainey loved that about him and all the security staff she harassed into paranoia where she was concerned. It was a necessity, as it turned out, because they had all learned trouble did visit the Bell-Meyers family often.

"Good evening, Agent McNally."

"Good to see you again, Cliff," Danny said.

Cliff looked over at Rainey. His expression registered the same concern as his tone, when he asked, "Ms. Bell, are you all right?"

"It looks worse than it is. I'll be fine in about ten minutes, when I have a very stiff drink in my hand and my feet are finally warm."

Cliff didn't hold them up any longer. "Glad you're home safe," he said, and pushed a button on the remote to open the gate.

Danny drove slowly through the neighborhood to the last house on the left, closest to the lake. The lights came on at their approach and the front door flew open. Through the wrought iron fence that separated them, Rainey saw Katie step onto the porch, with Molly and Leslie flanking her. The thought of never seeing Katie and her children again left a prickle of pain in Rainey's chest from that moment in the van until now. It vanished with the sigh of relief that escaped from her, loudly enough to draw Danny's attention.

As he applied his fingerprint to the biometric lock on the gate, he said to Rainey, "She's the reason you breathe, isn't she?"

Rainey never took her eyes from Katie, when she responded, "You'll catch her if I fall, won't you, Danny?"

As the gate crawled open, she heard him say, "You appear to be immortal, so I doubt my services will be needed, but yes, I promised to take care of your family and I will."

"When I thought I was a goner, all I could think about was how she and the kids would make it without me," Rainey said, finally letting her emotions run wild. "Causing them pain is the last thing I ever want to do."

Danny reached over and squeezed her hand. "Rainey, if anything ever happens to you, your family will be safe and loved, trust me."

She squeezed his hand and watched Katie come down the steps toward the driveway to greet them. "I do trust you, Danny. I always have."

Katie reached for the door handle before the vehicle came to a stop. It wouldn't open until Rainey pulled the handle on the inside, which she did, but put her hand out in front of her to stop Katie from leaping at her.

"Whoa, don't smack me in the nose," Rainey said, warning Katie off.

191

Katie stopped in mid-lunge and took a good look at Rainey. "Oh my, God. That must hurt like hell."

Rainey stepped down from the SUV and opened her arms to pull Katie to her. "Yes, it does. Just stand still and let me hold you a second."

Katie slid her arms around Rainey and squeezed her tight. "I was so scared I'd lost you."

Rainey leaned back so she could look down at Katie's upturned face. "You do know that you can't lose me, right? I will always be with you, always."

Katie didn't smile. She looked stunned and said, "You thought you were going to die, didn't you?"

"Only long enough to remember why I had to survive," Rainey said, hugging Katie to her again.

"Don't you ever forget that," Katie replied, nuzzling into Rainey's chest.

"I won't," Rainey said, and smiled over at Molly and Leslie, cueing them to walk over to where she stood.

Molly spoke first. "Glad to see you, even if you do look like you went a couple of rounds with Laila Ali."

"No, just a homecoming queen with bad intentions," Rainey said, smiling and accepting a handshake from Molly.

She couldn't hug her because Katie wasn't letting go and Rainey wasn't going to make her.

Leslie spoke up next, apologizing, "I took Joey home, but we did speak about the video game. He really did not know it was wrong to help with it. He knows now."

"It's okay, Leslie. Joey was taken advantage of," Rainey explained.

Leslie wasn't finished. "I'm sorry about Theodore spying on you, too. I would never have brought him into your life if I knew he would do that."

Rainey reassured her. "He's not a bad guy. Just a little misguided. He meant no harm. He's going by his old name now, Graham Dean Colde."

"What old name?" Leslie asked. "He's not Theodore Suzanne?"

"No, and it's a long story. I promise to fill you all in as soon as I've had a hot shower and put on socks."

"Socks?" Katie said, still clinging to Rainey's waist.

"I will probably sleep in socks for the rest of winter," Rainey said, and started moving everyone toward the house. "In fact, I may never be without socks again in my lifetime."

Danny, following behind the women, piped up to say, "I think the lavender hippopotamus you were wearing on your head when I found you should become part of your signature look."

Molly's summation of Rainey's last two days rang true. "Only Rainey Bell could go to a funeral and end up with a story encompassing a misguided stalker, a murdering homecoming queen, and a lavender hippopotamus."

#

1:51 a.m.
Clear, 34°F, Windchill 27.2°F

"Hey," Katie's whisper tickled Rainey's ear.

She was standing behind the couch, leaning over near Rainey's reclining head. Rainey sat up and realized she had fallen asleep leaning on the cushions in the corner of the couch. Her hands went straight to her nose that began to throb with the sudden movement.

"Ouch," she said, stretching the protective mask away from her face.

Coming from behind the couch, Katie crossed to stand in front of Rainey. "Come on. Let's go upstairs. There is an ice bag waiting for you and you can take the mask off for a while."

"Where did everybody go?" Rainey asked, still holding the mask away from her face.

"Molly and Leslie went home and Danny went to bed. You passed out pretty quickly after you sat down. I'm surprised you made it back down here after your shower. Danny told us what you went through today."

Rainey gently returned the mask to her face. "I think the van got the worst of it. I wonder if our insurance covers murderous intent."

"Not sure, but maybe we should look into a floating car," Katie said with a chuckle.

"Not a bad idea," Rainey replied and then added, "By the way, I will never again tease you about stuffing our vehicles full of emergency supplies. Thank you."

Katie held out her hand, offering Rainey an assist off the couch. "And thank you for being so hard to kill."

Rainey took the offered hand and stood up. She pulled Katie into a hug. "I knew you were looking for me. I'll always come back to you, Katie. As long as I'm breathing, I will never stop trying to come home to you. Don't ever count me out."

Katie stood on her tiptoes and kissed Rainey ever so gently on the lips. "Rainey Blue Bell," she said, "that was Ellie Paxton's mistake. It will never be mine."

They held hands walking up the stairs together. Rainey started laughing about halfway up to their bedroom.

"What's so funny," Katie asked.

"Look," Rainey said, pointing at the second floor landing.

The large stuffed bear from the kids' room sat on the first step to the third floor. He was wearing socks on his feet and on his head rested Weather's pink tee shirt, with the lavender hippopotamus smiling back at them.

#

5:53 a.m.
Clear, 28°F, Windchill 20.8°F

The phone rang out loudly on the bedside table by Rainey's head. She bolted upright, remembered her nose with the first throb, and covered it with one hand, while she reached for the phone with the other. She didn't take the time to look at the caller ID, fully expecting the person on the phone to apologize for the wrong number at such an ungodly time of morning.

"Hello," she said, in her Edith Ann voice.

"Ooo, it sounds like that nose of yours is really painful."

The female on the line was no stranger calling a wrong number before the sunrise.

"Hello, Ellie," Rainey said, sitting up at full attention now.

So was Katie. She was up and moving fast toward the door. Rainey assumed she was running to get Danny, which was a very smart move. Danny had access to Brooks; the computer genius at Quantico with tools to track phones most people didn't even know existed.

Ellie sang out in her nonchalant style. "You have no idea how hard it was to crack your phone, but a few drinks and a blow job can get you a lot from a lonely geek on vacation."

"I see you haven't missed a trick, pun intended. I suppose he thinks you're Sally Sue from Peoria or some other unsuspecting former friend, whose identity you usurped along the way."

"I probably should have pulled the trigger on you while I had the chance," Ellie commented. "I'll not make that mistake again."

"Fortunately for me, you will not have a second chance," Rainey said, calmly.

An airport announcement for a connecting flight to Los Angeles sounded in the receiver. Ellie was on the move. It would be too easy to suggest she was headed for LA. Ellie wouldn't be that stupid.

Rainey pretended not to hear the boarding call and continued, "I'm sure you are long gone. You better work on that accent, though. It's hard to mistake that eastern North Carolina drawl for anything else."

Accommodating Rainey's suggestion with the skill of a practiced character actress, Ellie dropped the drawl for a perfect French/Canadian accent, saying, "Parlez-vous français? Connaissez-vous le Québec?"

"My father always said not to get too far from the truth on your fake identity. The Canadian thing might work, unless you run into a real Québec resident. Then it might get a bit dicey."

Katie returned with a disheveled Danny, who was, as Rainey predicted, already on the phone. He made a hand gesture to Rainey, asking her to keep Ellie talking.

"I had some time, while I was traveling. I did a background check on you. Man, they've got your personal life locked down like Fort Knox, but I did find some articles about your father's death. How sad. Oh, and that article from the Y-Man about your attack, that was really dark. Not much happy in Rainey Bell's life."

"I'd be happier if crazed killers didn't call my house before sunrise," Rainey remarked, while watching Danny in the hallway speaking quietly to someone.

"I saw pictures of your wife. You were right, she is gorgeous, and that family of yours is picture perfect. I'm almost glad you survived to keep the family intact."

"Almost?" Rainey laughed. "I suppose you're wondering if I'm going to look for you now."

"Don't bother, Rainey. As you said, I'm long gone."

"New life, new name, new lives to ruin—is that it? You're on to the next. Must be tough starting over with nothing."

"Nothing? You don't believe that, do you? Surely you know I was smart enough to have an out." Incredulous, Ellie continued, "I doubt that was your assessment of me to your FBI colleague. Danny, wasn't it? Super-cute ginger man. Is he a good fuck? You know you had some of that, Miss 'I have my principles.' Or was he part of your sport-fucking days before you switched teams?"

"Danny? No, I never slept with him. Never kissed him, either. That would be like kissing my brother." Rainey chuckled for effect. "Oh, that's right, you don't have a problem with that."

Serial killers had boundaries, warped ones, but boundaries nonetheless. These boundaries were crossed without compunction, yet the depraved minds still knew the societal taboo of their actions could not be overcome. Ted Bundy didn't want people to know he practiced necrophilia, but had no problem talking about decapitating his victims. He didn't want to talk about the little girl he raped and murdered either. Ellie's boundary line was drawn at incest. She wasn't bragging about that dirty deed. Her tone darkened.

"Forget you met me, Rainey Bell. Don't come looking. I won't make the same mistake twice and you'll never see it coming."

"Are you trying to make some kind of deal, Ellie? If I don't look for you, you won't look for me, is that it?"

Ellie resumed her sunny disposition. "Yes, I'd say that's it. I'd rather not look over my shoulder and I'm sure you have better things to do than wonder if I'm watching you through a rifle scope right now."

Rainey replied to the threat with no emotion. "Well now, that's interesting."

"What's that?" Ellie asked, taking the bait.

"You're afraid of me," Rainey said, making sure her smile could be heard in her tone.

"Ha! Me, afraid of you? I'm giving you the opportunity to live your life with that hot wife and those adorable triplets. You got lucky. Take advantage of your second chance."

"Second chance? Oh, this is at least a fourth or fifth attempt on my life. There have been so many I've lost track. I'm hard to kill, they say. So, give it your best shot, Ellie."

"Game on, then," Ellie said, trying to sound confidant, but Rainey could hear a crack forming in her adversary's veneer of indifference.

By now, Rainey knew the phone call would bring few clues to Ellie's whereabouts. She was too smart to have stayed on the line without a plan. The trace would lead to a location far from Ellie Paxton Read's final destination. She wasn't coming after Rainey. She was testing the water to see if Rainey was going to knock on her door one day. Rainey decided to plant that seed of doubt deeply in Ellie's brain.

"Run, Ellie, run. This should be fun. When I find you, be a good sport and come peacefully. Like Graham said, people that fuck with me end up dead. You know the funny part is, I didn't kill any of them. Kind of like the people around you, they just don't live long."

"Remember, Moby Dick did not end well for Ahab," Ellie said, trying to be witty.

"Call me Ishmael," Rainey countered with wit of her own. "Good bye, Ellie. See you soon."

Rainey hung up before Ellie could.

"Did Brooks get a fix on my phone," she called out to Danny.

She heard him giving instructions to whomever he was talking to on the phone. "Send the picture to TSA. Check the rental car counters too. She probably dumped the phone." He waited and then said, "Call me if they find anything." One more pause before, "Yes, I'll tell her."

Danny stepped into the bedroom from the hall. "The ping registered near Charleston International Airport."

Rainey climbed out of the bed. "She was in the airport. I could hear the paging system. I'm guessing my phone will be located in a trashcan near a ticket counter she never approached. You can check flights, but I'll bet she keeps driving to another departure point."

Katie came to stand beside Rainey and asked, "Is she a threat to us?"

Rainey put her arm around Katie. "No, honey. She was calling to see if I was coming after her. Ellie Paxton is putting as much distance between us as possible. She hasn't dealt with many people like me, ones who saw the beast beneath the beauty. In the past, I'm sure she ran from them as well."

"Or killed them," Katie commented.

Danny lightened the mood with, "Brooks said you need to go ahead and have that tracking device implanted. It would make finding you so much faster."

"They have those?" Katie inquired. She didn't wait for an answer, adding quickly, "Where can I get one put in her and how fast can it happen?"

Rainey and Danny laughed.

Katie's hands flew to her hips. "I'm serious."

Rainey shook her head. "That's what's so funny. I am quite sure that you are, but the technology isn't quite perfected yet."

"Well, let me know when it is and you'll be first in line."

Rainey yawned as the sun broke the horizon and peeked through the blinds.

Katie put a hand in Rainey's back. "Go back to bed. I'll make you some breakfast and bring it up to you."

"No, I'm awake." Rainey looked at the baby monitor on the bedside table. "I can't sleep through sunrise anymore, even when they don't wake us up. When I stayed at the Wise house, it was too quiet. I missed hearing them breathe."

Danny chuckled. "I never in a million years pictured you with a family, Rainey. Hard core single woman to the end, I truly believed. And here you are almost four years later all sappy and lovesick because your children aren't at home." He faked tears and goaded her like the brother he was, "It's beautiful man, I tell ya'."

"Hey, don't laugh too hard," Rainey teased back. "Ellie thinks you're hot, but then she slept with her brother. You attract the strangest women, but one day we'll find that special someone just for you."

Katie pushed them both toward the door. "I will pray that her first four years with you are less fraught with peril."

Rainey and Danny said in unison, "Amen to that."

\#

6:51 p.m.
Mostly Cloudy, 45°F, Windchill 41.2°F

Danny caught a flight out of Raleigh-Durham International Airport just after lunch, but not before the reports came in on the airport lead. Rainey's phone, located in the Charleston airport, was still on and waiting to be found, as Ellie meant it to be. Security tapes showed a dark haired female, in a big floppy sunhat and facial feature-concealing large sunglasses, drop the phone in the bin on her way to the rental car garage. The cameras followed her to the express lane, where she hopped in a waiting convertible and drove away. She used the credit card of the geek that cracked Rainey's phone to pay for her expensive ride. They found the clueless man passed out in a motel room, not far from the Charleston Airport. He became completely unnerved when informed he had a drunken one-night stand with a serial killer. Lucky man was all Rainey could think. The rental car and the credit card were found down at the Charleston docks, where the rich yacht owners played. Round one to Ellie.

After Danny left, Rainey napped most of the afternoon with Katie spooned into her back and Freddie curled in the bend of her knees. Ice bags came and went at intervals, between Ibuprofen doses and sleep. The romantic getaway reservations were cancelled before breakfast, after Katie got a good look at the state of Rainey's face. It even shocked Rainey when she saw the two black, puffy bruises under her eyes.

Her comment to Katie had been, "At least my nose is straight."

Despite all their amorous intentions leading up to Valentine's Day, the hours ticked away while they caught up on much needed rest. Rainey woke up once and decided that this was true romance, cuddled together, warm and secure. The spa day and romantic dinner would have been nice, not to mention the promised of unbridled, children not in the other room, passion they teased each other with for days. But the intimacy of being held while she slept peacefully was more than enough show of affection for a tired woman with a broken nose. This was the romance Rainey always dreamed of and it was hers every day. Besides, her face throbbed at the thought of raising her blood pressure.

They rose together about four thirty, showered, and then went their separate ways in the house. Katie went to the kitchen to make dinner, while Rainey took Captain Wise's file to her office, and Freddie went outside to survey his grounds. Rainey took the protective mask off and placed it on the corner of her desk. The swelling had gone down considerably through Katie's constant care. Her nose still ached, but the stuffiness had gone with the aid of a bit of nasal spray. Rainey no longer sounded like a six-year-old with bad sinus drainage.

After opening the mail, she checked in with Junior. All was well and he was staffed for the romance weekend fiascos that filled jail cells with drunks and anger management intervention candidates. Junior kept up with Rainey's abduction and recovery through Katie, and had in turn informed Mackie of her safe return home.

"Mackie said you were the only person he knew that could go to a funeral—"

"And end up abducted," Rainey finished for him. "Honestly, did Katie call everybody?"

Junior chuckled. "I heard the phones on the hill were ringing off the hook. I guess doing time as a politician's wife came in handy."

Rainey laughed with him. "She does have access to some private numbers not available to the public. See you Monday, and don't forget to romance that new wife of yours. The criminals can sit in jail a few hours longer if need be."

"See you Monday, Rainey. Glad you're okay."

After talking with Junior, she checked her email. Ernie, who was oblivious to any of the drama, sent the message, "Wish you were here," with pictures of glaciers and eagles attached. Rainey sent a reply encouraging more photos to show the kids and did not mention her recent brush with death. There would be time to share the incident with Ernie without interfering with her dream vacation.

Caught up with correspondence and her business duties, she turned her attention to Wellman Wise's file. With a new perspective and a different agenda, she started taking notes for her quest to find Ellie. It was going to take weeks and possibly months to process all the data. That's where her team of computer geniuses was going to help. The notes she took included ideas for a program that could sort through information and search for the woman they all would like to see behind bars.

Rainey had her head down in the file for almost an hour when there was a knock on the open office door.

"Agent Bell, can I tear you away from your investigation for a romantic dinner for two?"

Rainey looked up to see Katie smiling at her. She put her pen down immediately and beamed at all she'd ever dreamed of.

"I'd love to have dinner with you. It smells delicious. My stomach caught wind of it a while back and began to talk about it."

Katie crossed to the other side of Rainey's desk. She had changed into a silk blouse, lacey bra, and freshened her hair and makeup. Her perfume crossed the room with her and swirled around Rainey's head. The effect was the same as the first time Katie batted those baby blues at an unprepared Agent on medical leave. The result found the woman she loved standing in front of her, in their home, the mother of their children, still flirting as if they'd only met. Every day, every moment, Rainey knew she was blessed. Katie confirmed it again, when she leaned over the desk,

201

exposing much more than the curve of her breast, but keeping enough hidden to make an observer want more. Rainey had to admit, the girl had skills. Her smile broadened, reminding her of the bruised condition of her face.

"Ms. Meyers, I'm afraid you're being quite forward," Rainey teased.

Katie's eyes sparkled with delight. She loved that Rainey could not resist her and used it to her advantage often.

"I made your favorite, cheese ravioli."

"Oh, now you're just fighting dirty," Rainey said. She glanced down at the corner of her desk at the mask. "I think I need to remind you that I'm on injured reserve."

Katie grinned. "You're going to need that mask when you see your Valentine's present."

Rainey stood up, grabbed the mask off the desk, and walked past Katie out the door.

Katie called after her, "Where are you going?"

"To look for a football helmet."

#

8:05 p.m.
Mostly Cloudy, 44°F, Windchill 38.6°F

Rainey pushed back from the table. "I can't eat another bite." She smiled at Katie, who was glowing in the candlelight. "I am so glad I married you. I mean you're beautiful, intelligent, and unbelievably sexy, but it's really all about your cooking talents."

Katie took a sip of the wine she nursed all through dinner, and winked over the glass at Rainey. "I have to keep my girl satisfied. Wouldn't want some young thing to come along and tempt her, would we?"

Rainey's one-sided grin appeared. "Did Danny tell you about Ellie's proposition to fulfill my fantasies?"

"He mentioned something about that, when her picture came up on the news this morning. You had gone upstairs to change out of your pajamas."

"Did he tell you what I said to her?"

Katie put the wine glass down. "He just said you brushed her off."

"I told her you fulfilled all my fantasies, all of them, and I am very happy right where I am."

"Is that so?" Katie said, rising from her chair. She moved around the table to stand next to Rainey. "You're not getting bored with the whole family and wife thing?"

"No, I think being a mother has made you more attractive." Rainey reached out and pulled Katie into her lap, so they were eye to eye. "If I didn't think my nose would explode from the increased blood pressure, I'd clear this table off and have you for desert."

Katie threw her head back and laughed. "You know just what to say to a girl, you sweet talking thing you."

Katie leaned in for a tender kiss, careful of Rainey's nose and her blood pressure. The doorbell rang, just as Rainey was deciding she wasn't that badly bruised.

Katie sprang off Rainey's lap. "Oh, that's your Valentine present. Wait here." Before she left the dining room, she turned back to say, "You're going to need the mask," and then exited with a wink.

It happened so fast, Rainey was late putting together that the person entering the gate had a biometric key. She had to know them, so it could be only a few people. Danny was back in Virginia. Mackie and Ernie were out of town. Only their parents and her half-sister, Wendy, were left, and Rainey couldn't see what they had to do with a Valentine gift. She was running this over in her mind, when she heard an unmistakable sound.

Tiny feet in tiny shoes pattered across the hall toward the dining room. The next sound made Rainey's heart sing. A chorus of "Nee Nees" rang out as the three loves of her life rounded the corner. The singing praise stopped abruptly when the children saw Rainey's face. She hadn't put the mask on yet, which might have freaked them out more, but she wasn't sure how. Mack turned to grasp Katie's leg. Weather plopped down in the floor and tuned up, but didn't cry. She appeared at a loss for what was required and just stared at Rainey. Timothy stopped, leaned forward to get a good look, and then ignoring the other's hesitancy, toddled forward.

Rainey took the chance he wouldn't smack her square in the nose, and knelt down closer to his level. He approached the last few steps with caution and then pointed a tiny finger at her face.

He said, "Boo boo, Nee Nee."

Rainey smiled. "Yes, Nee Nee has a boo boo."

Timothy turned back to the others. "Boo boo. Ouch."

This seemed to appease the reluctant ones and all three charged at full speed. Rainey stood up quickly and let them wrap around her legs. Katie walked over to the table, picked up the mask, and held it out to Rainey.

"I told you to put this on," she said, smiling. "Mom and Dad dropped them off. They said tell you they are happy you are home safe. They didn't want to intrude on the reunion, so they went back home."

Rainey patted her children as they giggled and squealed at her knees, saying "Boo Boo" and "Nee Nee" loudly.

She turned to Katie, "Thank you. This is the best Valentine's present ever. I'm sorry yours is around some other woman's neck, but I'll get you something else."

"I know you love me, honey. When I see you with them, I know." Katie chuckled. "Besides, if I had you to myself, I'd probably give you a nose bleed."

Rainey leaned over and kissed Katie. Then she slipped on the mask and stepped back from the kids so they could see.

Katie helped out by pointing to the protective shield and saying, "Nee Nee has a boo boo. Be nice. No hitting."

The triplets were back to being stunned by yet another strange thing on Nee Nee's face. Rainey smiled under the mask to ease their anxiety and dropped to her knees.

She threw her arms open and said, "Rugrats."

The giggling trio stormed her, and though her nose was in jeopardy, Rainey wrapped them in her arms and hugged them tight. "I missed you guys."

"Nee Nee home," Mac said, looking up at Katie.

Katie knelt down beside Rainey and brushed a stray hair from Mac's forehead. "Yes, Nee Nee is home."

Rainey sighed the breath of total relief. She survived again. The luck had to run out sometime, but for now, she kissed each child and then her wife.

"Yes, Nee Nee is home."

Chapter Eleven

May 10, 2014
Elysian Fields, a beachfront bar west of
Cozumel, Mexico
2:43 p.m.
Scattered Clouds, 86°F, Heat Index 91.8°F

The bartender, Bren, as it identified him on his nametag, came by to check on her again. "Would you like another beer?"

"No, thank you. I'm still nursing this one." She kept her back to him, watching the waves crash into the shore.

"If you can tell me who you're waiting for, maybe I can help you locate them." The bartender laughed easily.

"She'll be along soon, I'm sure."

There were only a few other patrons in the beach shack bar. The bartender—a young American, freckle-faced, surfer type on his quest for endless summer—hung around to talk to her. Apparently she was an anomaly.

"We don't get too many high-end women like you in the shack. Most of the women with money are at the resorts closer to town."

"What makes me high-end?" She sipped her beer and waited for his reply.

"That black credit card I saw in your wallet when you paid for the first beer. Our clientele are mostly locals and the expats down here, working like me. Let me try to guess where you're from. Accents are kind of my hobby."

Another sip. "I've lived in several places, but go ahead. This could be interesting."

"You're definitely southern. Even if you are educated and cleaned it up, you still have a touch of drawl."

She sat up a little taller on the barstool, but remained facing the ocean, with Bren at her shoulder. She glanced at him from time to time, but focused on the waves. Behind the shades and under the ball cap, her features were indistinguishable. Still, she didn't want to give him a good long look, just in case. This had to be a surprise.

She responded to his assessment of her origins with, "Southern can mean a lot of places. It's the largest accent group in the United States. You'll have to get closer than that for the prize."

Surfer boy took that as a suggestive statement, as all twenty something men might do. "How close do I have to get for a date?"

"Oh please, I could be your mother."

"That's hot," was Bren's witty reply.

"Hey Bren," a voice called out behind the bar.

Bren turned away to greet the newcomer. "Good afternoon, boss lady. Hey, I want you to meet my new southern friend. I'm trying to guess where she's from."

Rainey spun slowly on the bar stool, while she removed the sunglasses and hat. She grinned at the boss lady Bren was so eager to have her meet.

"Hello, Ellie."

Bren was confused. "Ellie? Who's Ellie?"

"Shut up, Bren, and go wait on somebody. That's what I pay you for. It certainly isn't your pencil-thin dick."

Bren objected, "Damn, who pissed in your cereal today?"

Rainey slapped a one hundred dollar bill down on the bar. "Here's your tip, Bren. Go find another job. This one is about to come to an end."

Ellie walked over to the cooler behind the bar, grabbed two cold beers, popped the tops, and slid one in front of Rainey. Bren, though mostly clueless, knew the telltale signs of a catfight he wanted no part of. He snatched up the hundred and bottle of tequila and hit the beach running.

"What shall we drink to, Rainey? Your good health? The nose healed nicely, by the way."

Rainey slid the freshly opened beer back across the bar. "If you don't mind, I'd rather not accept a beverage from you after that last time."

"Suit yourself. Drink the hot one. So, to what shall we toast?"

"I'm drinking to my father. He was murdered five years ago today."

"You picked today to come see me. I'm honored and I will drink to that," Ellie said, tipping her bottle in salute.

She tilted her head back for a long draw. Rainey took another sip of her safe, but warming beer.

"Here's what I know," Ellie began. "You're in Mexico, so if you're armed, it's illegally. Bounty hunting is illegal also, so unless you have the local police or an FBI agent with a warrant in his pocket, you can't detain me. I know you don't have the locals with you, or I would have known. I pay them handsomely to watch my back. Damn, I enjoyed this life. Oh well, on to the next."

Rainey saw the glint of the diamond pendant around Ellie's neck. "I came to collect my wife's necklace."

Ellie reached for the clasp at the back of her neck. "I guess if you came all this way to get it, you deserve to have it. I was saving it for a rainy day." Ellie laughed. "I guess this is a Rainey day."

"You could call it that," Rainey said, glaring at the woman that tried to kill her.

Ellie removed the necklace and laid it in front of Rainey on the bar.

"So, does that conclude our business?" Ellie asked, and then sipped her beer.

"Not quite," Rainey answered. "Aren't you curious how I found you and who else knows where you are?"

"I could use the info, so I don't make that mistake again."

"For someone who claims not to make mistakes, you've sure made a lot of them."

Ellie had lost none of her arrogance. Faced with being caught, she maintained her superior attitude. "Not putting a bullet in your head was probably my biggest one, but do tell, what other mistakes have I made?"

"For starters, you should have made sure Graham Colde was dead. He is the one who wrote the program that found you. He spent two months combing through every moment of your life, compiling data. He's going to be working with the FBI now, using the program he wrote to analyze evidence. You've actually made him quite the star in criminal investigative code writing."

"Good for him," Ellie commented, as she eyed the exits.

Rainey continued. "Using Cassie Gillian's identity was a stroke of genius, but ultimately your undoing. You built a whole life for her, after you took hers. We found her bank accounts, real estate holdings, and the deed to this bar she bought from Ely's estate long after her death."

"Hmm, probably should have let that bitch die back in 2001. It was just so easy to be her. I knew everything I needed, family and medical history, important dates, and of course having her social security card and driver's license helped immensely. Her parents always wondered where her wallet went."

"Yes, we talked to them and everyone else you've ever associated with. The wives in Wilmington were more than willing to spill all they knew about you. Nobody knew too much, but all together, it was plenty. One of them in particular hates your guts, especially after you befriended her and then slept with her husband. It might have been a mistake to mention your brother owned a bar down here."

"That had to be Katrina. She was such a spoilsport."

"You leaked, Ellie. Your narcissism compelled you to delight in your duping of others, too much, as it turns out. You leaked information like a sieve and we just followed your trail."

"So, what now?" Ellie inquired, growing bored with Rainey's tale. "Where is your backup? Where are the badges and guns to take me in? Or did you come down here on your own to exact revenge."

Rainey's one corner grin crept onto her lips. "Did I mention that my wife is independently wealthy? She was very willing to pay any sum to the local law enforcement officials to cooperate in locating you. It didn't take that much to buy them off. I can pretty much do whatever I want at this point."

"Oh, really?"

"Rainey, are you ready to go?" Katie's voice sounded behind her.

Ellie looked over Rainey's shoulder and commented, "My, she is more striking in person."

Rainey did not turn around. She kept her eyes on Ellie, especially her hands. "I'll be with you in a second, honey."

Ellie's sarcastic, "Aw, isn't that sweet," compelled Katie to come closer.

Rainey felt Katie place a hand in the small of her back. "So this is Ellie Paxton. I was sure she'd be better looking, but then the sun does age a woman rather quickly."

Rainey chuckled and said to Ellie, "She doesn't like you very much."

"Hey, are you guys coming?" Molly's voice filled the bar.

Katie spoke to her. "We'll be along in a minute. Rainey's just finishing up in here."

Rainey watched Ellie's reaction, as Molly and Leslie came to stand beside Katie at the bar. Her armor began to melt away with each passing moment. Her eyes betrayed her fear.

"Is this your posse?" Ellie asked, sizing up the group. "Do the criminals just give up so they can be frisked by these gorgeous women?"

Rainey shook her head. "No, they're just friends. We're all here on vacation. I didn't come here to take you down, Ellie. As you say, bounty hunting is illegal in Mexico. Besides, you aren't out on bail, you're a fugitive with outstanding warrants in nine murders, and of course the charges resulting from our last interaction."

Ellie had been eyeing Molly. "Aren't you that defense attorney from Durham? Kincaid, I think it is."

"Yes, but you can't afford me," Molly replied. "In fact, with the evidence they have on you, I'd just go with a public defender

210

and throw myself on the mercy of the court. You're going to prison for hundreds of years, with or without expensive legal representation."

Ellie challenged with, "Circumstantial evidence at best. OJ walked with blood on his hands."

"But he left no witnesses," Rainey countered.

"So I do a little time for trying to kill you. Any confessions you claim I made can be disputed because of the drug I gave you. Graham is a total mess as a witness. He didn't even remember his name for years. They'll have a hard time proving I killed anyone."

Katie leaned closer to Rainey and asked, "May I please be the one to tell her."

"Yes, you may," Rainey answered, enjoying Katie's vengeful desire to sink the dagger in Ellie Paxton's life of crime.

Katie reached to lift the diamond pendant from the bar and held it up, pinched between two fingers like a dirty diaper. "It's very pretty, but I hope you know it has to be reset or traded in."

"Katie doesn't wear seconds, eh?" Rainey teased.

"Not her seconds," Katie said, indicating Ellie with a head nod in her direction."

Rainey laughed and took the necklace from Katie. She slipped it into her shorts pocket, saying, "I'll remember that."

Ellie wasn't impressed with the light banter. "If you two are finished, I've got a plane to catch."

Katie focused on Ellie with a look Rainey hoped she never used on her. "In a hurry? Let me make this short and sweet for you then. When you drove my van into that sandpit with my wife handcuffed inside, you actually solved a murder, one you committed."

Rainey saw Ellie flush red. She was on the verge of bolting any second.

Katie continued, "Do you know why she survived? The van came to rest on something on the bottom, which kept it from rolling into the deepest water. Just ten more feet and your plan might have worked."

"I'm not in cuffs. I don't see badges or warrants. Enjoy your stay, ladies. Drinks are on the house."

Katie wasn't deterred by Ellie's attempt to dismiss her. "Pour yourself a shot. You're going to need it."

Ellie glared at Katie. Rainey kept watch, ready to spring should Ellie make a move.

Ellie instead smiled at Rainey, "She's cute, real spunky. I bet she's a firecracker in bed too. Spicy. I like it."

Molly and Leslie chuckled quietly, but Katie didn't. She leaned in closer to Ellie for her reply. "She turned *you* down, didn't she?"

"Oh, is that what she told you, that she turned me down? My, aren't we trusting," Ellie said, trying to unnerve Katie.

Katie waved a dismissive hand and laughed. She smiled at her adversary and said, "Trust? I do trust her, but really, this is simply a matter of a cheap knockoff you can buy on the corner versus haute couture."

Rainey nearly fell off her chair. She'd never seen Katie in a girl fight. It was amusing, but at the same time, Rainey had to make sure Ellie wasn't hiding a weapon or planning to jump the bar and start pulling hair. Pretty girls fought differently. The usual dance of taunts before the first punch could turn violent in a flash. When one of them ran out of words for a witty comeback, she could go from mad to "I'm going to snatch you bald" in zero-point-two seconds. Ellie, it appeared, was out of her league with Ms. Meyers. Hair flying was imminent.

Katie left Ellie no time to respond. "Back to the van and your attempt to murder my wife. As it turns out, you saved her. When you dumped Adam Goodwin and his car in the sandpit, you should have made sure it rolled to deep water. The van stopped on the bumper of his car, just fifteen feet from the surface."

Ellie tried to play dumb. "I always wondered what happened to Adam. Who knew he was in the sandpit the whole time?"

"You did, Ellie," Rainey said.

Katie shushed her. "I'm telling this."

Ellie interrupted, "There isn't a speck of evidence in that car that links me to his disappearance."

The sly smile on Katie's face was priceless. "Really? Did you check the glove box?"

The expression on Ellie's face was proof positive that she had not. She began to take on the wide-eyed look of a caged wild animal. Her eyes darted around, as she planned her escape.

Katie plunged the dagger deep. "You didn't fool everybody, Ellie. Adam saw you for what you were. In his glove box, in the water tight plastic bag the car manual came in, he slipped a three page document outlining your crimes, with a note explaining he was confronting you with what he knew and warning that if he disappeared, you were responsible."

"That's all you got," Ellie said, feigning indifference.

Katie twisted the knife. "Well, there was that tape he made of Ely's drunken confession. Did I forget to mention that earlier?"

Ellie was stunned.

Molly chose this time to step forward. She plopped some papers on the bar. "Ellie Paxton, you have been served. I represent the families of your victims in the civil suit they are bringing to make sure you have not a dime left of your ill-gotten gains."

"Good luck with that. I'd have to be in the US for that to have the least effect on me."

Rainey jumped in. "We'll see you back in Carolina. Time for us to continue our vacation."

Before Ellie could react, Danny stepped into the shade of the bar, followed by six local law enforcement officers and the Chief of Police. They had been outside listening to the conversation through the microphone on Rainey's hat, which she had placed on the bar.

"I believe that's my cue," he said, grinning at Rainey.

He turned to Ellie as the locals cuffed her behind the bar. "Ellie Paxton Read, you are being taken into custody for extradition to the United States, which the Mexican government is more than willing to do. I have warrants for your arrest on nine counts of first degree murder and three counts of attempted murder."

Ellie resisted the cuffs, but was not successful. She cried out, "Three attempted murders? Who else are you accusing me of trying to kill?"

Rainey stood, put on her sunglasses, and answered Ellie's question. "You tried to kill Graham twice. It counts. Enjoy the plane ride back. It will be the last time you see more of the sky than the solitary exercise yard allows."

Mask of normalcy gone and desperate, Ellie screeched, "I should have blown your head off."

"But you didn't. I wasn't looking for you, but you came looking for me. That was your biggest mistake. My father shared with me some ancient Chinese wisdom years ago, which might have benefitted you before you tried to kill me. 'The supreme art of war is to subdue the enemy without fighting.' You should have just kept driving, Ellie, and left me alone."

Ellie ran out of witty comebacks and bellowed, "I hate you! I hope I never see you again."

"Oh, Ellie, don't be like that. I'll see you from the witness stand. You'll barely have time to miss me," Rainey responded with a laugh. She put her arm around Katie, and called over her shoulder as they exited, "Be sure to soak up this last bit of sun, before you leave. I believe the forecast at home is cold and rainy."

About the author:

2013 Rainbow Awards First Runner-up for Best Lesbian Novel, *Out on the Panhandle,* and three time Lambda Literary Award Finalist in Mystery with *Rainey Nights (2012), Molly: House on Fire (2013)*, and *The Rainey Season (2014)*, author R. E. Bradshaw began publishing in August of 2010. Before beginning a full-time writing career, she worked in professional theatre and also taught at both the university and high school level. A native of North Carolina and a proud Tar Heel, Bradshaw now makes her home in Oklahoma with her wife of 26 years. Writing in many genres, from the fun southern romantic romps of the Adventures of Decky and Charlie series to the intensely bone-chilling Rainey Bell Thrillers, R. E. Bradshaw's books offer something for everyone.

Learn more at www.rebradshawbooks.com

Made in the USA
San Bernardino, CA
13 May 2014